T0357260

NAHIA

EMILY JONES

HOLIDAY HOUSE  NEW YORK

THE SEA PEOPLE

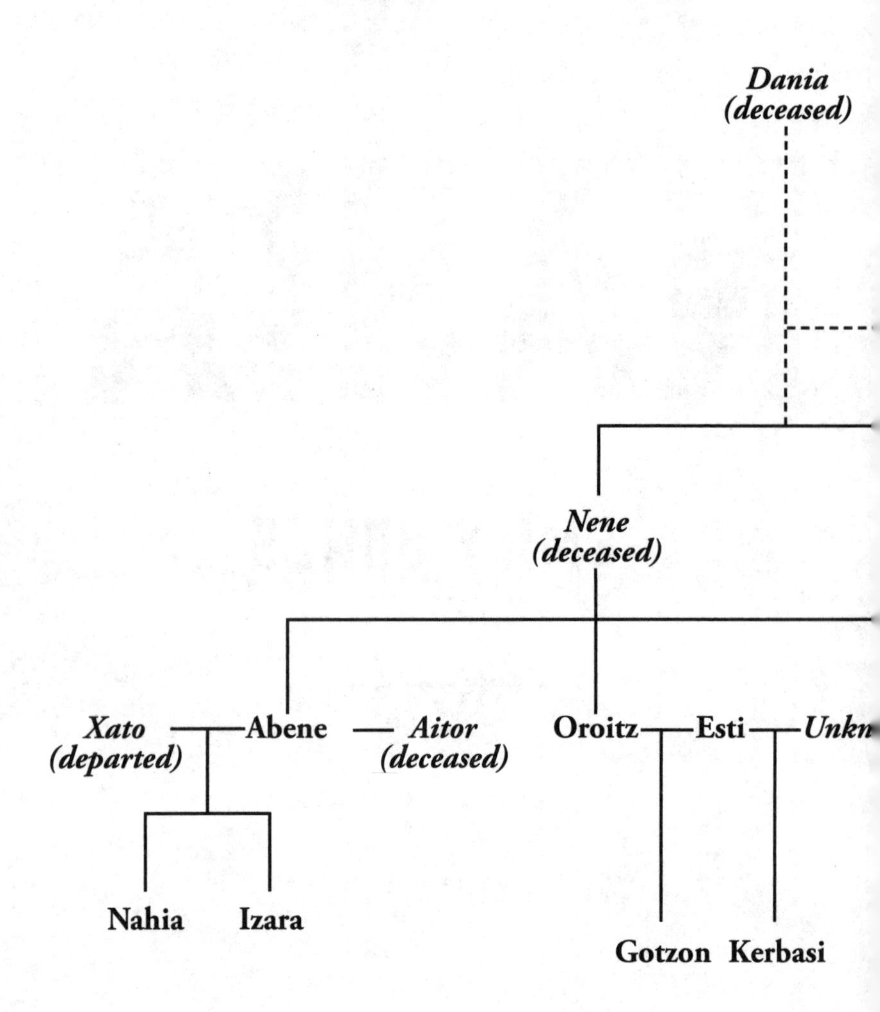

Other bands:

The Acorn Gatherers
The Deer Hunters
The Ibex People
The Salamander People

Other hunters:

Gogor
Hanu
Maru
Omer
Osaba
Pes
Tello
Urko
Zumar

Copyright © 2025 by Emily Lena Jones
All Rights Reserved

HOLIDAY HOUSE is registered in the U.S. Patent and Trademark Office.
Printed and bound in February 2025 at Sheridan, Chelsea, MI, USA.
www.holidayhouse.com
First Edition
1 3 5 7 9 10 8 6 4 2

Library of Congress Cataloging-in-Publication Data is available.

ISBN: 978-0-8234-5835-6 (hardcover)

EU Authorized Representative: HackettFlynn Ltd., 36 Cloch Choirneal,
Balrothery, Co. Dublin, K32 C942, Ireland. EU@walkerpublishinggroup.com

For my niblings: Julia, Ben, Evie, and Juni

ONE

The path was littered with remnants of the winter's storms. Izara and I went single file, picking our way slowly through broken tree limbs. She cursed under her breath as she stumbled, grabbing an oak branch to right herself.

Despite the strenuous trail—and the gnawing hunger in my belly—my heart was light. I had a day in the woods, a day away from the rest of the band, ahead of me. The tensions of the gatherers' meeting we'd left behind were melting away. The tall trees soared high overhead; the damp air cooled my skin. Even the light rain gently trickling down was refreshing.

Izara dropped back to walk beside me, her footsteps muffled by the damp leaves blanketing the forest floor. She snapped a twig from a shrub as we passed, then broke it again, and again, before scattering the pieces on the ground.

"Where should we go?" she asked.

I considered, reaching my senses farther into the forest. "There's not much to be found this close to camp," I said. "If we want to fill our baskets with anything besides acorns, we'll need to go deeper in."

"We'd better come back with more than acorns," Izara said darkly. "But we can't go too far. If we're back late, Abene won't like it..."

I heard the unspoken half of her sentence: *And you're in enough trouble with her already.*

Abene was our mother, but she was also the headwoman of our band, the Sea People. And Izara wasn't wrong: after this morning, I definitely shouldn't push Abene any further. I sighed. "How about Big Forest Hill? No one's gathered up there in ages, have they?"

A dimple came and went in Izara's face. "You know they haven't."

I did know. Abene had kept everyone close since we came to winter camp. No one had been allowed farther than the shore or the forest's fringe all season, as I had so tactfully pointed out this morning.

Why *was* she keeping such a tight leash on us?

"If we're doing this, let's hurry—we have a lot of ground to cover to be back by nightfall." My sister adjusted the straps of her gathering basket so it hung straight between her shoulder blades, then set off at a brisk pace.

I rushed after her, struggling to match her speed. I didn't know where Izara got her energy. We were all tired and hungry.

Traditionally, winter was when we ate mussels and seaweed, supplemented with greens and roots from the forest's edge. But for the past few years, there had been fewer and fewer shellfish, and those we caught seemed smaller and smaller. Worse, Abene was less and less willing to let us forage in the forest instead of along the coast. Worst of all, she kept us at the shore longer and longer into the spring, putting the move to summer territory off later every year. People were going hungry, but Abene was inexorable. Last year, we'd stayed at winter camp so long, I'd worried the shell-sickness that comes in the warm months would arrive before she allowed us to depart.

Shellfish, shellfish—it was always shellfish, always the gatherers in one big group, spreading along the shore in search of mussels and barnacles, both increasingly difficult to find. If it hadn't been for Izara, I would be with them again today. When I'd proposed that I go into the woods to try to find some fresh, unpicked greens, Abene had glared at me as if I'd suggested I spend the day lazing about the fire. I'd stared back, my cheeks flushed. And then Izara had come to the rescue, taking my side, and Abene had relented. I was still baffled by our mother's obstinacy.

I looked at my sister, trudging along beside me, and I was filled with warmth. "Thank you, Zari."

Izara dimpled at me again. "You were right," she said. "We *do* need something besides mussels. But you have to manage Abene better. You know it's not our place to speak at the fire, yet you do it anyway."

"I'm first daughter. I can speak." But even as I said it, I knew it wasn't true.

Or at least, it wasn't true enough—a first daughter might be excused for speaking, under extreme circumstances, but that wasn't the same as having unconditional approval to do so. Yet if I hadn't insisted that we needed food from the forest as well as the shore, who would have?

"You're not mated," Izara said, "and you won't be counted among the women until you are. You know that. You should have asked Abene about gathering inland at our tent this morning. *Privately.*"

I shrugged. "I guess I thought she'd be less likely to say no in front of everyone else."

Izara shook her head, as if I were so hopeless it wasn't worth saying more. She changed the subject. "So, when do you think Garbi's band will come for a visit? Soon, maybe?"

There was a mischievousness in her voice. Izara had enjoyed a dalliance with one of the hunters from Garbi's band, the Salamander People, when we visited with them last summer. She'd been hoping for another encounter ever since.

I curbed my impatience. "Not soon, I hope. We don't have enough food for ourselves."

"We'd manage," she said. "Really, Nahia. It's almost spring. You don't need to worry so much."

I thought Izara's thin, hungry face belied her words. "Spring is at least a month away. I have to worry. We should all worry."

I didn't look at her, but I knew Izara was shaking her head at me again. "What good does worrying do?"

It was a question with no answer.

When we reached Big Forest Hill, we separated, spreading out to cover more area. Some gatherers didn't like the deep woods; they preferred the beach, where everyone could always see everyone else. Many were afraid of the spirits of the forest. But my mother, Abene, had little use for ghost stories or tales of spirits. "It's all foolishness," she would say.

Unlike her, I loved the stories. But like her, I wasn't afraid: not of spirits or ghosts or of *tsairiu*, the half-animal, half-spirit beings said to roam the woods. I adored the forest. When I was alone among the trees, I felt *real* in a way I never did when surrounded by people.

My enthusiasm was ground down as the day wore on, though. There wasn't much food to be found at Big Forest Hill, even though no one had been here all season. I only uncovered a few early spring greens, their tips poking up through the leaf litter, and some roots. Still small, and I hated to harvest them now, since it meant less later in the season... But we needed the food, so I went ahead and dug them up. The customary prayer of thanks I offered felt brittle.

The rain intensified as I worked, making it harder to see. Water streamed over my forehead and into my eyes. My hair clung to my neck like seaweed, and my fingers were numb from grubbing through soggy leaves. As the day waned, my delight in being in the woods and away from the rest of the band completely faded. I wanted to be home. But I couldn't go home yet: the painful emptiness in my belly was matched by painful anxiety about my half-full basket.

I wiped at my forehead, trying to rub away some of the water. I succeeded only in smearing mud across my face.

How could this patch of forest be so empty of food? Had the winter storms done so much damage? Surely, there must be somewhere I could find more roots, more tender greens, something besides acorns. Somewhere I must find something that would fill my basket, fill the Sea People's bellies—maybe even earn a little praise from Abene. But my mind was slow and stupid, filled with fog. All it showed me was places I had already been, and fantasies of coming home with a full basket.

I became aware of a rustling in the brush to my right. It wasn't the sharp sound of a squirrel, but a softer, more subtle noise. It stopped, then began again.

I put my basket down, propping it against a tree, and went to investigate.

It was a rabbit, small and brown, caught by the leg in one of the hunters' snares. As I approached, it froze, as if by going still it could escape my notice. It was pitifully thin. I thought of Gotzon, one of the band's children. He had the same look these days: his eyes too big for his face, his head too big for his body.

It would be days before the hunters came this way, if they did at all. The rabbit wouldn't be good to eat anymore by tomorrow. The traplines were really meant to trap predators, not game, and they were rarely checked; in the cold weather, the hunters mostly went out fishing in their canoes.

The gnawing sensation in my belly, so familiar these days, suddenly was inescapable. I couldn't remember the last time I'd had fresh meat. Even this skinny rabbit, stewed with mussels and the meager greens I'd collected, would be a feast.

But still I hesitated. There was something too uncanny in the way the rabbit met my eye. Looking at it, I was drawn in to its world:

a warren, filled with other rabbit-folk; darting through grasses at the forest's edge; the spike of fear as a raptor's shadow darkened the sky . . .

All this I saw in the rabbit's eye, clear as a reflection in still water.

I shook my head to empty it. I'd never heard of a *tsairi* that took the shape of a rabbit—of bears and wolves, yes, but not rabbits.

The rabbit was perfectly still. The only movement was its shallow breathing, the tiny chest pumping in and out. Its ribs protruded, ridging its brown fur.

I reached out and loosened the snare.

The rabbit fell to the ground. It froze in place for a moment, as if it couldn't believe this wasn't yet another trap. Then it bounded one leap away and stopped again.

Why couldn't the thing take its freedom and leave? I was unreasonably annoyed. But I quashed my irritation—*I've wasted enough time*—and turned away.

As I moved, something on the ground caught my eye. It was smooth and flat and completely unfamiliar. I picked it up.

It was a polished red-brown on the outside, slightly curved, with some sort of design impressed along one edge. Neatly triangular in shape, it seemed like a piece that had broken off from something larger. The fragment was heavy, solid in my hand. It wasn't wood or bone; it felt more like a rock, but its texture was too regular.

A memory surfaced: my hands, much smaller, wrapped around a little bird figurine. The figurine had been like this—heavy as rock, but regularly textured. I remembered the strange smooth heaviness of it lying in my hands. The same as the fragment that lay in my palm now.

I'd held the figurine years ago, when I was a tiny child at summer meeting. Summer meetings were not formal affairs, just gatherings of a few bands at midsummer. But that summer meeting had been big: five bands. And there were many shamans that time . . . which was strange, now that I thought of it. They'd held a ceremony, something about protection . . . and they'd asked several of us to hold those figurines. I remembered Abene's stiffness, how she went rigid when one of the shamans, a tall man wearing a necklace of wolf teeth, handed me the figure. I'd asked him what it was made from. He'd cast a sharp eye on me. I'd shrunk back, but then he answered: *hardened clay*.

This broken shard was the same, I was sure. But it was smoother and harder and flatter than the clay of the figurine, and the design along the edge, too, was unfamiliar.

The stories say the *tsairiu* give presents to those who help them.

The hairs on the back of my neck stood up. I looked around to where I'd last seen the rabbit, but it was gone.

"Nahi?"

Izara. I started, quickly tucking the strange object into the small leather pouch hanging at my waist. Izara was like Abene: she had no patience with stories of spirits.

"I'm here, Izara," I called, and scurried back to my basket.

"Are you ready to go?" she called back. Her voice was closer now, and after a moment, I glimpsed her making her way through the trees. It was hard to see her through the gloom. "We should have headed back ages ago. Is your basket full?"

"Almost," I said, boosting it up on my back. I wiped my face with my sleeve and walked toward her, waving so she would see me.

Izara was neat and rosy-cheeked despite the rain. *How does she stay so tidy?* My own hands were covered with dirt, and I could feel that my hair was tangled. But Izara's dark waves hung perfectly around her face, the strands sparkling with raindrops. Her basket, like mine, was not quite full, but her eyes were shining and she was smiling.

"Guess what I found?" she asked. "A few hazelnuts! The squirrels must have missed them." She peered into my basket. "Roots... and acorns? Ugh, better than nothing, I suppose. I have a bunch of them, too." She set off in the direction of winter camp. "Come on, we'd better get back or we'll be late."

The fragment of hardened clay, the *tsairi*'s gift, had turned sideways in its pouch. Its hard edge dug through the soft leather of the bag and thudded against my leg as I walked, poking me. I ignored it and followed Izara.

We were about halfway back when we heard sharp crackling sounds—someone, or something, moving swiftly through the woods. Izara looked at me inquiringly. I listened. The footfalls were light and quick, but heavier than deer. It was a small person, running.

"Tora, I think," I said. "Tora or maybe Kiria." Tora and Kiria were the daughters of Abene's sister, our aunt Udane, and the other two unmated girls of the Sea People.

We waited, and soon enough, Tora dashed onto the footpath, skidding to a stop when she saw us. She pushed her large cloud of black hair back from her face, gasping.

Izara touched her shoulder. "Catch your breath."

Tora shrugged her off, wheezing. "There's a visitor! Abene sent me to find you." My cousin's eyes darted sidelong toward me. "She says Nahia should bring firewood! And Izara, she says you should come right back with whatever you managed to harvest."

My shoulders slumped. I was exhausted already, my body aching. Gathering a load of firewood would put at least another hour between me and the evening meal.

Izara raised an eyebrow at me. I could hear her thinking: *This is why you shouldn't cross our mother.*

I narrowed my eyes at her. *If you're so wise*, I thought back, *why didn't you say something yourself? Why am I always the one who has to ask?*

"All right, all right," Izara said aloud. "Tora, what's the visitor like?"

Tora shrugged. "I *think* he's a shaman," she said doubtfully. "But I didn't see his pendant. And Eneko didn't say, when he introduced him to Abene."

I took off my basket and knelt beside it, rummaging to extract the hide wood-carrier from the bottom. If Tora was right, it would be an interesting evening; shamans always had stories to tell. And if the visitor had gone straight to Eneko, rather than to the hunters or Abene, he probably *was* a shaman.

For Eneko was a shaman himself. He had been with us almost a year, which was an unusually long time. Shamans were outsiders, solitary, coming and going among the people as no one else did. Hunters sometimes traveled, but they moved from band to band in search of adventure and knowledge, and eventually they chose a home. Shamans—well, they mostly lived on their own, in the wilds. A shaman might take up with a band for a season or two, but then he would leave, disappearing in the middle of the night as if he'd never been there at all.

Shamans were strange creatures. Some were dangerous. All the shamans I had ever seen were men, but my favorite stories were of the woman shaman Benare, who could speak to spirits as easily as she could people—more easily, even. When the spirits were angry, they would send her, disguised as an ordinary woman, to join a band. And then she would enact the spirits' vengeance, drawing their punishment down: siblings would fight, lovers would quarrel, hunters would rage, children would sicken. Such things did happen, even now. The Salamander People had been cursed by a shaman they'd offended, so the elders said. For years after, their band had suffered from infighting, one faction after another leaving, until there were nearly none of them left. They'd had to find another shaman to reverse the curse.

I had never known a shaman to curse anyone. But every shaman I had met was strange, cold, sunk too deep into the spirit world to care much about the rest of us. It was important not to offend them—even Abene, who mocked most superstitions, agreed. Shamans had power, and wherever that power came from, it demanded respect.

Eneko wasn't as strange as most. He was young, and maybe that was why. Like all of them, though, he was remote—unreadable.

"Is the visitor good-looking, Tora?" Izara asked.

I stared at her. For the last couple of years, Izara seemed to think of nothing but sex, but still. "He's a shaman!"

Izara shrugged.

Tora giggled, turning bright red. "He's old," she offered.

"How old?" persisted Izara. "If he's not a new hunter, like my last lay, so much the better. I prefer a man who knows what he's doing." She gave a little shimmy.

"He's a *shaman*," I said again, not patiently. "Shamans don't take mates."

Izara gave me a wicked smile. "It's not a mate I'm looking for. And anyway, we don't *know* he's a shaman. If he is, well, it wouldn't stop me from having a good time for a night, would it? I've always wanted to try a shaman. See how I would hold out. Make him work for that *bizi*." She winked at Tora.

Tora was still giggling, her hand over her mouth, her eyes wide at Izara's audaciousness. I shook my head. The tales said shamans slept with people only to collect spiritual energy, *bizi*, but Tora was too young for this kind of talk.

"You are outrageous," I told my sister.

"I know," said Izara unrepentantly. "But I'm fun, no?"

I couldn't help but laugh. Izara was so—so—so *Izara*. I held my basket out to her, and she accepted it, waving away Tora's offer of help. She looped the straps over her shoulders so the two baskets hung side by side along her back. "Oof," she said. "I'll save you a seat by the fire!"

And she and Tora set off for home.

I moved in the opposite direction, searching out dry wood—or at least, less-damp wood—and piling it into the wood-carrier. I was hungry and tired and eager to get back to camp so as not to miss any of the visitor's stories, and I moved quickly, selecting wood less carefully than I might otherwise have done. My carrier was nearly full when I heard a voice—a voice speaking quietly, so softly I almost didn't hear it.

I froze. I was off the main trail, behind a stand of brush, so I didn't have to worry about discovery. A good thing, since in the next moment, I recognized the voice as belonging to Kerbasi, one of our band's hunters.

I'd never liked him. He was a bully; he and his friend Omer had made Izara's and my lives a torment in childhood. They were older than we were by at least five years, but that didn't matter to them. No one had been too young for their rough teasing. Now that they were hunters, they were mostly too busy to bother with us, but I still stayed away from him.

"There's a visitor," Kerbasi said. "He stays with the shaman tonight."

Another voice responded—that of my uncle Oroitz, Abene's brother. Oroitz was both head of the hunters and the mate of Kerbasi's mother. "It is of no concern," Oroitz said, dismissive.

"But does he *know*?" Kerbasi asked, even more softly, but insistently. I could hear the anger in his voice beneath the softness, like a current lurking just beneath the surface of the sea.

Was "he" the visitor, or was it Eneko?

And what might he know or not know?

A chill crept over me. Were the hunters keeping something from us? Times had been hard among the Sea People. The weather was bad and food was short. These were exactly the kinds of problems which led to infighting . . . and to fracture. The dissolution of a band.

This wasn't the first time I had worried about the hunger or the storms, but it was the first time I'd worried about the hunters. No one ever *wanted* fracture to happen, but it did anyway. And it had been happening often in recent years. Not to us, but to other bands. A good number of the bands we'd visited with when I was a child were no more, their members scattered to other groups, where they had no status.

Abene said fracture happened when there was a rupture between hunters and gatherers. "But we have the hunters in hand, with my own brother born as head of hunters," she always said.

I stood still, listening. The leaves rustled beneath the falling raindrops. Kerbasi and Oroitz passed me by. I could hear the staccato rhythm of Oroitz's reply to Kerbasi, but not the words. Whatever he said, it seemed to quiet Kerbasi, for after Oroitz spoke, I heard only their footsteps moving away from me, back toward winter camp.

TWO

My wood-carrier was bulging and my muscles burning. The forest was dark but for cloud-filtered moonlight, dark and damp and full of the soft noises of late winter. There were ducks at the stream, clacking sleepily at each other as they settled for the night. As I drew close to winter camp, I saw the glimmering of the bonfire through the trees, heard the hum of conversation. The fire and noise were light and bright, a contrast to the silky darkness of the trees. The evening meal was underway.

Three of the hunters who had joined our band last fall, Hanu and Gogor and Osaba, stood eating together at the very edge of camp. Hanu's dog hovered nearby, hoping for scraps. I nodded to them as I passed into the heart of our home, heading for the woodpile. Most of the other men were eating in detached groups as well: Pes and Tello by the hunters' tents; Zumar, Urko, and Maru over on the southern edge. Only the elders, the women, and the children were at the fire.

I felt a familiar pang of unease. There were fewer women among the Sea People than there had ever been. Abene had accepted four new hunters this past year, while the number of gatherers continued to shrink. Several of the older women had died, and Abene had allowed matings for first

Andi and then Lorea that took them to other bands. This was another of Abene's actions that I couldn't understand. There were now only four grown women in our band: Abene, Udane, Esti, and Lorea's sister, Alaia. Until Izara and I mated, that was all.

When Lorea had gone, leaving so few of us, I'd asked Abene why. All she'd said was, "Too many mouths to feed, and no need to keep girls from Lili's line." But if there were too many mouths, why had she accepted new hunters? It felt wrong to have the band so unbalanced. When I pressed Abene on it, she refused to answer.

Kerbasi and Omer were beside the woodpile, their heads together, talking. Kerbasi and Oroitz must have come straight back to camp after I'd heard them in the forest, for Kerbasi's wooden bowl dangled from his hand, already empty. I kept my head down and my ears open as I drew near—might Kerbasi be talking about his conversation with my uncle?—but they fell silent as I passed them. I glanced up and saw them both looking at me, Kerbasi with an unpleasant smirk on his face. I looked away and unloaded my wood quickly before drawing toward the fire.

The visitor sat eating with the band elders—Abene, her brother Oroitz, and her sister Udane—and with Eneko, close to the flames. From that distance, I could see he had a handsome, narrow face. His hair was tied back at his neck, in the way of men from the north. He didn't look so old, despite Tora's words. He was certainly much younger than Oroitz, to whom he seemed to be listening attentively.

Oroitz was expounding on something, thumping his leg to emphasize, and I stifled a chuckle. He was powerfully built and seemed imposing when sitting, when one couldn't see how short he was or how he limped from an old injury. Izara always said Oroitz sat as often as he could so people would think him taller.

Udane didn't look at the visitor directly, but her bent head, how she considered him out of the corners of her eyes, the way she rolled her walking stick back and forth before her—she was sizing him up. Though she seldom spoke, Udane was imposing, too, standing as well as sitting. And when she did speak, her words carried weight.

But no one looking at the trio of elders, I thought, could mistake who held the real power. There was something in Abene's posture that spoke of authority. She was as firm and rooted as the oldest oak, and about as swayable.

A little farther along, in the spot with the best view of the visitor, sat Izara and Tora. Next to the rosy-cheeked Izara, Tora was tiny and frail, a bundle of curly dark hair and big blue eyes in a brown face. Their bowls, already empty, sat on the ground beside them, and their heads bent toward each other as they whispered and giggled. My stomach ached as I looked at them, a stab of loneliness beside the ever-present pain of hunger. Izara was so much easier with people than I was.

I pushed the thought away. It was finally time for me to eat. Oroitz's mate, Esti, was at the cooking pit. The long light hair that marked her as a foreigner, a northerner, hung loose down her back.

"Thank you, Esti," I said as she filled my wooden bowl with mussels and seaweed.

She smiled at me. "We missed you today," she said in her throaty, accented voice. "But it is good to be in the woods when you can."

I looked at her, confused, but she just smiled placidly. I shook it off. Esti was always enigmatic, and Izara was waving at me, gesturing at the space next to her. I glanced surreptitiously at the visitor as I made my way to her side, trying to get a better look.

Everything about him was long and thin—his body, his face, his fingers. His northern-style pulled-back hair made his bearded face look even longer, but in an appealing way. His eyes were keen in his narrow brown face, his gaze as cool and appraising as a hawk's. But was he a seer? A small skin bag, suspended on a leather cord, hung around his neck. The bag might hold a shaman's pendant, or it might not. I checked for a tattoo, but his tunic obscured his upper arm.

Still, those watching eyes... and the way he and Eneko sat companionably... he *had* to be a shaman.

Just then, he looked up and caught my eye, and my stomach fell out of my body. His gaze was a sharp bright blue, piercing. I couldn't move—I just stood there, pinned.

After a moment, Eneko, beside him, looked up too. He glanced at me, then whispered something to this visitor, who raised his eyebrow and—at last—turned away.

My face was hot, and I felt conspicuous, but no one else seemed to have noticed anything. I scurried over to Izara, my cheeks flaming, and sat. She smiled in welcome. "Finally!" she teased. "Did it take that long to find firewood?"

"Dry firewood is not so easy to find in winter," I said stiffly. Tora, predictably, giggled. I quashed my irritation and began to eat. The food was no longer hot, but it was still warm enough to be comforting.

It was a wonder that Izara had apparently not noticed my exchange of glances with the visitor. For all her conversation was focused on Tora, she was trying mightily to attract his attention: smiling across the fire, arching her back, tossing her shining hair over her shoulders so it caught the firelight. I felt another pang, envy joining the loneliness and hunger. My own hair was wild and unruly, not likely to reflect light, and right now it was snarled and probably full of twigs. Izara and I were twin-born, but so unalike we might have come from different bands, let alone different births. Our one similarity, the deep brown eyes, came from our southern father. We'd never known him; our grandmother Nene had arranged the mating, and it hadn't worked out. Our father departed for his southern home before anyone knew we were on the way.

Izara couldn't really mean to seduce a shaman, could she? Shamans did take lovers sometimes, people said, but those foolish enough to lie with them even once were weakened for a fortnight or more. Izara knew the stories as well as I did. But then, like Abene, Izara had little patience for stories; her feet were fully planted in the here and now. *Bizi* meant nothing to her.

Izara was asking Tora, "Did Gotzon go out with the hunters today?"

Tora glanced over to where the elders sat. "No. The hunters passed while we were on the beach, and Oroitz tried to take him, but he wouldn't go. Then Esti told Oroitz to let him be for now; she would keep him."

Izara shook her head. "Foolish. He'll have to go sometime."

"Why push him, though?" I asked. "He'll go when he's ready."

Izara scrunched up her nose at me. "It'll get harder the longer he puts it off."

"But…" I began, but then Abene spoke and the whole band quieted.

"As you all have seen," Abene said, rising, "we welcome a traveler this evening. Zigor, lately of the Deer Hunters, a people of the mountains, is traveling to the band of his birth, the People of the White Cliffs. We welcome him to the Sea People. Nahia, first daughter?"

She glared at me. She might as well have said it aloud: *Do not fail me, daughter.*

The weight of all the eyes on me was crushing.

I should have been used to it: I'd been first daughter all my life, after all. But then, most of our visitors were people we knew already. There was rarely any call for this particular ritual. Zigor was a solitary traveler from far away. There was no help for it; I would have to recite our history.

I stood, cleared my throat, and began.

"In the time before time," I began, "Dania, mother of the Sea People, came to these lands." My voice was too high, and it trembled as I spoke. Zigor leaned closer, his piercing eyes focused on my face. I flushed and spoke louder.

"Dania and her sister, Ina, were children of the south. They came from a large band, where Ina was headwoman. The years passed and the band prospered, growing larger and larger. They prospered so much that the day came when they were too many for their territory. Ina had strong land-sense, and she heard the earth's message: *The band must split, and soon, or the land will suffer.* So Ina said to her sister, 'Dania, you, too, are daughter to the headwoman's line. We must split the band, and you will lead one half away from here. I will give you the best of the hunters and the best of the gatherers, and you will take them north in search of a new home.'

“Dania was a proud woman. Though she did not have land-sense as strong as her sister’s, she had sight. She told her sister, ‘I will take the split, yes, but only those who choose to go—only those called by the north—will accompany me.’ And so Dania stood before the people, and the gatherers and hunters who most wanted to see the north flocked to her, while Ina and the others remained in the south. Dania and her brave ones passed through the deserts, the forested cliffs, and the marshy delta of the birds.”

I paused, momentarily lost. All the eyes, pressing on me. My throat was scratchy and raw. My mind was blank. What came next?

Izara whispered loudly, “*All the bands asked her to stay.*”

Of course. I let out my breath and continued. “Dania and her brave ones met many other peoples in their journey. Each band they met asked them to stay, to join with them. But Dania told them no. She was meant to be headwoman; her mother’s mothers had been leaders since time immemorial. She would not submit to any other woman’s authority, and she would not rest until she found a land that called to her—a territory that would support her people, no matter how they grew.

“After many months of travel, Dania and her band arrived here, on this coast. Dania’s land-sense had gained in strength as they walked, and when they reached this shore, the earth tugged at her sharply. But it was late winter, the starvation time, and there was little food to be found. Dania and her people had been traveling a long time, and they were weak and hungry.

“Still the land told Dania, *This is your place.*

“So Dania went to the Cove of Rocks, the same Cove of Rocks we know now, leaving her people to wait in the forest. She sat by the sea, and she said, 'Spirits who guard this land, send me a sign. If you show me how to keep my people fed, we will remain as people of the sea for all time. If you show no sign, we will continue our journey.'

"Dania felt the land thrumming beneath her. And then her eye rested on a strange formation on the rocks. It was a bed of mussels, clinging to the promontory. She saw that the Cove of Rocks was full of shellfish—that food which is rich in the season when all else is poor.

"And Dania had her answer. She returned to her people, and brought them to the Cove of Rocks, and told them, 'The spirits of this land, the spirits of forest and sea, they have brought us home. See the bounty before us. The sea will feed us throughout the winter, in the fat years and the lean ones sure to come as time passes, while the coastal forest will feed us and be our home in summer. We are a new band: we are the Sea People.'

"The Sea People feasted on mussels and seaweed. And they stayed, and as Dania had said, they were supported, in both lean times and plentiful ones, by the fruits of the sea. And so the Sea People we remain."

I stopped speaking and sat, my face burning. It was silent for a moment, but then chatter rushed in, filling the space.

Abene was staring at me fixedly. She muttered under cover of the noise, "Remember that, girl—we are the Sea People."

I wanted to answer back: *When did you last look out over the Cove of Rocks and see mussels strung across it? This isn't Dania's time.* But I thought of Izara's warning, earlier today, about handling our mother better. I reached out to grab Izara's hand. She squeezed mine in return, then let it go.

Oroitz said to Zigor, "And now, visitor, tell us of your journey." The band leaned forward, eager for a new story.

"As your headwoman said, I was born to a people south of here," Zigor began. "But I wished to travel, and so I did. Eventually, I came upon the Deer Hunters in the northern mountains." He gazed across the crowd toward Esti; her long fair hair and ghostlike skin shone in the light from the bonfire. "They took me in. I was content with them and had no thought of leaving. Eneko here knew me as one of them, eh? But then my mate died this past fall."

He was mated? Maybe he wasn't a shaman after all. As if in response to my thoughts, Izara's elbow dug into my side.

Zigor continued, "I found in myself a great craving for the sea, and the land of my birth. And so, when the weather warmed, I set out for the coast, and have been making my way home. It has been a disturbing journey."

An expression I couldn't read passed over Oroitz's face—something between anxiety and annoyance. He glanced quickly at Abene. I did, too, but Abene's face was still. Udane, next to her, didn't look up at all, just rolled her walking stick across her lap, back and forth, back and forth.

This was odd. What would make Zigor's journey disturbing?

Beyond the occasional disagreement or minor raid—and there had been no raids in a long time, not that we had heard of, anyway—the coastal territory was quite peaceful. Our hunger wouldn't alarm a traveler, either. Late winter was always hard. It was only those of us who knew that *every* season had been hard these last few years who were concerned. Some of us, not even then.

"Disturbing?" Alaia asked, a little self-consciously. I was grateful to her for speaking. Alaia was only a few seasons older than Izara and me, and new to being counted among the band's women. She'd been like an older sister to us while we were growing up. But last fall, Abene had arranged a mating between her and Bakar, one of the new hunters, and ever since then, Alaia had been stiff and distant, trying to earn her place among the women.

"Ah, you haven't heard?" Zigor said. "It's well I happened here, then. You are on the coast; you need to be prepared. Bands down the shore have been attacked, and the young women taken away. Sometimes the rest of the people are slaughtered and left for the carrion birds; sometimes they are left alone, but barren and doomed without their girls. The attackers are not of the bands, so they say, but strangers, strangers who have come from far away, strangers who..." and here he paused, letting the silence lengthen.

I knew what he didn't want to say. Strangers with bad spirits, dangerous powers. It was better not to mention spirits, especially bad ones—speaking their names aloud could catch their attention.

Beside me, Izara twitched uneasily. A peculiarly alert stillness told me the rest of the band was thinking the same thing I was.

Zigor continued, "Many have moved inland, to seek new territory or to join with other bands. Truthfully... I had wondered, at finding you here, whether you were brave or foolish."

Maybe it was growing up in Abene's tent, but stories of bad spirits rarely moved me. This was different. The lack of food, the stormy weather... Abene's refusal to move despite the dwindling supply of shellfish... the threat of fracture... And now this.

Zigor's story seemed one more warning, one more pebble on top of a pile that was becoming a mountain.

Something is wrong, very *wrong. Abene, you are headwoman. Don't you see the signs?*

The tension inside me was mounting. I was a river flush with snow-melt, about to breach its banks.

Kerbasi snorted. "Of course! Every visitor must arrive with scare stories."

Zigor smiled at Kerbasi. His smile was cold, his voice tinged with detached amusement. "I have seen it myself. When I left the band of my birth, I traveled with my brother. He joined a band along the coast some distance north of here. During my journey, I searched for them, hoping to find him. I found no band—no living people at all, in fact. What I found were bodies. Not my brother's, and indeed he may have moved on many years since. And no women or girls. But everyone else was dead, abandoned to the scavengers. They must have been attacked not long before; they were still recognizable." He touched the skin-pouch at his throat, then let his hand fall back to his lap. "And, like a fog, evil hung over that broken camp. I left as quickly as I could."

The silence was thick and heavy, almost tangible.

And inside me, there was another kind of pressure. Words were beginning to emerge from the rushing torrent within me, words that demanded to be spoken.

But I *couldn't* say anything. I might be first daughter, but I was still unmated, as Izara had reminded me earlier. A girl, not a woman. I'd violated the rules about speaking out too often. And I'd already attracted Abene's ire today, several times.

I stared at my mother, thinking at her instead of speaking: *Abene, what are you doing? Don't you hear this? Why don't you move us inland?*

Finally, Kerbasi broke the silence. "Pfft!" The noise was weak, swallowed immediately by the heaviness. "All nonsense! Who is this fool? Why are we listening to this?"

Oroitz moved his hand in a swift sideways gesture. "*Enough*."

Kerbasi looked mutinous, but subsided.

Still, the exchange was enough to loosen the silence. The band murmured; Oroitz and Abene looked at each other. Udane watched the two of them, her eyes traveling back and forth between them, her fingers wrapped tightly around her walking stick.

Udane is an elder, and a master gatherer besides—she *knows we need to move. She must. Surely, she sees the lack of food, the omens, the risk in staying here? Surely, she understands what Zigor is saying? She will speak.*

But Udane remained silent, watching, her eyes narrowed into tiny slits. When she finally did speak, she didn't challenge Abene. "Eneko, you have traveled much these past months. Have you heard news of these strangers?"

I turned my hopeful eyes to Eneko.

He was sitting quietly beside the fire, as he always did, his black eyes serious. At Udane's question, he wrapped his strong, graceful fingers around the perforated boar tooth that hung at his neck, his shaman's pendant.

The firelight accentuated his high cheekbones and firm jaw and flickered along the edges of his wolfskin cape. Like Udane, Eneko could speak out at the central fire without fear of censure. Those who communed with the spirits had their own status, their own power—even if it was a frightening power. I didn't know what Eneko might think of Zigor's story, but surely, he must have noticed that the coast wasn't providing enough food to feed us.

But maybe he didn't care. He likely wouldn't be with us much longer; he'd already stayed far longer than most shamans ever did. Perhaps to him it didn't matter if we all died, whether in a raid from one of Zigor's strangers or from starvation.

Whatever his reasons, Eneko did not challenge Abene, either. He said calmly, "I told you there was much movement among our neighbors. Many are moving inland." He nodded to the elders. "I told you also there was talk of new people."

My heart sank again. If neither Udane nor Eneko would stand up to Abene, who would?

Zigor said, "The bands I encountered on my way here said these strangers are building camps—large ones. They mean to stay."

Abene's eyes raked over the band, coming to rest on Eneko. The muttering died away. When it was perfectly quiet, she turned to Zigor and said, politely and coolly, "Thank you for your warning, visitor." She leaned on the word *visitor*. "But we are the Sea People. We will always remain in this territory—this land my mothers have held from the time before time, this land that keeps us safe against starvation. This territory that is tied to my line through land-sense."

Land-sense. Abene never spoke of it, except in circumstances like these.

I didn't know what her land-sense might have been telling her, but my own told me a different story. And it wanted to speak; the words were ramming themselves against my lips, fighting to be freed.

There is no food on the coast anymore! Already, the hunters are rumbling. If we stay, we risk fracture! If we stay, we risk being raided!

Abene, it is time. We must move inland.

We must.

Thickly, I swallowed. *Abene will be angry*, a voice in my mind warned. *This is much worse than speaking out before the gatherers; this is challenging her before all the Sea People—challenging her land-sense, even. And with a visitor present, too. She'll be so angry.*

I knew the voice was right, but the words would not be denied.

"Abene . . ." I leaned toward the fire. "These strangers are raiding along the coast, he says. If they go along the shore, we're bound to come in conflict with them."

I did not look at my mother as I spoke these words. I didn't have to. I could feel her glare, boring into me like a dagger of ice. Zigor, too, had turned toward me, staring. Beside me, Izara stiffened. I could hear her thinking, *Shut up, Nahi—shut up.*

But I have to, Zari.

I tried to gather my thoughts. It would be better not to speak of bad spirits, even if it might sway the rest of the band. Abene would have little patience for that. I took a deep breath, trying to control my trembling, and then more words tumbled out again, one after another, almost of their own accord.

"What if they have sea-traveling boats, like in the stories?" The band murmured to each other. I spoke over them. "Boats better than our canoes? If they survived the open ocean, they are strong enough to dominate us, on sea and on land. Let the strangers have the coast! If we go inland now, we will live to find a new territory for the Sea People."

The heavy silence returned. I heard the fire snapping, but nothing else.

And then, suddenly, there was a light, soft touch on my hand. I started. Eneko was sitting beside me, his hand resting lightly on mine. *How did he get here? Wasn't he across the fire?* My heart beat so fast I thought it might launch me into the air.

Zigor spoke to Abene, though his eyes still rested on me. "There is truth to what she says, headwoman. Farther north, the bands who survived the raids are already fighting over territory."

"I said, *thank you, visitor*," Abene snapped. She turned to me, her voice frosty. "And thank you for your thoughts, *daughter*. But rest assured—we elders will make the best decision for the band."

I don't know why I continued; I should have known better. But the words were still in me, shaking me like a rattle in their eagerness to get out. "Abene," I said. My voice was rough and uneven, and there were tears pricking at my eyes again. In a distant, observing part of my mind, I thought, *What am I doing?* But the speech flowed out, unchecked. "We cannot stay here. The land is exhausted. We are starving—and now there are raiders, bringing bad spirits with them? If we are to survive, we *must* move."

Abene turned away, ignoring me. She spoke across my words, saying to Zigor, "You have surely heard many interesting stories in your travels. Share one with us."

Eneko's hand encircled my wrist for an instant, and then he let go.

And with that, all words left me. I was empty, shaking. Abene's anger was palpable, a chill worse than any winter storm. I was in for it, that was clear.

But maybe she'd heard me, somewhere beneath the anger. I clung to the thought. *If Abene decides to move us, it will be worth it, no matter the punishment.*

Zigor didn't say anything further about the strangers. Instead, he embarked on a long story about a haunted wood and an evil bear spirit, up in the mountains. I barely heard him.

After Zigor finished his tale, it was time for the children to be sent off to bed, while the rest of the band shared gossip and old stories. Usually, Izara and I, so close to adulthood, would stay, would listen to the conversation. Tonight, Oroitz said, "Children—Izara, Nahia, all of you—the meal is over. Go to your tents. Nahia, take Gotzon back to his mother's tent first."

My cheeks warmed, but I was relieved even as I was embarrassed. *She was bound to punish me, and being sent from the central fire like a child is not so bad as punishments go.*

Beside me, however, Izara stiffened. At first, she didn't move, but glared at Oroitz. After a moment, she stood and began to slowly gather her things.

Gotzon was asleep, his pale head burrowed in Esti's lap. She lifted him up to me, not meeting my eyes, and I gathered him carefully in my arms. He did not wake. I walked out of the circle of light into the damp night air.

THREE

Esti's tent was in the middle of camp, only a short walk from the central fire. I touched the ground outside the tent to honor her ancestors before propping the leather entrance flap up with my free hand. Now that the clouds had cleared, moonlight streamed inside. Gotzon's bedding, just next to the entrance, was a tangle of furs. He was still fast asleep, his body a limp, heavy weight. I smoothed the bedding as best I could as I tucked him in and waited a moment to be sure he wouldn't wake.

In the moonlight, everything was drained of color. Each moment passed so slowly. My heart still pounded with the aftershock of the meeting, and everything around me—Esti's tent, the moonlight, Gotzon—seemed far away, distant.

Gotzon turned over and said, sleepily, "Nahia?"

I reached out and stroked his head. In the strange colorless light, his hair looked white as an elder's, but it was soft beneath my fingers. The sensation was grounding. "Shh. The evening meal is over. Go on back to sleep."

He was quiet for a moment. I leaned back, withdrawing my hand, but he grabbed at it. "Don't go."

"What's wrong, little rabbit?"

"Why do I have to go out with the hunters?" he asked.

"That's just how it is," I told him. "We each have certain responsibilities, to band and family. Yours is to be a hunter. Mine is to be headwoman's first daughter."

"I don't want to go with them. I don't like them."

I squeezed his hand. "What do you mean, you don't like them? You like your father. And what about Bakar? I saw you playing with him just yesterday. And," my throat caught, but I went on, "what about your brother, Kerbasi?"

Gotzon wrinkled his nose. "They're mean. Well—not everyone. But when they're all together, they're awful. They say horrible things, and sometimes they fight. I don't like it."

I sat next to him, holding his hand. I didn't know what to say.

"Why do I have to go with them?" he asked again. "Couldn't I just stay with the gatherers instead? Why do I have to be a hunter?"

A bubble rose within my chest. "I remember asking Abene almost the same thing when I was your age," I said. "I asked, 'Why do I have to be first daughter? Why can't I travel?' " It was still as clear as yesterday; Abene's words echoed in my mind's ear. *The world is how it is, girl. Don't kick against the snare.*

Was it only this afternoon I'd set that rabbit free from the snare? If the *tsairi*'s piece of hardened clay was supposed to bring good luck, it had surely failed.

But I couldn't tell Gotzon that. Instead, I said, "The world is how it is, I told you. We have to go along with it."

"Did Abene tell you that?" he asked.

"She did. And I grew to see she was right."

"You didn't want to be first daughter?"

The bubble in my chest erupted in an unexpected sound, half-laugh, half-sigh. "I didn't," I said. "I wanted to spend all my time in the woods... and I wanted to see what lay beyond the mountains. But it was foolish of me, rabbit. I'm not a hunter. I can't travel."

"You could be a shaman," suggested Gotzon. He couldn't say it straight-faced, though; he began to giggle.

"I'm a girl, silly!" I told him, ruffling his hair. "No, I have to stay here, with the gatherers. Take a mate," I swallowed the lump in my throat, "and be first daughter to Abene, then headwoman after her. Just like you have to go out with the hunters."

Abene's long-ago words were still rolling through my mind. *What would you do instead? Roam the forests like a deer?* I ignored them and told Gotzon, "Someday you will be a hunter, and you can travel for me."

"Hmm," he said, snuggling down in his furs. "I don't want to travel. I wouldn't mind being first daughter instead. I wish we could trade."

I kissed his forehead. "Well, we can't. We don't get to choose. Now go to sleep."

"Goodnight, Nahia," he said, closing his eyes.

The entrance flap fell shut between us, and I stood up. Esti's tent, the tall trees, even the flickering light from the direction of the central fire—they were all pale. I looked up into the sky. Dark branches crossed overhead; I could see stars and the moon between them.

There was a pressure behind my eyes, a pressure that warned of tears. *Why should I cry? I accepted I was first daughter long ago. I'm doing the best I can.*

Even speaking out against Abene for the good of the band.

She would be honor-bound to discipline me for arguing with her in front of the others. I would be in for an unpleasant few days, or even weeks.

Well, it won't be the first time. And I did the right thing. A good first daughter should *speak, when things are wrong.*

Still, the tears pushed at my eyes. It was dark, and there was no one to see me, so I gave up trying to stop them.

Izara was in bed when I reached Abene's tent. She was a motionless shadow on the mat of rushes we shared—tense, and so still I knew she wasn't sleeping. I crawled in next to her, tucking the furs around me carefully.

I'd only been lying there a moment when her anger pierced the silence.

"What got into you?" Her voice was harsh as our mother's had been.

I struggled to find words. "You know we have to move, Zari. But no one speaks out, no one says anything. I had to."

"Right. You *had* to act like a child and make a scene—in front of a visitor!—because it was the *right thing to do*."

"What do you mean? It was. He said there are raiders!"

"He was telling a *story*, Nahia. A story, nothing more. And you believed it. You got all worked up, and you shamed Abene. You shamed all of us! Don't you ever think of anyone but yourself? Do you want attention that badly?"

"No! Zari, I never even thought of such a thing! It's because I'm worried about the band that I had to speak!"

"If you were really worried about the band, you would hold your tongue. I've told you a thousand times. I told you today, even! When you embarrass Abene, you shame our line, and you guarantee she will close her ears. Think about it! Are you trying to make her look weak to the hunters? How much harder is it going to be for her to manage them, with you behaving like that? Do you *want* a fracture?" She rolled away, toward the fringe of the mat.

I propped myself up on my elbow, indignation rising in me. "It's because I *don't* want a fracture that I acted! Zari, I heard Oroitz and Kerbasi when I was gathering firewood—they're keeping something from us—"

Izara interrupted me. "Do you really think they have business that Abene doesn't know about? Oroitz is her brother. Our *uncle*. Honestly . . . it's like you don't care about me at all. I was hoping to get Zigor's attention—you knew that. You'll be the next headwoman, so you don't have to worry about anything. Maybe you don't care, but *I* am ready to be mated. *I* want to be counted among the band's women." And then she added, bitterly, "I don't have anything else to look forward to."

"I'd give it to you if I could, Zari—"

"Be quiet, Nahia. I'm going to sleep."

I lay on my back, staring into the blackness above me. My cheeks smarted, as if Izara had slapped me.

How could she think I was angling for attention? Why was it so hard for her to see the danger we were in?

She was right that I had likely failed, though. Only Zigor and Eneko had shown any sign of hearing what I was trying to say.

I had never known how to speak what was in my heart—not to Izara, not to Abene, not to the band. Everything I said came out wrong. I was trying so hard to be good: to keep Abene happy and look after the Sea People, both. And I was a catastrophe.

Maybe, like Izara said, I was only making things worse.

I rolled to my side, tears leaking from my eyes again. It was cold, and I felt so alone. I wished I could snuggle up to my sister as we used to when we were small, could bridge this distance between us. But I couldn't.

I lay still, willing myself not to sob aloud, while Izara's body stayed rigid at the far edge of the sleeping mat. She was as far away as my childhood dream of seeing the world beyond the mountains.

In the morning, the tent was silent, the atmosphere thick and charged.

Izara stoked the fire and placed the cooking rocks within it, not speaking. I filled the cooking basket with water and herbs for an infusion, also without speaking. We ate our rootcakes silently. When we finally joined the rest of the gatherers by the central fire, everyone else was quiet, too—quieter than normal, it felt like.

When Abene finally spoke, it made me jump.

"Alaia," she announced, "you will lead the gatherers in my place this morning. My sister and I have matters to attend to in camp. The shellfish need rest, but land snails are plentiful."

Alaia flushed, but I could see pleasure on her reddening face. I snuck a look at Esti—who, as the eldest of the gatherers, should have led the group—but she just smiled, apparently unperturbed. Perhaps Abene meant to reinforce Alaia's position as a woman... a position neither Izara nor I had attained.

It was a long, quiet morning's foraging. The rain had returned while we slept, and it was windy, wet, and miserable. We spread out along the rocky shore, looking for snails. There were some, but they were hardly plentiful. There wasn't much else to gather, either. I felt only a weak thrum of life here. I wished I were in the deep forest.

If Abene knew the shellfish needed rest, why were we still here? *Why?* This question I could not ask hounded me, as it did every day.

We returned to camp at midday, when the sun was high, or would have been if it were sunny. Abene, Udane, Oroitz and Eneko were sitting around the central fire, deep in conversation, their heads bent together. Zigor had departed long since, presumably. The elders and the shaman looked up as we entered the camp. Abene and Oroitz appeared smug, Udane, angry. Only Eneko seemed placid and undisturbed.

Abene sent Izara and me to clean out the tent, but as we were crossing the camp, Tora called to my sister.

"I'll take care of the tent," I told Izara. "You can go with her."

Izara's face brightened. "Truly? Thank you, Nahia," she said, giving me a brief hug before bounding off. My heart lightened at her touch, relief washing over me, though I wasn't really surprised at her change in mood. Izara's temper blazed up and down; it was as quick to cool as it was to flame.

Abene, on the other hand... Abene's anger lasted.

I had plenty of experience with that anger. Maybe it was my fault. I never seemed to understand what would make her angry. It had been that way for many years. I tried to please her, she came down hard on me, and Izara acted as peacemaker: that was our cycle.

It hadn't always been this way. When my grandmother Nene was headwoman, Abene had been more relaxed. She had been as strong and stern as she was now, yes, and as formidable when angry, but she had also laughed a lot.

Once, when Izara and I had been tiny, Kiria's age or younger, a hunter new to our band had come to the tent. He was from the far north and still unfamiliar with our language. He had asked Abene, very respectfully, if he could pleasure her with fresh deer meat at the central fire. She had collapsed to the ground, laughing so hard that she could not speak. The hunter had turned red, realizing his mistake and stammering an apology, but she had wiped the tears from her eyes, still gasping for air, and assured him that it was all right—although she'd started howling again as soon as he was out of sight. I had clamored to know what he'd said, what he'd meant, and she'd pulled me into her lap to explain.

She became much more serious when Nene died. She'd become harder on me, then, too. But she had still laughed. It was only after Aitor died that she stopped. Aitor and Abene had mated when Izara and I were in our eighth year—Abene had met him at a summer meeting, and he'd come home with us. He was a cheerful man, tall and round and always willing to play games. Izara and I had adored him. So had Abene.

But he died in a hunting accident, gored by a boar, and after that, Abene became ill. A week she lay in the tent—unmoving, not even speaking. Udane came every day. She brought herbal infusions, and then stronger medicines, but nothing helped.

Finally, Udane brought Anai, who was shaman to our band then. Ancient Anai had terrified me. He was old, older than anyone I had ever met, and had a piecing stare like an eagle's. Every time he looked at me, I felt like prey, like a tiny mouse desperately racing to escape a raptor's claws. I lurked outside the tent the whole time he was there, trying to stay out of his sight but desperate to know if my mother would recover. Anai gave Abene more medicines. When they didn't work, he chanted for her, but still she did not get up.

Late one night, I was awoken by loud moans from Abene's bed. "Is she grieving?" I asked Izara.

Izara had been asleep. It took her a moment to respond. "No, it's the baby," she said, sitting up.

"The *what*?" I asked.

"Don't you know? Oh, never mind. Go get Udane, then get the fire started." She was already at Abene's side.

Udane came. I built a fire just outside, piling the wood high so it would burn bright. Abene's moans grew louder and louder. After a time, Udane sent me to fetch Anai.

When I got back to the tent, I stood frozen by the flames. Izara was calm, hurrying between tent and hearth, carrying water, bringing infusions. I knew I should be helping, should be doing *something*, but I could only stand unmoving. It was like a dream, a bad one. How could Abene—my strong, stubborn mother—be making those awful sounds?

I did manage one journey into the tent, but after that, I stayed outside. Abene's pain crawled inside me, overwhelmed me as though it was my own. Udane had touched my shoulder sympathetically. "Your mother will be all right, little one. Babies do this to us, but she is strong."

This is normal? I remember thinking. *How can this be normal?*

As it turned out, it wasn't quite normal. Our little sister was born dead, the cord wrapped around her neck, her face a sickening blue-gray color.

Anai chanted a prayer, then held the small, stiff blue figure out to Abene. Abene turned away from him, staring at the tent wall.

"But you must," Anai said. "You must. The spirits of forest and sea demand it. They will be angry—will wreak havoc on us all if you do not do your duty!"

"Pah," Abene said, her voice weak. "What do the spirits care for us?"

Udane said to her, "Hush." She turned to Anai. "I am her sister born. I will do it." She took the baby's body from him. Anai shook his head and stalked out of the tent.

And so it was Udane who prepared our sister for burial, who made the offerings that would carry her to the world beyond. Abene laid in the tent.

Things didn't get better for a long while.

Abene sat, staring, day after day. Izara and I took turns making infusions with strengthening herbs, bringing her food, but she ignored us. The way she looked right through me gave me chills. In desperation, I even went to Anai to ask for help, but he turned away and would not acknowledge my presence.

Izara was concerned about the hunters. "They are fighting amongst themselves," she told me one night. "This is very bad. They don't have Abene to guide them,"

I thought she was coldhearted. "How can you care about the *hunters*?" I snapped. "Abene is sick, so sick, and she's not getting better. Udane can take care of the band."

"Nahia, don't you understand?" Izara's usually lively face was solemn. "When hunters are restless, when they begin to squabble... that's when bands fracture."

Izara and I were young, but not so young we didn't know about fracture. Abene had drilled it into us: preventing fracture was the greatest responsibility of the headwoman's line. When bands fractured, their members were scattered, forced to beg admittance to neighboring bands. It wasn't as bad for the hunters, but women lost all their status. Especially the headwoman and her family.

And now Abene was too ill to bring the hunters into line. New fears crashed over me in an unexpected wave. There was so much to worry about—how could I take care of all of these problems?

"Can we stop it?" I asked Izara. "What can we do?"

Izara tilted her head to one side. "Udane is trying to control them. Maybe she can." She sounded doubtful.

But then our uncle, Oroitz, returned to us from the north. How he knew to come, he never said, but come he did, and he brought his mate, Esti, and Esti's son Kerbasi, too. He took charge of the hunters, sending the worst troublemakers away and settling the lingering arguments. Anai left, disappearing in the middle of the night as though he'd never been with us.

And, after a time, Abene had come back. She was, essentially, her same old self, but she was also different: a little thinner, a lot harder on me, and humorless. Sometimes she unbent with Izara, or with Udane, but never with me. At most, I'd see a glint in her eye or a twitch of her lip that told me she found something funny, but that was the closest I ever saw her come to laughing again.

The world changed for me, too. The Sea People, who had been in my mind indestructible, suddenly seemed fragile. I realized it took work, every day, to hold them together. And as strong as Abene seemed after she recovered, I no longer fully trusted her not to disappear again.

Izara was sitting with Tora and Kiria when I arrived at evening meal. I made to join them, but Udane beckoned me to sit with her. As I did, she patted my knee, a tender gesture utterly unlike her usual brusqueness.

Uneasiness crept over me.

I looked at Udane, really looked at her. Her brow was creased and her body tense.

My uneasiness grew.

What had the elders been discussing, earlier today, while the rest of us had been out gathering? Was it *me*? The way Udane looked at me—and the way Abene didn't—suggested my true punishment was more serious than I was expecting. Maybe I was to be silence-bound, forbidden from speech for a day or even a week. I'd been silence-bound before. It hadn't been announced at the central fire—Abene had simply sentenced me at the tent—but when Kerbasi was silence-bound last summer, she had announced it at evening meal. So maybe that was it.

I'll bear it, whatever it is, I told myself. *I'll do anything—anything she wants. Then I can try to speak reason to her again.*

Eneko cleared his throat. The cheerful mealtime chatter died instantly.

He looked over the group, his face impassive as always. He met my eyes, and I quickly looked away. Whatever this was, it couldn't have anything to do with me. A shaman would not announce a silence-binding.

"I am glad to announce my new apprentice," he said, very calmly. "Nahia."

The words echoed through my head.

Apprentice . . .

Nahia.

Apprentice . . .

Nahia.

I was looking at the ground, but I didn't see it. My vision had gone hazy, grayness creeping across it in strange wispy tendrils. I was dimly aware that there was noise around me—maybe Eneko said something more—but I couldn't make sense of it, didn't even fully hear it. My ears were full of the sound of rushing waves.

I'm not a shaman's apprentice. I can't be a shaman's apprentice. I have a band, a family. I'm headwoman's daughter. Headwoman's first *daughter.*

At least I was *headwoman's first daughter. Am I still?*

Is this *Abene's punishment!?*

I raised my head, looking wildly about. Abene was watching me, her face hard and angry. The message was clear: *If you will not obey me, you will learn obedience elsewhere.*

I swallowed.

Udane reached out and laid her left hand over mine. She didn't meet my eyes.

Eneko held a pendant, a drilled boar's tooth on a strip of leather, identical to the one he wore around his neck. He walked around the fire, sunwise, until he reached me.

Udane drew her hand away. I didn't move. I felt like a tree.

Eneko leaned over me, tying the cord around my neck. I felt the light touch of his hand on my head for a brief instant before he returned to his place by the fire.

"And now," said Abene. The band's rustling quieted. "And now, let us sing the blessing song in honor of our new shaman's apprentice. First daughter Izara, you lead the song."

The band's attention withdrew from me and descended on Izara. She began to sing in a strong tuneless voice.

Izara was first daughter now?

I looked at my sister, the firelight flickering across her face, her mouth open in song. Her expression was solemn, but I thought I could see pleasure in her eyes.

Had she known?

A brief flash of anger, mixed equal parts with hurt, sparked deep inside me, but it disappeared as quickly as it came. Izara couldn't have known. She would have told me. Wouldn't she?

She *had* always wanted to be first daughter.

When the song was over, the conversation started. Gotzon snuggled up next to me, his pale head in my lap, and I stroked his hair dully. Alaia asked again, timidly, about Zigor's strangers, and if we shouldn't move now. Oroitz mocked her; Abene said there had always been strangers, and these would prove to be no different than the ones who came earlier. No one raised any further concerns.

I was too numb to even care.

After a time, I extricated myself from the sleeping Gotzon and slipped into the trees around the clearing. No one took any notice of my leaving.

I went to the sea. It was only a short walk from camp, maybe fifteen minutes, though it took longer in the dark. There was barely enough light for me to make my way across the Cove of Rocks without tripping.

At the center of the beach, I stood and looked out across the rippling sea, its surface lightly pocked by raindrops. The wind was cold. It felt good.

I had never heard of a shaman's apprentice. I'd never thought about how someone became a shaman. I didn't want to think about it now. And I certainly didn't want to spend time with Eneko.

He was deeply strange, as all shamans were. He had appeared out of nowhere; the elders had welcomed him readily, as our previous shaman had left us a few months before. Izara—who always seemed to find out everything about everyone—told me that even though Eneko was so young, he was already well-known for his healing skills.

Everyone was surprised that he had stayed with us so long, nearly a year. Shamans weren't part of the bands they stayed with; usually, they remained only for a season. Eneko would leave, sooner or later, maybe taking up with another band, maybe going off on his own, disappearing into the woods as if he'd never lived with the Sea People. That's how shamans were. Separate. Bandless. Without ties to human beings.

They were the way they were because they spent so much time in the spirit world. If I were to be a shaman's apprentice—even if it were just for a time, until Abene cooled off and set things right—would I, too, spend time in the spirit world? Would it make me as cold, as distant as he was?

I'm not a shaman. I'm not strange, I'm not bandless, I'm not half-human. I'm first daughter. And I'm a girl.

No women were shamans; at least, I had never met one, had never even heard of one outside of stories. If Benare, the woman shaman from the legends, had existed, it was a long time ago.

This is a punishment, no more.

With that thought, my racing heart began to settle. It *was* just a punishment. It would fade in a fortnight and be withdrawn. No one could ever mistake me for a shaman. I *couldn't* be one. Still, this was a brilliant stroke by Abene—if I wasn't first daughter, I would have no voice at the fire at all. And I'd been worried about being silence-bound!

I'd thought Abene angry. But she must have been beyond angry, beyond furious even, to do this to me.

It is a reprimand, no more. I can bear it.

It is temporary, like all punishments.

Temporary.

I watched the water. There must have been a storm out on the sea, for the waves were rougher than usual. After a time, I noticed my face was wet, raindrops and tears running together across my cheeks.

I stood there, gazing at the surf, until I was shivering too hard to stand.

⁂

Camp was quiet, the central fire extinguished, when I returned.

My footsteps slowed as I walked toward Abene's tent. The rain had ended, and our family's little fire was burning brightly. Izara and Abene sat next to it, not talking, drinking from wooden cups. A gathering basket—mine; I recognized the fraying edge, the extra-long leather straps—was beside them, overflowing with what looked like furs.

I stood, awkwardly shifting my weight from foot to foot. Izara looked up, her eyes meeting mine. Hers were big, and she was not smiling.

Abene rose and faced me. She was stern and cold, as unmovable as stone. She bowed, as if I were a visitor like Zigor, and then lifted my basket and pushed it into my arms. I took it, staggering under the sudden weight.

"Blessings and fortune go with you, Nahia." Her voice was crisp and formal. "Here are your things, to take to your new home with the shaman."

I took an involuntary step backward. It was as if she'd struck me. The hearth, the tent, the trees all whirled around me, and I thought I would fall.

And then the world steadied, and I knew where I was: standing before Abene, holding my basket, being cast out of my home.

"I—I have to live with him?" My voice was hoarse and scratchy.

Abene said, "You are his apprentice." She returned to the fire and sat, her back to me.

Izara was watching me. She shook her head—sadly, I thought—and then she looked away, back to the fire and our mother.

I stood rooted to the spot for some time. Abene was taking no chances. If I were living at home, it might have happened that my so-called apprenticeship would quietly disappear after the initial humiliation. The band would forget. Maybe even Abene would forget, when some time had passed.

If I were living at Eneko's, no one would forget. No one would mistakenly go to me as first daughter. I would seem like an outsider. My disgrace would last until Abene took steps to reverse it.

What if I *didn't* go to Eneko's?

Different scenarios ran through my mind. I could scream I wouldn't do it, as a child would. But I was old enough to be mated. And I knew Abene. Any rebellion from me would only make her more determined.

I could stay with Udane, maybe, or with Alaia and Bakar. But they would not want to go against Abene. No one would. And even if someone dared to take me in, I would still be disobeying my mother. Any chance of reconciliation would burn away in the face of her displeasure.

If I obeyed . . . if I went along with this farce . . . then Abene would see that I was a good daughter, and she would relent. Maybe she would even consider what I had been trying to say.

But stay with Eneko? With a *shaman*? With a *man*?

It's too wet, and too cold, to sleep outside. And if I don't go to him, that's my only other choice.

The leaves overhead rustled, shedding raindrops. The fire hissed and spat. Neither Abene nor Izara looked up from the blaze.

Eventually, I lifted my basket onto my shoulder, and I crossed the camp to Eneko's tent.

I didn't know what else to do.

FOUR

Eneko's tent sat at the very edge of winter camp, by the little-used trail leading to the northwest. It was more in the forest than part of the scatter of tents around the central fire. Our previous shaman had insisted on setting his tent in the middle of camp, where he could see everything—and everyone could see him. Not Eneko. His tent was so far from the others that you couldn't really see it from anywhere else in camp.

It was a long walk from Abene's tent to Eneko's. The distance gave me too much time to think. With every step, I worried more, until my numbness was almost fully overtaken by panic. I tried to calm myself, but the back of my throat burned and my heart beat faster and faster. What was I doing? Eneko spoke to *spirits*. I was only an ordinary gatherer, just a girl of the Sea People. I had no protection against the spirit world, no power to stand against the forces he dealt with every day.

Why did he even agree to this?

And then, another thought, accompanied by a sinking feeling that intensified my already-acute panic: *Does he even know I'm coming? Maybe he expected me to stay with my mother. What if he tells me to leave? Where will I sleep then?*

The shaman's fire was still burning, and Eneko sat beside it, his hands folded in his lap, his eyes closed. He didn't stir as I approached. I stopped at the very edge of the circle of light.

The flames crackled. I waited, forcing myself to be still, to keep from fidgeting.

He opened his eyes. When he saw me standing at the edge of his clearing, he jumped. Laughter nearly bubbled up inside me—a shaman, startled!—but I hastily choked it back.

A long, awkward silence followed.

He stared at me, his expression blank. I stared back, conscious of the load on my back, my dripping hair, my reddened eyes.

Say something, Nahia! If you say the right thing, maybe he won't turn you out.

But what can I say? "Abene has sent me to stay with you"? I can't say that.

Eneko's eyes came to rest on the basket strapped to my back. His face went still and hard. Then the moment passed, and his expression settled back to its usual state of distant-but-friendly.

"Welcome," he said, and stood. He bowed, then lifted the tent flap and gestured me inside.

Relief washed over me. I wouldn't have to explain. I didn't have to say anything at all. I wouldn't have to sleep in the weather, either. Eneko might have been surprised to see me, but he understood.

So my new life began.

Eneko made space for me on the north side of his tent. He even brought out a deerskin and helped me to set up a screen for privacy—something

I'd never had before. And in the morning sunshine, he split his stores with me: smoked fish and rootcakes, more of each than I'd ever had at Abene's.

I'd been worried about getting mixed up with spirits and magic. But the first task Eneko set me was easy and unthreatening.

After we ate, he brought out a large number of leather bags and began teaching me the names and properties of his medicinal plants. I knew many of them already—every tent had basic medicines on hand, and I'd always liked the challenge of the rarer and harder-to-find plants—but Eneko knew many more uses than I did, and there were some plants in his collection that were completely unfamiliar to me.

That first morning passed pleasantly enough. It was a little uncomfortable; before yesterday, I'd exchanged no more than a handful of words with him, and now I was living in his tent. But he was carefully formal with me, which helped. He didn't seem to expect me to talk. He just explained the plants and their uses to me, simply and one by one.

We worked our way through all the bags before the sun was halfway up the sky. I found myself thinking that perhaps this punishment wouldn't be as bad as I had feared. If all Eneko expected of me was to learn about his plants, I could do that. Maybe he thought that I would gather for him. Clearly, he needed a large supply on hand.

But when he finally put everything away, he gave me an altogether different task.

"I would like you to go to the Cove of Rocks," he said. "You should stand at the edge of the water and look out at the horizon. For as long as you can."

I stared at him, uncomprehending.

Stand on the beach and watch the horizon? That sounded innocuous enough. But why? Surely, if he didn't need my help at the tent, and he didn't yet trust me to find the plants he needed on my own, it would make more sense for me to go foraging with the women?

I didn't know Eneko well enough to ask. I didn't know him at all. I had never spent so long in his presence before.

Abene's voice echoed through my head, reminding me of the rules I was raised with: *Don't ask questions. Don't be disrespectful. Do as you're told.*

Eneko nodded at me and disappeared into the tent.

I did as he asked. I rose, followed the twisty path down to the cove, and stood on the pebbly beach, right at the edge of the water. It was still gray and chilly. I wrapped my arms tightly about myself and looked out across the waves.

What am I doing *here?*

I answered myself: *I'm taking my punishment without complaint, as I swore I would.*

My attention had wandered. I turned it back, gazing fiercely at the horizon. The sea was quiet today, the waves just small swells, one after another after another.

I felt stupid. I didn't know what I should be seeing or doing.

After some time, I heard singing, and a shout of laughter. I looked back across the beach, to the other end of the Cove of Rocks, and saw Abene's tall, upright figure picking its way around the boulders. Behind her came the rest of the gatherers.

I'm not doing anything here; this is a waste of time. Should I join them? Get something worthwhile out of the afternoon?

Gotzon caught sight of me. "Nahia!" he shouted. I smiled and held my arms out, expecting him to run to me as he always did.

But before he could move, Alaia grabbed his shoulders. "Shh, Gotzon!" she hissed. "You know better than that!"

Abene turned her back to me. I heard her say, "Turn away."

She retraced her steps, picking her way across the rocks into the south cove. There was a steep and therefore usually ignored path to camp there—one that wouldn't require her to pass by me.

The gatherers followed her. No one—not Izara, not Gotzon—looked back to where the waves reached the shore, to where I stood, alone, watching them go.

That encounter was a harbinger of what was to come. No one but Eneko spoke to me, not on that first day, nor the next, nor at any time in the weeks that followed.

I tried to keep my head high. *Soon this will be over, and I will go back to my real life. Abene will see that I'm obedient, that I'm a good daughter, and she'll forgive me—better, she'll finally consider what I said. And then we'll move upcountry, away from danger, where there is more food.*

But the days passed and nothing changed.

My hope began to fade. And I began to wonder: If I was no longer first daughter, then who was I?

I couldn't be a shaman. Women were gatherers, not shamans. And even if that weren't a problem, I was a failure at almost everything Eneko tried to teach me.

At first, when I'd thought my apprenticeship was only learning about plants and standing on the beach, it wasn't so bad. Every morning, he taught me plantlore. And every afternoon, he sent me to the beach to watch the waves. I had no more uncomfortable interactions with the rest of the band; it was just me and the sea, alone together. Standing in the cove was often boring, but it was peaceful. And every evening, I listened to him perform the ceremonies for protection. These consisted of a long series of songs, to be sung in a specific order, each night and each dawn. I'd never known shamans did this, but I gathered from Eneko this was actually their primary responsibility when with a band.

Maybe he communicated with the spirits while chanting the songs; I didn't know. He was always so absorbed in them, and his expression became unguarded, animated, totally unlike his usual self. His voice was strong, compelling, even breathtaking. I couldn't keep my eyes from him when he sang—in truth, I stared. The wind rifled his dark hair, as if his songs were so alluring that it, too, couldn't stay away.

But then Eneko told me I must sing as well. And immediately the chants went from occasions of awe and wonder to occasions of horrifying embarrassment.

My own voice was thin and weak, and I fumbled both words and melody every time I tried to join him. Eneko seemed unperturbed. When I made a mistake, he stopped and gestured at me to begin again. And so I would sing along uncertainly until the next mistake; and again, and again.

It was mortifying.

But the ceremonies weren't the worst part. Once I learned why Eneko sent me to the beach, the afternoons, too, became torment.

I learned the truth one evening after he took me through the protection chant. We were sitting by the fire, and I was waiting to be dismissed so I could go to sleep. But instead, he said, "Nahia, this world is not the only one. There are more worlds than there are stars in the sky."

I started with the unexpectedness of it, then squinted across the flames at him. His voice was offhand, but I could see him looking at me intently.

"I do not mean," he said, "those worlds are physically in another place, though they may be. There are other worlds everywhere—in the mountains, in the forest, in the sea. In the past. In the future. They are here in this camp, even on the tip of a finger. But one must learn to see them, else one will never know them. Most people know only the world before their eyes, no more."

He gazed at me expectantly.

I didn't understand whatever it was he was trying to tell me. I felt dense and slow. I tried a question. "If we learn to see these other worlds, can we visit them?" I asked. "Or... do we only know they are there?"

Eneko was silent, considering me carefully. My face burned, and I writhed inside.

I am worthless. I'm failing at this. I fail at everything.

He didn't answer my question. Instead, he cleared his throat and said, "Look for those other worlds when you are at the sea. See what you can see. This practice will help you find them."

I swallowed nervously as I realized the afternoons watching the horizon did, in fact, have a purpose—a purpose which I had not remotely satisfied. How was I supposed to do what he wanted? I stared at him, frustrated.

He must have sensed my feelings. He leaned forward and said, "Look for the worlds the same way you saw the sea-traveling boats at the central fire."

Sea-traveling boats?

I had said something about sea-traveling boats the night I'd challenged Abene, I remembered, but... it had been nothing. Just something that tumbled out in the rush of words. Just an image in my head gleaned from fireside stories. Was *that* why they'd made me shaman's apprentice? Because they thought I had visions?

My heart sank. *Does* Eneko *think I have visions?*

"But," I said aloud, and stopped. *I don't have visions, Eneko,* I wanted to say, but the sentence stuck in my throat. If he realized how hopeless I was and threw me out, where would I go?

Eneko inclined his head, his face calm and unreadable, and briefly gripped my shoulder.

The afternoons on the beach had been boring before that conversation. After, they were agonizing. I never had a vision, never saw another world. I tried hard to see something that would earn my place, but all I ever saw were the waves and my own thoughts and memories. I didn't understand how I was supposed to see anything more.

My frustration was beyond trying and failing. I found I wanted to please Eneko, who was kind to me, who had welcomed me, who did his best to make me feel at home. I wanted to find a place for myself in this new life that seemed to be mine.

But I *didn't* want to see spirits. The idea filled me with a creeping horror. I couldn't have explained it to anyone; I didn't understand it myself. Their power had always frightened me. They could be benevolent, and we relied on them, but their unseen forces could cause life or death on a whim. Or, worse perhaps, they might draw a person away from the mundane world, ensnaring her so tightly she could not escape, using her as a tool to enact their caprice. And those were just the stories I knew. Who knew what else the spirits could do?

Every day I approached the beach with apprehension, fearful that I would see something—and equally fearful that I wouldn't.

Eneko had me try other ways of visioning, too. Some evenings he asked me to gaze into a bowl of water, others a flame; once, he even gave me a crystal to look at. But these worked even less well than staring at the waves. All that ever happened was my nose, or my toes, or my elbow would begin to itch—a little at first, then intensely. Soon I would fidget, and Eneko would take the scry away.

As the days passed, I expected him to lose patience with me, to say this was a mistake and I'd better go back to Abene (*and what would Abene say then?*) but he never did.

I did, eventually, work up the courage to speak honestly. After he tried me on the crystal—again unsuccessfully—I took a deep breath and said, "I hate to disappoint you, again and again. Since I can never be a shaman, can't I just focus on the plants? I'm good at that, and I can start gathering for you."

Eneko smiled at me, lightening his features. "Why do you say that you cannot be a shaman?"

I stared at him. "I am a woman. Women are gatherers."

"I am a man, and I am not one of the hunters."

I let out my breath impatiently. "But there *are* men who are shamans. There are no such women, not outside of stories."

He shook his head, still smiling. "How do you know?"

"Are you saying they exist?" I asked, shocked. "Where?"

He was laughing now, lightly. My cheeks went hot.

And then he stopped, and met my eyes, his face serious again. "I know the feeling of *I cannot be a seer*. Do not pay it too much heed." He gestured at me to build up the fire. "Now we will try again."

I swallowed my frustration. But the feelings of failure stayed with me.

Early one morning, after yet another discouraging session of chanting, I set out for the woods. Eneko had sent me to replenish the herbs we'd used in this morning's protection ceremony.

I passed through camp, something I had not done for several weeks. There was a crowd near Esti's tent; I could hear Oroitz shouting angrily. One of the eager onlookers called, "*It's your own fault, Oroitz!*"

I craned my head, but I could only see the crowd, not the conflict. Should I stop? No—I couldn't face the sudden silence that would descend if I joined the throng. I continued on my way. Most of the hearthfires were dark and cold—they all must have rushed to Esti and Oroitz's immediately upon waking. Abene's fire was bright, though. Why weren't she and Izara intervening in the fight? Maintaining order was their responsibility.

Well, it wasn't my concern. Not anymore.

I plunged into the trees. My connection to the forest had shifted since I'd been with Eneko. Maybe it was living so close to the deep woods, on the furthest fringe of camp; maybe it was all the time I spent alone. When

I lived with Abene, escaping into the woods was an explosion of relief, like scratching an itch I'd had to ignore while people were watching. But now—now being in the forest was a slow, swelling joy, like being lifted by a wave while swimming. I was not escaping anymore: I was joining. It was as if I were not just *in* the forest, but part of it.

It was hard to explain, even to myself.

That morning the forest was misty and cool. I heard the trumpeting call of cranes as they flew overhead, moving toward the mountains. The early spring smells, sharp and green, surrounded me. I let my eyes roam across the path, looking for spiky tips that would indicate new growth. It would be good to have some onionweed or oyster thistles.

I don't know how long I'd been roaming the woods when I became aware I was uneasy. The feeling crept over me, slowly, until I could no longer ignore it. My skin shrank and crinkled, as if someone were watching me. I glanced around, but I saw nothing, heard nothing.

It was oddly quiet, though. *The birds have stopped singing. Why?*

I paused on the trail, listening.

A squirrel chattered angrily behind a stand of brush.

There must be something nearby. An injured animal, maybe? If it were a human being, the squirrel wouldn't dare to scold so—it would run away instead.

Carefully, quietly, I made my way toward the angry squirrel, investigating. As I approached, the squirrel quieted, and I heard a scuffling, as if something were scurrying around the brush to hide from me. I ran, abandoning my attempt to keep quiet.

I found Gotzon, on hands and knees, scrambling away from me.

I dropped to the ground beside him, wrapping my arms around him. "Gotzon! What are you doing here?"

He stiffened, resisting me. "I won't go out with the hunters. They're cruel, Nahia. They say terrible things about... about everyone. When I tell them not to talk that way, they say I'm soft and useless, that I'll never be a real man. I won't go with them anymore. I won't!"

"Oh, Gotzon," I said sadly. I rolled back so I sat cross-legged among the leaves. He wiped at his nose defiantly, looking up to glare at me. His eyes were red.

What could I say to him? I, who was in this nowhere land: disgraced ex-headwoman's daughter, inept shaman's apprentice, girl without a role or a place?

The birds had resumed their singing. Gotzon and I sat quietly, not looking at each other.

After a time, he sniffled. "You're not going to make me go back to them today, are you? You won't tell anyone where I am?"

"No," I said.

"Why not?"

I sighed. "They wouldn't listen to me, anyway." Then I smiled at him. "You know that. Even you don't talk to me anymore."

"They told me I couldn't!" he protested.

I tickled him. He squirmed away, fighting the smile that was erupting over his face. "I know, little rabbit."

"Nahia?" he asked.

"Hmm?"

"Do you like being a shaman?"

"I'm not a shaman," I said. "I'm not even an apprentice, not really. Abene only sent me to Eneko to shame me."

"Oh." He tilted his head up at me. "I thought maybe...you said you wanted to travel..."

"It's a punishment, no more. Girls aren't seers, you know that." I pushed away the sound of Eneko's voice saying, *How do you know?* "It's just how things are," I finished firmly.

"I hate the way things are," he said, snuggling against me.

I hugged him closer. "Me too," I admitted.

"Why can't we change them?"

I had no answer. I stroked his hair, and we sat, leaning up against each other, till the sun was high in the sky.

FIVE

I stood at the edge of the water and watched the sea. The sun reflected off the water, filling the sky with light. It was warm, the first hot day of the season, and the air shimmered. A dolphin's body arced out of the waves. Birds chattered lazily in the forest on the slope above the beach.

All this I noticed only with a hidden part of my mind; my attention was on the horizon.

The hunters had gone out in their canoes, exploring off to the north. With luck, they would bring back fresh fish. The gatherers were in the next cove. When they'd passed me, Gotzon had sneaked a surreptitious wave in my direction; he must have convinced the elders to let him stay with the gatherers, at least for now. The rest of the gatherers—and the hunters, too—had pointedly ignored me, as always.

I'd become used to it, but still it stung. I told myself I'd never liked being surrounded by people, that I was glad to be alone. This was true... but I was still lonely. Since the night Abene had sent me away, the only people who had spoken to me directly were Eneko and Gotzon.

Izara's silence hurt worst of all.

Like everyone else, my twin behaved as if I didn't exist. I saw her—boisterously laughing with the gatherers, whispering with Tora at dinner—but she didn't see me; if she chanced to look in my direction, her eyes went straight through me. I tried to think about it rationally: if Izara spoke to me, if she even reached out to me, she'd risk Abene's fury—and a punishment of her own. But as rational as I tried to be, my sister's abandonment was a constant ache.

Well, I'm not completely alone. I have Eneko. I have Gotzon, even if all we can do is exchange waves. And I have Udane, kind of.

Because Udane had made it clear: she wasn't pleased with my punishment. She never spoke to me, but unlike the rest of them she would meet my eyes; she even touched my hand once. And at night, at the central fire, she made barbed comments to Abene about "so-called apprentices," about flouting tradition, about the shortage of gatherers—even about Izara's ineptitude, which caused a mean gladness to come over me. I knew it wasn't true. Izara was better at being first daughter than I ever had been. She was never flustered; she was always at our mother's side, supporting her, enacting her wishes without ever seeming to hesitate. Izara displayed an effortless authority I had never managed. But when Udane complained, at least I knew I wasn't invisible.

My hope of returning to Abene's tent had entirely faded. If her anger had lasted this long, she wasn't going to forgive me anytime soon. (*But why?* I still wondered. Her reaction seemed even more extreme as time passed.) No, I was with Eneko long-term.

Only a few months ago, I would have been devastated by this. But now I found myself strangely ambivalent.

I wasn't unhappy living with him. I'd become used to the chants (though I still made mistakes more often than I got things right), and I liked herblore. The visioning was a stumbling block, true, but Eneko hadn't pushed me on it. I just . . . spent time on the beach.

I'd never really wanted to be first daughter, either, if I was honest with myself.

Izara had.

But for three things, I would have truly been content as Eneko's assistant. The first, of course, was losing Izara. The second was my future. I tried not to think about it too much, but if I wasn't a shaman, and I wasn't going to be headwoman, what was I? One day Eneko would leave—*he* was a shaman, even if I wasn't. And then . . . ? Would Abene take me back in? Would I drift between tents, a status-less ghost in my own band? Or would I be driven out, into the wild? These were the fears that woke me up in the middle of the night and would not let me sleep.

The third was Abene's continued refusal to move. In the bright light of day, I could suppress the nagging disquiet about my own future, but I was haunted with worry for the Sea People. I brooded over Zigor's warning of raiders drawing ever closer; over the growing atmosphere of tension among the hunters; over our continued presence in winter territory, even as summer drew near. It was the very end of shellfish season now. When the hot weather arrived, mussels and oysters wouldn't be safe food anymore. Even Abene wouldn't have us eating them through the season of shell-sickness, surely?

We had to leave. The land was depleted, both on the shore and in the woods. I was in the forest every morning, looking for the plants Eneko wanted, and it was spent. Greens and root plants were scarce, and I hadn't seen any game at all. Worse, there had been a cold snap, and the trees had lost what fruits they had set.

I stretched, coming back into the present. The sun was getting lower; soon the hunters would return, and I could leave the beach. I thought idly about boats. *What would I do if the strangers appeared* now, *in a sea-traveling boat?* Our boats were just canoes, made of hollowed-out logs. The hunters never ventured far from the coast; they fished along the shoreline. A boat had been swept away once, years ago, when the hunters within had tried to ply deeper waters. It happened before I was born, but it was a story sometimes told around the fire when young men went to the sea for the first time.

Being on a boat that could travel on the open ocean . . . what was it like? Was it like being a caterpillar on a tiny nut in a big river, completely controlled by the action of the water? The boat would be like a separate world, one encased by sea and sky. I could almost feel the glare on my face, sense the rocking of the waves . . .

Many worlds, Eneko had said.

There was a scraping noise followed by some shouting, and I jumped. The hunters had arrived and were pulling their boats ashore at the far end of the Cove of Rocks. I could identify most of them easily, even from this distance: Oroitz at the head of the group, short and broad; Alaia's mate, Bakar, so big that the rest of them looked like children beside him; Kerbasi and Omer, the one tall and angular, the other shorter and stronger.

No one saw me. They lowered the boats carefully. Then Bakar swung around toward Kerbasi. Kerbasi straightened up, looking the older man full in the face—insolently, I thought.

Bakar grabbed Kerbasi by the shoulder and shouted at him. "What do you think you were doing?" he boomed, and then something that sounded like "Oroitz"—and then, "... *bakai*!"

Oroitz had come to stand behind Bakar. He was favoring his left side, leaning like a tree dead at the roots. His arms were folded across his chest. Something in the way he stood made him look hesitant... nervous, even. I strained to hear him. "The headwoman and I have the matter in hand."

But Bakar bellowed at Kerbasi, "Your behavior is insupportable. Apologize to the head of the hunters!"

Kerbasi turned away. His words I heard clearly: "Things are different now, and you *hari* know it. What use is your *bakai?* With all that has happened, the *bakai* is dead. I won't be bound by your rules. Why should I?"

The bakai *is dead? What does he mean?*

The *bakai* was the code of order that the hunters followed, but it was hunters' knowledge; I didn't know anything more about it.

I thought of the conversation I'd overheard between Kerbasi and Oroitz the day Zigor had come to visit, and I was seized by a cold dread. Izara's voice echoed through my mind: "*When hunters are fighting... that's when bands fracture.*"

Bakar grabbed Kerbasi and turned him around. He spoke quietly this time, but the anger in his voice was evident.

And then Kerbasi struck Bakar in the face.

Chaos erupted.

The hunters rushed over to Bakar, holding him back. Omer grabbed at Kerbasi, trying to restrain him, but to no avail. The group of men became a jumble of arms and legs, of angry shouts and the sound of blows.

Oroitz stood to the side, hunched, shaking his head, watching. He looked old and frail.

I couldn't help it. I cried out.

The shouting ceased instantly. The hunters' heads all turned, looking up to where I stood.

Fear shot through me, swift and sharp as an arrow.

I ran.

I was shaking—at what I had seen, and at having been caught watching something I shouldn't have witnessed. Gatherers weren't allowed at hunters' meetings. And even if it hadn't been a meeting exactly, I still shouldn't have been there.

What would the hunters do to me for watching them, for seeing?

"Nahia?"

It was Izara's voice. I'd been so absorbed in my thoughts that I hadn't been looking where I was going. I saw that my feet had led me not to Eneko's tent, but to Abene's.

Izara stood in front, her mouth slightly open, staring at me in surprise. A recently filled water bag sat beside her. She looked over her shoulder quickly and then grabbed my hand, pulling me into the woods. When we were far enough away that it was unlikely we'd be overheard, she stopped, dropped my hand, and asked, "Are you all right? Has something happened?"

My throat was tight with emotion—fear and agitation from what I had seen, and then a totally incongruous joy, to be with Izara, to hear her speaking to me. I swallowed, hoping I would not cry.

Izara's frown deepened. "What happened, Nahi? Did—are you hurt?"

"No, no, not hurt. It's something else." I swallowed, trying to put my thoughts in order. How fortuitous was this? My feet had served me well. Abene needed to know that the hunters were fighting. I would tell Izara what I had seen, and she would tell Abene, and Abene would take action.

Izara was looking at me, her expression somewhere between concerned and wary.

"I was at the beach. Standing—you know—Eneko sends me there every afternoon? And then the hunters came home." I hesitated.

Izara had crossed her arms over her chest, definitely more wary now than concerned, but she was listening. I plowed on, telling her of the fight—everything. When I finished, silence fell sudden as a summer's night.

My sister's arms were still crossed. She nudged her toe into a pile of leaves, working her foot beneath them. "So they were fighting?" she said. "I'm sure it's nothing. Hunters fight sometimes. Like gatherers." She smiled, but her smile was un-Izara-like—brittle.

I stared at her. "This was serious, Zari! Out of control! And Oroitz couldn't stop it; it just went on—"

"Until they saw you," Izara finished. "And then they dropped it. So, clearly, it wasn't *that* serious. Listen, what is it that you said Oroitz said? *The headwoman and I have the matter in hand*, no?"

"Yes, but—"

Izara shook her head. "You need to trust Abene." She wouldn't meet my eyes. "I have to get back to the tent." She shook her hair out of her face, then looked at me. Her face was calm and serious, utterly unlike my sister's usual lightheartedness. "Take care, Nahi. You don't know everything that's been happening."

And she turned and left me in the woods.

I watched her go. I wanted to scream. How could she not see the danger? How could she—and Abene—just sit and *watch* as the Sea People fell apart?

What would lead my mother to ignore fights, to let the hunters run wild? What could make her so passive? So *uncaring*? Last time, when she'd retreated from life, she'd had reason; she'd lost Aitor and our little sister.

But this time?

I began walking, slowly, but not toward Eneko's tent—not yet. There was one other person who might listen, who might be able to untangle this knot.

"My brother said *what*?"

Udane's voice was quiet, but no one could miss the sharpness. Relief shot through me. If she was shaken, the end of this was in sight. Abene would listen to her, I was certain.

It had not been easy to approach my aunt. I knew she didn't approve of my punishment, but I had never known her to go against her sister. To my surprise, though, she hadn't seemed upset when I'd neared her tent. She'd beckoned, instead, and I spilled out the story of the hunters on the beach.

"So you will speak to Abene?" I pressed. "If we move inland, where there is more food, the men will be busy again. They won't feel hungry, and they won't argue."

Udane sighed heavily, looking to the side. "I will try," she finally replied.

I made a move to speak again, but she raised her hand. "My sister is the one with the land-sense, not I," she said. "There is only so far I can go, if she feels the coast calling her to stay. And as you know, she is very stubborn about protecting this territory." She looked closely at me, and she must have read disappointment on my face because she said, "I *will* try. You were right to come to me with this, headwoman's daughter."

Udane stroked my hair, and then she guided me out of her tent.

I stood there, staring at the ground, discomfited. Udane was going to talk to Abene; she said she would try to convince her; and, no matter what she said, I was sure Abene would listen to her.

So why did I feel so forlorn?

I slowly made my way back to Eneko's tent, going the long way around. I did not want to encounter anyone more.

He was sitting by the fire. He raised his hand in greeting, then gestured for me to join him. An assortment of tools and objects were laid on the ground. Three singing stones, the lines drawn across them bright; arrowheads; a basket woven of seagrass, a few dried-flower stalks poking out. I recognized *mixu*, which was used in the protection chant, but there was also a stalk of *itsar*, a plant we'd never worked with before.

I nodded and sat beside him. I wished I could go in the tent and lie down, think through things, but I sensed that he had something important to discuss.

After a time, he asked quietly, "Has something happened?"

I opened my mouth, then closed it again. He was looking at me sidelong, silently waiting.

"I saw the hunters fighting," I said, finally. "On the beach."

Silence.

He spoke quietly. "Did they see you?"

"Yes."

"Did they say anything?"

"No. No, as soon as they saw me, I knew I shouldn't be there. I ran."

"Ah," said Eneko, and then nothing more.

A thought that had been bothering me tumbled out, unbidden. "Eneko, if the protection chants are to keep the band safe, why aren't they working now? We do them every morning, every night. But everything keeps going wrong."

His mouth quirked up in a half-smile.

"Perhaps the songs are keeping things from becoming more wrong." But then his face was serious again, and he shook his head. "The songs have power, but they are only a few of the many forces acting on the Sea People at this time. It is like healing: our medicines can only heal so much. Sometimes, all they can do is keep the illness from getting worse. Right now, there is a great disturbance in our world. If the songs can ease the disturbance at all—even a little—they will be helping. And easing may only mean making things easier for a few people... or even one person."

As had become my habit, I reached into my leather pouch and wrapped my fingers around the *tsairi*'s gift, the piece of hardened clay. The broken edge was rough against my palm. I'd shown it to no one; I wanted to keep it private, somehow, and anyway, the only person I could have shared it with was Eneko.

I could show it to him. Suddenly, I wanted to show it to him.

Eneko knew the spirits. Maybe he would be able to explain it, read its meaning. Maybe it would even tell him why the world seemed to be falling apart around us. I had found it the day everything changed, after all. The day Zigor came to visit, bringing news of death. The day I dared to use my voice.

I pulled it from the pouch and held it out. The reddish-brown shard rested in the center of my palm. It caught the afternoon light, its surface shiny, the impressed decorations along its edge dark.

Eneko was quiet. He reached out a cautious fingertip and tapped its face. "Where did you come across this? And when?"

"When I was foraging, before I came to you. At Big Forest Hill." I swallowed. "I set a rabbit free from a snare—I don't know why, I just had to. And then I found this. I thought— " I stopped short.

Eneko looked from the fragment to me. His gaze was sharp and direct, completely unlike his usual mild teaching expression. I drew back, startled.

And then the moment passed. "I thank you for showing me." Carefully, he folded my fingers around the object, saying, "Keep it safe—and hidden." His hand closed firmly over mine.

I swallowed again. His hand was warm, hot even. My skin tingled beneath it, a sparking sensation that ran up my arm and through my body. I both did and didn't want to pull away. But I drew back and tucked the piece back into the pouch, busying myself so I didn't have to meet Eneko's eyes.

I needn't have worried. When I raised my head, he was looking beyond me, his expression distant. Our conversation was clearly over. I shifted uncomfortably. This was the worst thing about Eneko. He never dismissed me—he just stopped speaking.

But then he surprised me by speaking again. "You have learned about the protection chant." His voice was quiet and formal, as if the previous discussion had never happened. "But you have not yet learned any variations. There are different versions, with different strengths. We will practice some of them tonight." He didn't smile, but his voice warmed as he added, "It will take some time. Rest now, if you like. After dark we will begin."

I thought maybe I should say something more, but my mind was blank. My hand still remembered the heat and pressure of his, an alien sensation. I had never touched a man so before. After a moment, I scrambled awkwardly to my feet, nodding to Eneko as I entered the tent. I crawled around the deerskin screen into my corner and lay down.

I did not sleep.

SIX

Eneko woke me several hours before dawn to practice new variations to the morning protection songs. There were three sets of them: one to protect from human envy and malice in a general sense, one that called directly on the spirits of the forest, and one that drew on the land itself. We went through all three sets twice. The sun was well up in the sky by the time we had finished.

I should have been exhausted after rising so early, and I was—but I also felt clean, whole, new, sparkling with life. *Is it the songs? Or is it an illusion born of lack of sleep?*

Either way, I had things to do. We needed more *bioli*. Eneko said not to worry, that he would replenish our supply later in the day, but I wanted to find it myself, to prove I could. He acquiesced, advising me that this herb usually grew close to oak trees. I took only a pouch into the woods. It was large enough for cuttings.

I paused under the arching trees. My heart lifted, filled with something I couldn't name—a rush of relief, of intimacy, almost euphoria. The voice of the forest seemed ever clearer. I closed my eyes, breathing deep. The scent of spring, the vigorous pungent smell of growth well underway, was all around. My ears were full of sounds. Birdsong, squirrels chattering, crackling leaves.

I felt the web of living beings all around me, and I knew myself to be part of it.

I don't know how long I had been standing there when my joy was overtaken by nervousness. It began as an itch between my shoulder blades, a small prickle of unquiet. I tried to dismiss it, but soon it grew into full-blown anxiety.

My eyes flew open, but there was nothing unexpected before me. The sun was shining. But for the fact the woods had gone silent, everything seemed ordinary.

From behind me came the sharp echoing crack of a twig snapping beneath a heavy foot.

I spun around, my heart in my throat.

Kerbasi stood, arms folded. A ray of sunlight fell directly on him; his face was sharp and hard as a knife's edge. Inevitably, half a step behind him was Omer. They were empty-handed; their fishing spears leaned against a tree within easy reach.

I should have been relieved to see them. It was only Kerbasi and Omer. *They're our hunters. They're sworn to protect all of us.* But my apprehension did not dissipate; I was, if anything, more anxious.

"*Ahai*, Nahia," Kerbasi said, smiling.

I wondered how a smile could look so disagreeable. But after all, it was Kerbasi. He was always disagreeable. "*Ahai*," I mumbled, my heart beating so fast and loud I could barely hear myself.

Suddenly, it occurred to me to wonder: *What are they doing here?*

Something about the way the two of them stood there—something about the way Kerbasi said my name—was threatening. I thought of a day long ago, soon after Oroitz and his family had come to us. Izara and I had been about nine years old. We'd discovered a cache of the straightest, most beautiful sticks imaginable at the edge of camp. We fell upon them with delight, never stopping to think to whom those sticks might belong; we weren't old enough to understand they were unfinished arrow shafts. We were happily engaged in the construction of a tiny tent, using the sticks as poles, when Kerbasi interrupted us.

"So, Nahia, you want to be a warrior?" Kerbasi's voice had been soft, friendly. I'd looked up, confused. He towered over us, smiling, his eyes as sharp and shiny as volcanic glass. Omer, shorter and plainer, lurked behind him.

I was frightened, but I pushed it aside. "No," I said. "We're making a camp, see?" I waved at the miniature shelter we'd constructed.

"Ah," Kerbasi had said. And then he'd struck me across the cheek so hard that my world went black.

I'd cried out in shock and pain. Izara cradled me in her arms. "You bully!" she had shouted, but her voice wavered.

"Don't play with warriors' things if you can't fight." His voice was still quiet and friendly, as if nothing at all had happened. I heard Omer's high-pitched laugh as they walked away. We never told Abene.

The two of them were older now: men, not boys. They should have been beyond tormenting those smaller than they. But they weren't, I knew.

I nodded to Kerbasi and Omer as coolly and distantly as I could. "I have to go."

"Why?" asked Kerbasi. "You don't have to be so unfriendly. You're not first daughter anymore."

They stalked closer. My hands were shaking. Kerbasi's words, rude as they were, were harmless enough. But they made me feel weak and unprotected—vulnerable. My heart pounded even louder. I hoped they couldn't hear it.

I won't say anything more to them; I'll turn my back on them and go.

I moved away. But Omer was quick. He was behind me before I managed even to turn. His hands came around and grabbed my wrists, hard. I fought against him, tried to break away, but my strength was no match for his. He turned me around, pinned my hands behind my back. He smelled of the days when sickness comes from the sea and the shellfish are not safe to eat.

My hair had come loose from the leather tie I used to hold it back. It was tumbling down over my eyes. "What do you want?" I cried.

"We just want to help our shaman-to-be." His voice dripped sarcasm. Omer giggled. "You need *bizi* to be a shaman. And we all know there's only one way you can get it. Let's see if you can take mine."

I don't know how to take bizi, I almost said, but of course they knew that.

I wasn't a child; I knew what this was.

Fear shot through me, fear and humiliation and dread. I kicked at Omer, hoping against hope that he would let me go, but instead, he caught my leg with his own, pinning me into place.

Kerbasi angled his head down so he could look through my hair and into my face. His gaze was glittering like a snake's. "You don't need to pretend you don't want it. If you're nice, I bet Omer will let you have some of his *bizi*, too."

"You can't," I rasped. "The elders will—"

Kerbasi laughed. "The elders will what?" he asked. "Who cares about you?"

"I'll scream. Someone will hear." My voice was little more than a whisper.

"You're boring me," Kerbasi said.

Omer's free hand stole around my face, covered my mouth.

I couldn't have screamed anyway. I was frozen, my mind shouting, *No no no no no no no*. But I couldn't move at all.

Kerbasi smiled at me, slowly, his smile creeping over his face as if it had all the time in the world.

And I thought of Esti—Kerbasi's mother, my uncle's mate, the woman who had been stolen from the north.

Esti came from deep in the forest and far from the sea. She had been captured in a raid and taken south by her captors. Oroitz had traveled when he was young, moving from band to band as hunters often do. When he visited the band with which Esti was living, he had taken her as his mate. Esti had come with him when he returned to us, along with their daughter—as well as the son who had been born while she was still with the raiders who had taken her from her home.

Esti was tall and remote. She had exotic light hair and pale ice-eyes, a combination she said was more common among the people of the north, and a glamorous throaty accent. From the time she joined our band, Izara and I were fascinated by her. We loved the stories she told of her homeland; we followed her everywhere, even risking proximity to Kerbasi to be close to her. For years, we begged her to tell us how she came to join our band, not really understanding what "captured" might mean. It wasn't until we were twelve or so, and nearing young womanhood, that she finally told us her story.

"All right, girls, I tell you what you want to know," Esti had said, smoothing her hands over her lap and sighing. We'd been visiting her tent, sitting with her by the fire. Both Izara and I were surprised, I think; we'd long given up expecting her to respond to our demands.

"My people live far, far north of here, in the deep woods, far from any salt water. We call ourselves People of the Deep Forest. Sometimes, visitors would speak of the sea, and my own father had been there once, on a journey, but he was the only one of our people who had.

"Not so many people live there as here. There are fewer bands in the north, and they are farther away from each other than your people are. But our band itself, it was large. Too large. Our headwoman had six sisters; my mother was the third sister, and I am youngest of four daughters.

"I was in my fifteenth year when the raiders came. And I, I did not know anything of raiding. I never thought about anything beyond life, every day. That day-to-day life, in some ways, it is the same as here. Our worries are simple things. Where we will find mates for our girls. We girls, we are always wondering, will we need to leave the band when we are mated? Always, we worry, how to find enough food. And finding enough food, it gets harder and harder. There is less food, and more and more of us.

"We worry about food above all else. And my older sister and I, we go out gathering, as we do every day. We begin fighting over where we go next—she wants to go to the valley, I to the toplands. We are fighting, and we are not looking where we are going. And then we stop, I do not know why, we stop and look up. There are four strange men there."

Esti's eyes turned distant.

I had been suddenly queasy. I thought, *Do I really want to hear this story?* I looked at Izara, trying to signal at her, but Izara was staring at Esti and did not see me.

Esti smoothed a wrinkle in her leggings and resumed her story. "Well," she said. "They caught us, marched us to a small camp. There were three more of them there, all men. They had their way with us. And then they took us south. We walked for many days, until the days became months."

"Didn't you try to escape, go home?" asked Izara, very quietly.

Esti had smiled at her and touched her cheek. "No, little one. At the beginning, they watched us too close. My sister, she tried to run away one day. They caught her, and then they beat her hard. And then, later, we were too far away from home. We did not dare to leave then, for we would have to travel far, without knowing our way, through unknown forest full of bears and wolves and other men. No, we could not leave." She shook her head. "After months of walking, we arrived in a camp, the camp of the band from which these men came. And I stayed there until I found Oroitz, and came away with him."

"Oh, Esti," I said, my throat thick with horror. "How did you bear it?"

Esti looked at me, her face blank. I was ashamed, but I didn't know why. She said, slowly, "We bear what we have to bear. But I tell you: I learned fast. If you act like a—what is the word?—if you act frightened, if you show your fear, they will own you. You will be their slave. My sister, she could not see this, and she became slave for the band. They walked all over her. For me, I saw they stole us because they needed us. So, always, I act like I am someone. Someone important. Someone who belongs. Soon, they forgot how I came there. I made allies. And when Oroitz came, visiting with Zaxi's band—I tell him I want to be his mate." She smiled. "For me, it all came right."

It all came right? How could winding up so far from family, with strangers, *be right?*

"And your sister?" Izara asked.

"I think that is the end of my story," Esti said, rising. For the first time, she sounded sad.

I was blinking back tears, but I was also filled with horror—horror and revulsion. For days, Esti's story hung over me, coloring everything I saw. I began to avoid her, so I could avoid thinking about the ugliness that had brought her to us.

I hadn't thought of Esti's story in years. But here in the forest, with Esti's son about to force me through what his own mother had suffered, it rose up before me, playing out in my mind's eye.

I'm not in that story.

I haven't been captured in a raid. These are hunters from my own band—*the band where my mother is leader.*

This can't be happening.

But it was. Impossibly, it was.

"That's better," Kerbasi said. "You're not bad-looking when you don't talk." He reached for my face, and I shrank back, but there was Omer behind me. Kerbasi gripped my cheek.

It was unbearable. Movement returned to me, and I struggled against Omer's arms. But I was caught too tight. There were two of them and one of me.

And then, from nowhere, there was a flurry of sound.

Omer buckled, groaning, and abruptly dropped me. I made to dash away, but not fast enough—Kerbasi grabbed my arm, hard. My fist swung and connected with his chin. He swore and seized my wrist with his other hand.

That's when I saw her.

Izara stood beside us, fierce, crouching, a wooden digging stick gripped in her hand. Omer had fallen to the ground. As we watched, he staggered upright—she'd used the stick to strike him in the back of the head.

"You bitch," Omer growled, and lunged up toward her. She pivoted out of his way, looking like the warriors who fought for sport at summer meeting. Her eyes were fiery and dangerous. She held the digging stick aloft, poised to strike again.

Kerbasi dropped my arm. Without thinking, I ran to stand beside my sister. The two of us faced the men.

As I watched, Kerbasi transformed from menacing to merely scornful: his posture relaxed into a slouch, and his snarl softened into his usual sneer. He wasn't looking at me anymore, but at my sister. He chuckled.

"So we have a fighter here?" he said. "You take things too seriously, Izara. We were just playing around. C'mon, Omer." He took a few steps toward the path back to camp, but paused, looked directly into my eyes, and added, “See you later, Nahia.”

Neither Izara nor I moved for a long time. I could hear her breathing hard, in and out, in and out. My own breath was ragged, a dull, irregular rasp.

At last, she turned. I couldn’t meet her eyes; I looked instead at the drifts of old leaves covering the forest floor. I was shaking so violently, I thought I might fall.

“Are you all right?” Her question seemed to echo, as if we were in a cave.

My hair was hanging in front of my face. It was tangled. Inside me, a pressure was mounting—tears, and something else I couldn’t name. It was a kind of wildness, a feeling I would burst apart, that I would shake myself into a thousand fragments of bone and blood.

Am I all right?

I looked up. Izara held my gaze. Her brow was crinkled with worry. She reached an arm out to me, as if she would take me into an embrace—

In my mind’s eye, I saw Kerbasi, reaching out to touch my face.

The pressure that had been mounting inside me broke through, and I shattered. I watched from above as the girl who stood next to Izara leapt up and dashed into the forest, as swiftly and silently as a deer. She was running, running away from her sister, away from what had just happened, away, away, away.

SEVEN

The girl ran through the forest.

I knew the girl was me, but I didn't understand how I could be running, how I could be doing anything but huddling in a tight ball, trying to hold the shattered pieces of myself together. I couldn't think, couldn't see, and yet the girl's body seemed to know where it was going. She dodged branches, leapt over downed trees. I wondered at the agility of this girl who could run. I hoped she would keep running forever.

But eventually, she—I—couldn't go any farther.

When she stopped, the sense of being outside myself faded. I leaned up against a tree, gasping. My heart was pounding, and my legs were trembling so hard I could barely stand. *I have to get away. I have to hide.* For a while, I was overwhelmed with dizziness.

When my vision cleared, I saw I had come to a place I knew: a remote outcrop of boulders, huge and close together, but with space to slip between them and hide. I'd come here before, when I needed to get away from the rest of the band. I couldn't think of a safer place anywhere in winter territory. I crawled between the stones and rested, my back against the largest of the rocks. There was a depression there, just the right size to support my head. I tilted my face up to the sky.

What just happened?

My stomach clenched, and I doubled over, vomiting.

When I could hold myself upright again, I crawled away from the mess. I wrapped my arms around my knees and laid my head down on top of them, curling into a ball, and I let myself cry.

I don't know how long I stayed there, sobbing; it seemed like hours. But eventually there were no tears left in me. I raised my head and looked out over the rippling sea. I imagined the waves were washing over me, washing me clean of everything that had come before this moment.

I was lucky. I was so lucky. If Izara hadn't appeared when she did...

My stomach clenched again, but this time I managed to fight the sickness back down. My cheek stung from Kerbasi's blow; my arm ached where he had grasped it. I would have ugly bruises on my forearm, although I didn't think my face would bear any marks.

My leather pouch had come loose. I tightened the strap, reaching in to wrap my hand around the *tsairi*'s gift.

I'm no one now. I have no status. That is why they dared.

And that is why they left when first daughter Izara appeared and threatened them.

I am no one's daughter. I'm under no one's protection.

For one brief moment, I imagined telling Abene. I imagined her righteous anger, imagined her exiling Kerbasi and Oroitz from the Sea People. But then sanity returned, and I had to fight down another wave of nausea. Abene might think this was my fault. If I'd been a better daughter, she'd say, I'd have been safeguarded by her standing.

I couldn't tell her. Even if I could find the words, too many times in the past she'd dismissed my feelings and concerns as foolishness. I could hear her voice in my mind's ear: *Enough with the stories, girl. Kerbasi is kin. He was raised by your uncle. Do you really think he would harm you? You must have misunderstood.*

And even if she *did* believe me, when would I be able to tell her? To Abene, these days, I didn't exist.

What was it Kerbasi had said to Bakar yesterday? *The* bakai *is dead.* And then he'd said he wouldn't abide by the hunters' rules any longer.

If the world was falling apart, if the hunters were no longer bound by *bakai*, then trouble might come from any direction. And I—a ghost within my own band—would be the easiest target, the first at risk.

How many of the hunters must I fear? All of them?

Tears were running down my face again. I barely noticed them.

How could I make the journey back to winter camp, when hunters free from the constraints of *bakai* might be anywhere?

I did go back, eventually. I didn't want to, but the idea of staying out all night was even more terrifying. I walked cautiously, carefully, alert for any unexpected sound that might signal a person nearby.

I skirted the clearing as I came into camp. The gatherers were skinning roots by the central fire, and the smell of smoldering seaweed filled the air. My stomach flipped over, but I couldn't tell whether I was hungry or sick. I caught a glimpse of Esti's pale hair, and quickly turned my head away.

I didn't see Kerbasi or Omer, or any other hunters.

I was grateful Eneko was not at the tent. There wasn't any shamanic paraphernalia out, either, which meant I wouldn't have to be up half the night failing at yet more versions of the chants. Unfortunately, it also meant we'd be joining the camp at the central fire for the evening meal.

Maybe I can say I don't feel well?

But what if he asks more questions?

Eneko's two water bags, made of cured leather and set by the tent entrance, were full. *Good, I don't have to make the trip to the stream to collect more water.* I crawled inside into my screened corner, and stripped off my tunic and leggings. I rummaged among my personal things for my second set of clothing. I felt better as soon as I had the new garments on.

I picked up the discarded clothes, holding them away from me. What could I do with them? They weren't really dirty. They looked ordinary, simply buckskin leggings and a tunic that had been worn during a foraging trip. But I didn't want to wear them again. I didn't even want them in the tent with me.

I briefly debated throwing them in the fire, but clothing took time to make. And Eneko would almost certainly see the scraps of leather in the ashes. And then he'd ask me about it. . . . I didn't want to talk about this afternoon with Eneko.

But then, maybe he wouldn't ask. Eneko was good about letting things alone. He'd see the smoking bits of leather, though, even if he didn't say anything. And burning perfectly good clothing would be a waste.

I carried my teasel brush, my sponge, and my wooden cup with one hand, my unwanted clothing in my other, and exited the tent. Outside, I hung the clothes on the stakes set up around our hearth. They would air out there, at least.

A strip of leather was wrapped around my brush. I unwound it carefully and bound back my hair. *Wash first,* I told myself, *then deal with your hair.* I dipped the cup into the water skin, filling it, and then dipped the sponge into the cup. I scrubbed hard at my face with the sponge. If my eyes were red and swollen, let everyone think it was the result of overly vigorous washing. When I was done, I freed my hair and brushed it, stroking hard. Somehow, it had become a solid mass of knots.

Don't think about it, Nahia.

I wouldn't think about it. I couldn't think about it. The brush pulled and snagged and crackled as I drew it through. The pain felt good. I kept brushing long after the tangles were gone.

When Eneko returned, I'd rekindled the fire and was sitting beside it, drinking an infusion of *kama.* I dipped a second cup into the cooking skin and offered it to him, keeping my face averted.

"Thank you," he said, accepting the cup as he lowered himself to the ground beside me.

After a moment or two of silence, I risked a glance in his direction. He was gazing across the hearth and into the forest. His face was tranquil and unreadable, as always. I wondered how to ask about staying home from the central fire.

Eneko cleared his throat. "I think there is enough dried fish left for tonight. If you would prepare the meal this evening, it would be a great help. I have too much to do tonight to attend the central fire."

I was so relieved that, at first, I didn't know what to say. "Of course."

It was getting dark, but Eneko caught me looking at him. I quickly dropped my eyes. "I need to pack. I am making a short journey," he said.

My relief fled. I shivered, and spots came over my vision. *Eneko is leaving me alone at the tent?*

Eneko had made several journeys since I'd come to stay with him. He never said where he was going, or why; he just said he'd be journeying for a time. I had never dared to ask for details. Usually, he was only gone for a day or two, and came back loaded with plants, both medicinal and ceremonial. Sometimes he brought other provisions, like furs or leather, and I assumed that on those occasions he'd been visiting with other shamans.

But sometimes he came back with nothing at all, and on one occasion, he had been gone for over a week. I was bored then—Eneko had left me with standard tent maintenance and provisioning chores, but I wasn't good enough at the chants to perform the protective ceremonies on my own. The days he'd been gone had been painfully empty. I tried going over to the central fire one evening, but it had been so awkward I had left as soon as I could.

I had been lonely while he was gone, lonely and bored and uncomfortable. Eneko might be distant, but he was kind. He talked to me, and he wanted me to answer. I don't think I spoke a single word the week he was gone.

And now—now being alone would be worse. Much worse.

"How long?" I asked. My voice sounded anxious.

"A few days—not quite a week, I don't think. I will visit with Hodei." Eneko paused, then said, "I will ask if the strangers' raids have continued, the ones Zigor spoke of. Hodei travels more widely than I do, and may have heard stories that we have not."

I was mostly trying not to panic about being alone, but I noticed with a kind of remote surprise that he had told me what he would be doing.

Hodei was another shaman, currently with Garbi's Salamander People, a short journey north along the coast. I had never met him. He had only been with the Salamander People for a few months, a little longer than I'd been shaman's apprentice, but Eneko spoke of him often. They had clearly known each other a long time.

A visit with Hodei would take longer than I had hoped, but not as long as I had feared. I looked out across the darkening camp. I couldn't see any of the other tents; I couldn't even see the central clearing. But there were small glowing lights I knew came from banked hearths in front of tents, and a larger, glimmering light from the direction of the central fire. They must have built a big blaze this evening. A burst of laughter drifted in our direction. I shivered.

If Eneko was traveling, I would have to plan my days carefully so I couldn't be caught alone. I could manage that during the day. But at night? Would I be safe then?

Surely, no hunter would dare to enter Eneko's tent, even if he isn't in it. Even if the bakai *is broken. Shamans talk to spirits, and spirits are dangerous.*

I'll be safe.

Maybe if I kept repeating it, it would be true.

Eneko said, so quietly I had to strain to hear him, "I would like you to practice visioning at the cove as usual, and to keep watch over the tent. But I would also like you to do the nighttime and dawn protection chants each day while I am gone."

I turned to him. "You—you think I can do it?"

The firelight from our hearth fire flickered across his face, highlighting his broad cheekbones. "Yes," he said. He met my gaze. His eyes were big and dark and sad. "You are ready. And I think the Sea People—and you—need protection."

His expression was open, inviting me to confide in him, but I looked away. I understood what he was doing. He knew something unhappy had transpired, so he was offering me the gift of his confidence in me. If I told him the truth, the full truth, all the ugliness of it, all the danger—would he stay, rather than leaving me here alone? Surely he would.

But I could not put words to what had happened to me. And so he would go.

EIGHT

When I woke before dawn the next morning, I was alone. I sat before the fire and chanted the morning songs as if I had never stumbled over the words or flubbed the melody. The notes came forth strong and clear, a contrast to my usual reedy voice.

It was as if someone else were singing for me. This voice couldn't be mine.

I watched the light spread across the sky as I sang. We had completed the full night protection chant the evening before, all three variations, and I'd slept deeply afterward, despite everything. I hadn't heard him as he left. When I rose, he was simply gone.

I felt different. It was as if some older, calmer, more capable Nahia had moved into my body overnight—as if she had come to protect me. The camp looked familiar, yet not, like the memory of a place in a dream. *This is my home, my family,* I tried to tell myself, but the remoteness persisted.

When I had tidied the tent and hearth, I made my way to the central fire. I didn't want to go into the woods on my own, and that left me one choice: to join the gatherers. I would not have dared before yesterday—I would have feared the awkwardness that was sure to ensue—but awkwardness seemed preferable to encountering any of the hunters on my own. And the peculiar detachment surrounded me protectively, like the shell of a snail.

If Abene yells at me, what do I care?

Still, I watched in amazement as no one said anything. The gatherers made way for me, not speaking, but acknowledging me nonetheless. Only Abene ignored me completely.

As we left the camp, Izara came to walk beside me. I cringed—I didn't want to talk about what had happened—but my sister didn't speak to me, just walked at my side. She called to the group, exchanging jokes, laughing, and joining in the occasional song. I might not have been there, for all she addressed me.

Even so, it was as if she'd taken me into her arms and was holding me close.

The gatherers didn't go to the cove; Abene must finally have deemed the shellfish unsafe. Instead, they walked to a stream above the Cove of Rocks and spread out to dig roots. I continued down to the beach, comforted by the sounds of the women and children just above me. When I heard them preparing to go back to camp, I climbed the slope and joined them.

It was harder back at the tent in the evening, but even there, the detachment persisted. I made a meal, then pulled out a few of the leather bags that I'd seen were getting worn. I would patch them, a difficult job that would take all my attention. I'd assembled all the tools—the prepared hides, some sinew, my awl—when I heard a rustling from the direction of winter camp.

My calm fled. My head snapped up, my heart in my throat.

Izara stood at the edge of the little circle, watching me. She was biting her lower lip, and her eyes were sad and uncertain.

I couldn't speak. I tried, but all that came out was a little mewing sound. I bent over, tears coursing down my cheeks. Izara's arms came around me, and I leaned back against her, letting myself cry.

When I got to the hiccupping stage, Izara drew back, taking my hands in hers. "I'm sorry, Nahi," she said. "I'm sorry I didn't listen to you. You tried to tell me about the hunters—I should have listened."

"It's all right," I whispered. "Thank you for..."

Izara shook her hair back. The anger in her voice came through strong. "It was nothing. We shouldn't have to worry about such things, not among our own people. Did they hurt you?"

I shook my head, even though it felt like a lie. My body was unharmed, and yet they *had* hurt me. I didn't feel safe anymore. But that wasn't what Izara meant, I knew.

"I don't know how they dared." Izara's rage was building. "I have to tell our mother about this. If Kerbasi and Omer would attack *you*, none of us are safe. She'll get Oroitz to send them away, I'm certain." Her voice softened. "You'll let me tell her, won't you?"

I nodded. I couldn't speak around the lump in my throat, so I sat staring at the leather bags.

Izara's arms surrounded me again. "Shh," she said. "I'll watch out for you."

And then she left.

Darkness fell and my fear grew.

I sang the evening protection songs, and again the strong, clear voice issued through my lips. *Where is it coming from?* My previous detachment had returned. I was still terrified, but the terror was behind the calmness, somehow. It was like I was two girls, one weeping in fright, and one who ignored all fear, too busy to be distracted by emotion.

And so it persisted. My calm other self stayed with me over the days Eneko was gone. I sang the songs, morning and night; I joined the gatherers to travel to the cove in the daytime. Izara didn't speak to me again, but every day she walked beside me, her presence a comfort and a support. I did not join the band for evening meal but ate at the tent instead, using the food from our storage.

The calmness deserted me only once in the days Eneko was gone, on the day the hunters came into camp with a rare ibex. They passed by our tent. I was sitting by the hearth, working on a basket. Omer led the group, strutting sturdily in front, his bow held proudly before him, his quiver slung over his back. My mind screamed *Run! Hide!* but my body had gone stiff as wood and I could not move. I sat, shaking, my heart racing and my stomach churning, long after they went by. It seemed hours before my heart went back to normal. I could have gone to the central fire to claim a portion of the ibex for Eneko's tent—I probably should have, as our dried-meat supplies were getting low—but I couldn't make myself do it.

On the fifth day, Eneko came home.

He was there when I returned from the cove, but he hadn't built up the fire. He sat quiet and still beside the cold hearth. His hair gleamed darkly in the afternoon light. There was a smudge of dirt along one of his cheekbones, but his leathers were neat and clean. At first glance, his strong, compact body seemed utterly relaxed, but one of the muscles in his neck jumped as he saw me.

My heart sped up as I recognized: *He's worried about something. Is he worried about me?*

In that instant, Eneko was dear and familiar—not strange, not remote, not half-human. He smiled at me, a gentle smile, but it didn't quite reach his eyes. They stayed liquid, black, full of thought.

I was flooded with warmth, with a tenderness I had never experienced. I felt my face light up in an involuntary smile. "Welcome home!" I cried.

Immediately, I wished I'd kept quiet. My exclamation seemed to echo across the clearing, and my cheeks flushed.

Eneko nodded. When I sat beside him, he briefly squeezed my shoulder. My heart skipped and my breath went suddenly shallow. *What is* wrong *with me?*

His gaze was direct, frank, without judgment. "Is all well with you?"

"As you see," I answered.

There was an awkward silence. My hands seemed large and in the way, somehow. I tucked them behind me and looked off into the trees.

"I learned much from Hodei," Eneko began, calmly. The moment in which I had seen him not as shaman but simply as my friend was gone. He seemed as he always did, pleasant and removed. And yet my pulse still thrummed erratically. "We will be attending the central fire tonight." He paused, and then said mildly, "You may wish to rest and wash beforehand."

I was suddenly conscious of my sweaty face and snarled hair, and I felt myself flushing again. I nodded at him, stiffly, and entered the tent, slinking behind the screen and rummaging through my personal items. My embarrassment faded, and I realized I was happy.

I am glad to see Eneko. I missed him.

I knew it was true, and the knowledge itself was warmth, a small sun radiating inside me. I had missed him, and more, I trusted him. He would have stayed with me, these past few days, had I asked him to. Now he was back, and a sense of rightness that I had not realized was missing had returned to me.

There was an edge of excitement to these feelings, but I did not interrogate it.

I hummed to myself as I retrieved my teasel brush and sponge. I left the tent, collected the water bags, and headed down to the stream to wash up.

Izara was already there, filling water bags for Abene. She looked up as I approached, and I smiled at her and waved.

She smiled back. "This was always *your* job, remember? I never had to fetch water until you left!" My twin laughed. "Can't you drop this apprentice thing? Come home and carry water!"

I laughed, too, and dipped our bag into the stream. "Now that," I said, "is something I don't miss. I only have to carry water for myself and Eneko." I bound my hair back with the leather tie.

"Over there, you don't have people running in and out of the tent, either," Izara moaned. "It seems like every time I have the bags filled, Esti, or Alaia, or Udane, or all of them, are over to chat and drink tea—and then it's always, '*Izara?*' " She mimicked Abene's piercing look.

I giggled. In that moment, she really did look just like Abene. Izara picked up the three large bags, adjusting them carefully, then met my eyes and hesitated. "I talked to her."

My stomach turned over.

Izara looked quickly over her shoulder, then back to me. "We can't talk here. I'll try to come see you tomorrow."

I nodded, my stomach twisting uncomfortably. If Abene were going to punish Kerbasi and Omer, Izara would just say so. If Izara wanted to talk, it must be more complicated than that.

I didn't even know what to hope for. For Abene to invite me back to her tent? That would would have been my hope, once... but now? The thought that arose in my mind was simple:

I don't want to go back.

I don't want to leave the songs, the forest, the horizon... or Eneko.

Though it would be safer in Abene's tent, probably.

I tried to keep my face calm. Izara seemed not to notice my inner turmoil, which was reassuring. "See you at the fire tonight?" she asked.

"Eneko is back. We will both be there."

"Good." She dimpled at me as she set off.

NINE

The hunters were scattered around the central clearing in clumps of two or three, as always. They fell silent as Eneko and I approached. I lifted my chin and averted my eyes.

The hunters always stand around like this. It is no different from any other evening meal, I told myself.

But it felt different.

Inevitably, I saw Kerbasi and Omer. Was it my imagination, or were they—were all the hunters—watching me? I wouldn't look at them, wouldn't glance to check. I moved closer to Eneko, and he gestured to me to pass and sit first. I breathed easier.

The central fire at the evening meal: the entire band, and the overwhelming noise of their conversation. Had it been only a week since I'd last come to eat here? I looked around me at the Sea People, and I almost didn't recognize them. They looked different, foreign. But what had changed, really? Gotzon and Kiria chased each other through the crowd, shouting. Izara and Tora had their heads together, whispering and giggling. Esti stood by the fire, distributing baked roots.

Eneko and I sat across from the elders. Abene didn't acknowledge me, as usual. I was still in disgrace, still disowned. But even so, something about Abene seemed different as well. Her expression was quieter, more thoughtful.

Something had changed. Something was going to happen. I could feel it. My stomach was tight with anticipation.

Eneko cleared his throat. The cheerful conversational din quieted.

"I am recently returned from the territory of the Salamander People," he began. "I had meant to visit with them, but they are not at their summer camp."

Oroitz interrupted almost before Eneko had finished. "That is not so strange. They have surely gone visiting themselves." He thumped his right leg with his fist.

Abene fixed her stare on Eneko. Any trace of softness that might have been there before was now gone. Her eyes were narrow, her lips pressed into a hard line.

I looked at her, and I looked at Eneko, and the tightness in my stomach, the uneasiness about an unknown future, darkened into foreboding. This had the looks of a confrontation. The *tsairi*'s gift was burning against my leg, its warmth radiating through the thick leather of the pouch I wore. I put my hand over it. *Something* is *going to happen.*

Whatever Eneko said next would alter my world. I didn't know how I knew it, but I did. Part of me wished he wouldn't speak. Another part wished he would hurry and get it over with.

Eneko's face was calm. I didn't see so much as a muscle twitch, but I knew he was angry at Oroitz. His eyes darkened as he responded: "Their territory was altered beyond recognition. Forest burned to the ground, replaced with a meadow full of plants I have never seen before. And I have traveled far and seen many lands."

Each word he spoke now was deliberate and distinct. "And then . . . there were the strangers."

Everyone's eyes fastened on him.

He waited a moment before continuing. "It was pure luck I was not captured. I was trying to learn where the Salamander People might have gone, when two men—short, lighter skinned, with cropped hair, as if they were in mourning—came by. They did not see me, so I hung back and followed them. They spoke an unfamiliar language, a language with sounds completely different from our own. I could not understand even a word.

"These men led me to a large clearing, in which they have made their camp. And their camp, too, is like nothing I have seen before. I do not know if 'camp' is even the word I should use. It contains many circular structures, built of wood and stone, not of skins. And those structures hold men—men I have never seen the likes of before. Many, many men. This is a larger group than our largest bands. I dared not get too close, but I could see this much: they have with them few women, and those I saw seemed to be of the bands.

"And yet this was not the strangest thing. In these camps, in these structures of stone and timber, they keep animals. They looked like deer, but hairier. These animals, they follow the men like dogs."

There was a stirring from the audience at this. I heard a few whispers—of disbelief, I thought.

"I backtracked, more carefully this time, in hopes of finding someone from the Salamander People. After some searching, I encountered their shaman, Hodei, in the forest, who spoke to me freely. The Salamander People suffered great loss from these strangers, and now are no more. Headwoman Garbi and those few that live have fled inland, toward the mountains. Hodei has parted ways with them, but now turns to the mountains, too, for the outlanders take more and more of the coast, and it is not safe. Just as Zigor warned."

The hunters' muttering became a rumble, like distant thunder; in contrast, the women listened quietly. Alaia's face was incredulous; Izara's head was cocked to one side, her expression calculating. Tora looked back and forth, from Eneko to her mother, Udane. And Udane was watching Abene. Her walking stick lay across her lap; she rolled it, back and forth, back and forth.

Eneko continued. "When the strangers first arrived, Hodei told me, they began by building their camp. Garbi and the elders decided to let them be. They had heard tales of raids, as we have, and so they posted extra guards. But otherwise, they only tried to stay out of the way of the strangers. This meant they lost territory, but Hodei said Garbi thought it worth it, to avoid the risk of conflict.

"The Salamander People had three girls at or near to womanhood, but not yet mated. One morning, Garbi discovered all three of them were missing." Eneko paused. "It did not take long to learn where they were. One of the girls escaped, made her way back—all three had been taken, she said, by the strangers. She had seen that all the women in the strangers' camp were, in fact, captured from the bands. I saw this for myself, as I told you.

"The elders of the Salamander People discussed staging a rescue to get the girls back. But as they spied around the strangers' camp, they saw how many there were, and how difficult it would be. The hunters fought among themselves, some arguing that to attack the strangers would be futile, others that honor demanded it. In fear, some of them left, as did some of the women. Those that remained did attempt a raid . . . but it was not successful. The strangers outnumbered them, and nearly all the Salamander People were killed or taken. Garbi survived and remains free, but she is one of very, very few."

The rumbling had ceased. The group was silent, listening. I didn't move, didn't think, just waited for the next words.

"I told Hodei I would pass this message on to you: *To stay here is certain death. All bands along the shore must move inland, or perish.*"

At this Abene stirred. Her expression was as furious as I had ever seen it.

Eneko ignored her. "One more thing I must say. On my journey back, I took a different route. And I discovered the beginnings of a new camp, not even a half-day's walk from here. A camp where men are building structures of stone and wood. A camp with those same furred deer. These strangers are no longer a distant threat. They are here. The time has come to move."

It was just like the night of Zigor's visit—only now, I wasn't the one speaking out. They had tried to silence me by sending me to Eneko, but here he was, saying the same thing I had. My heart beat faster.

I was right.

Will they hear it now that it is not just me, but him?

Abene stood up. "So, shaman," she said, dangerously cold, "you think you know better than my land-sense? You think we should abandon our territory, this jewel of the coast my mothers have held since time immemorial? That we should scuttle, cringing, to the mountains, to try and claim a bit of inferior dirt there?"

"I do," Eneko said. His voice was even, but I could see the tension in his shoulders. "The alternative is capture—or death. Garbi, too, had land-sense, and she, too, chose to keep her band in the territory of her ancestors. The Salamander People paid the price. The Sea People will meet a similar fate, should you stay. You have been short of food these past seasons. The spirits of forest and sea have been trying to warn you. The first daughter," he nodded at me, "shared their warning with you months ago."

I felt, rather than saw, all the heads turning toward me.

I swallowed and stared straight ahead, looking at the air before my eyes. A gnat danced there, moving in a hypnotizing rhythm. I tried to keep my face immobile, like Eneko's, but my body pulsed with apprehension.

Anger edged Abene's voice. "Nahia is your apprentice. Not first daughter." The word *apprentice* sounded dirty.

Eneko replied, coolly, "Then you might consider yourself twice warned by her."

"You overstep, shaman! What do you know of the Sea People? Who could oust us? Our territory is the richest, our women the most skilled, and our hunters the strongest of any!" Abene turned to face the rest of the band. "Anyone who is frightened of these newcomers may run away." Her mouth was set in a straight, hard line. "But I will stay. We are shore people. What would we do in the hills?"

Our hunters are the strongest... I looked from Abene to where the hunters stood. Kerbasi was in their midst, tall and strong as a reed, his chin up proudly, his hands gripped round the shaft of his spear.

Abene won't send Kerbasi and Omer away, I realized. *Not if she's relying on the hunters to defend the Sea People's territory from invaders.*

She won't even discipline them. They're free to do as they choose, without any constraints of bakai.

The knowledge was like being stabbed. I sat, motionless, bleeding inside.

Eneko rose too, facing Abene. The band waited breathlessly.

No person has authority over a shaman. Everyone fears their power. To challenge a shaman was to risk being cursed.

I knew Eneko as no one else in the crowd did, though. I knew he would not call a curse on Abene, or the Sea People. No, he would leave, retreat into the forest, to wherever shamans went when they were not with a band.

And when he was gone... I would be alone. I'd have no one and nothing.

My fears were coming true.

The warmth I'd felt, hearing Eneko support me, was replaced by cold panic.

"I have given my warning." Eneko turned his back on the crowd and walked in the direction of his tent.

I hastily stood up to follow him, tripping over my own feet. As I did, I glanced at Abene. She was looking straight at me—not through me, but at me. Her blue eyes were sharp and watchful in her brown face.

The *tsairi*'s gift burned like it was on fire.

And in that moment the final piece of information dropped into place, like the last stone set in a fish weir.

Abene knew the strangers would come for us.

This is why she accepted so many hunters this past year. Why she let the band become so unbalanced.

She knew it all, before Eneko told the rest of us. Before Zigor, even.

She knows. *She has known for some time—the first warning must have come many months ago, and she never shared it. She will fight the strangers to keep the land, even if it kills us all.*

In a flash, I grasped her thinking. If these strangers were so numerous, moving to our accustomed inland territory would not save us; it was not far enough away. We would have to find an entirely new territory, deep into the uplands, as I'd urged.

No—most likely, we'd have to join another band to survive, like Garbi had. Not only would we no longer be Sea People, but Abene would no longer be headwoman. None of us would have status.

If the Sea People were to remain ourselves, our only chance was to fight. And we *did* have many hunters. Too many for ordinary times, but enough, perhaps, to keep us safe now.

I looked to where the hunters stood muttering, jostling each other. They seemed nervous and uncertain. I thought of the brawl on the beach. "*The headwoman and I have the matter in hand*," Oroitz had said.

He knows, too.

Why hadn't they told the rest of us that this struggle was coming? Why had they lied?

Surely, abandoning the shore was preferable to what awaited us if it turned out the hunters could *not* defend the territory?

I looked at my mother's haughty, angry face, and I knew that to her, it wouldn't be preferable. She would stay here, condemning us to hunger and war, so she could keep her pride, her ancestors' land, and the life she'd always known. *We are the Sea People, girl,* she would say. *It's better to be headwoman of a broken band than subservient in a new one.*

Fury crashed over me, a breaker of anger so strong it was almost serene. I was Abene's daughter, yes. But I had already suffered from her choices. For once, I didn't look away from her glare.

Eneko was right. *I* was right. And she was wrong.

TEN

Eneko and I didn't speak after the confrontation at the fire. He was withdrawn; I was preoccupied. I stumbled worse than ever on the evening songs and was relieved to go to bed, but then I couldn't sleep. I fidgeted and tossed, my body thrumming with panic and fury.

How could she? How could she? How could she? my heartbeat drummed in my ears. *She knows I'm right. She cast me out of the tent, stripped me of my rank,* knowing *I was right.* Knowing *the strangers were coming!*

All these years, I had done as Abene told me, followed her orders, struggled to earn her approval. And she was betraying us—me, Eneko, Izara, all of the Sea People.

I should challenge Abene. I should tell her that I know her mind. If Eneko is leaving anyway, I have nothing to lose. If I stand up to her, if I threaten to expose her before everyone, she'll have to change her plans.

I will *stand up to her. I'll do it right now.*

I sat up and listened. From the other side of the deerskin screen came a brief rustling as Eneko rolled over, then silence. I waited, but there was no further sound. I pulled on my clothes and peered carefully around the screen. Eneko was an indistinct dark lump at the other end of the tent, his breathing smooth and regular. I lifted the tent flap and crawled outside.

It wasn't so late. As I crossed the camp, I saw the flickering light of hearths still lit. When I drew near to Abene's tent, I saw her fire, too, was burning. Two figures sat beside it: my mother and my twin.

I stopped short, outside the circle of light. I hadn't thought of Izara being there. But of course, where else would she be?

"Gotzon needs to go out with the hunters," I heard Izara say. "I'll go talk to Esti; I don't mind."

I felt a sharp stab of protectiveness for Gotzon. *Why do you care, Izara? Why not let him be? It's not your concern.*

Abene didn't answer right away. After a time, she said, "That is Esti and Oroitz's choice, not ours."

That's right, I thought fiercely, surprised to agree with her.

Abene's tone hadn't been inviting, but Izara persisted. "But Abene, isn't it headwoman's business to care for the band? What use will he be when he's a man if he won't hunt?"

I drew in a long breath, then let it out slowly. Surely, Abene would reprimand Izara for contradicting? *Wait—I'm angry at Abene, not Izara.*

When Abene spoke again, it wasn't a reprimand. It wasn't even about Gotzon. "You remember Nene."

Nene. My grandmother. She had died when Izara and I were very young, some years before Abene met Aitor. My memories of her were hazy—a ferocious gray-haired woman, her presence filling the entire tent. Mostly I knew her from stories about the rivalry between her and Lili, her younger sister.

"A little," Izara said. I heard the indifference in her tone.

"She never wavered," said Abene. "Always, she knew what was right.

So she mated me to Xato, and Udane to Zek. And she sent Oroitz off, when he was first made a hunter, at fifteen."

Oroitz left when he was fifteen? I was surprised. Usually, boys stayed with their mother's band until they were twenty or so, moving on only when they were strong enough and experienced enough for another band's hunters to take them in—and often not even then.

I did know about Zek, Udane's mate. He was the father of her sons Miki and Alde, who had left us to travel after they became hunters. Zek himself had left years earlier, when Miki and Alde were still young boys, before I was old enough to remember him. Udane hadn't mated again after he'd departed; Tora and Kiria were from summer meeting.

"It is not so easy, to never waver," Abene continued. "But to be a leader, you need to appear strong, even if you do not feel so. Otherwise, the band will worry; they will lose faith in you; and soon enough, fracture will come. You must show only your strength, never your doubt. But it is not easy. Sometimes, you try and try, but you cannot turn water to stone. Sometimes, you make the wrong choice, but you stick with it anyway." She shook her head. "If you must make a change, you must make it in a way that no one sees it as wavering, but instead sees it as part of your strength. You are a good daughter, Izara." She patted Izara on the knee, and Izana leaned up against her. My eyes were suddenly damp. "A good first daughter."

My stomach churned. What did she mean, *you cannot turn water to stone*? Was she talking about me? I'd always tried, always done as she asked. How could she brush all my effort aside?

Underneath my anger, a small forlorn voice cried, *Why does Abene never caress me that way? Why won't she love me as she does Izara?*

I couldn't confront her; I couldn't do it.

I melted back into the darkness.

The next morning, Eneko brought out a roll of hide, and unfurled it on the ground before me. Inside, sinew had been sewn up the hide at regular intervals to make pockets. Tucked into those pockets were long branches of herbs—*itsar*, *mixu*, *bioli*, all the protection plants. In the upper corner of the hide, three short horizontal lines had been burned into the surface. I ran my finger over them, slowly, and looked up at him.

His forehead was creased, his eyes distant. "This is the protection bundle, for traveling," he said. "You know all the protection plants now, I think. Please, will you make sure each one is there in plenty?"

He's leaving now. My stomach roiled, as if a nest of snakes were squirming around in it. *I have to ask him if he's leaving forever, so I know for sure, and I can plan what to do next.* But I couldn't speak around the lump in my throat; I just nodded.

"Thank you, *maiti*," he said.

Maiti. Dear one.

He'd never called me that before. No one had.

The tenderness of it—the knowledge of all I had to lose if he left—overwhelmed me. My eyes filled with tears. I couldn't look at him with my eyes overflowing, couldn't let him see. I nodded again, staring at the bundle, chewing the inside of my lip so the tears would not spill down my face.

Eneko touched my shoulder lightly, a quick butterfly touch. There was a soft thump as he dropped his cup to the ground beside the water bag, and then his footsteps faded into the forest.

I was still blinking back tears when I heard the sharp crack of a twig snapping beneath a sandaled foot. My head whipped up, but it was only Izara. I waved her over, surreptitiously wiping at my eyes.

She squatted beside me. "What are you doing?" she asked, looking curiously at the protection bundle.

"Oh, just sorting medicine," I said vaguely. I could feel her eyes on me, trying to look into my face. I cursed my tears. "I like working with the plants." I began organizing the herbs, for something to do with my hands.

After a moment, she began, "Nahia, about—"

"I know," I interrupted her. "I know she won't send Kerbasi and Omer away. She needs hunters."

"No," said Izara. "I mean yes, you're right, she said no. But I'm working on her. She must see it's worse for all of us to have them here."

"She won't," I said again. My voice was curiously flat. "Not if she wants to stay here, on the coast. And that's more important to her than I am. Than any of us are."

"That's unfair," Izara protested. "You know Abene—it takes her a while to adjust to something new. I don't think she fully believes me, to be honest. She doesn't want to think Oroitz would let the hunters get so out of control. I tried to tell her, it's just Kerbasi—"

"It's not just Kerbasi."

"Oh, come on, Nahi," Izara said. "Of course it's just him. It's always him."

I shook my head, my throat thick.

Did Izara understand why Abene needed so many hunters? *I should tell her. About Abene, about her plans to fight for the territory, about her needing men for that.* But I couldn't speak.

"Anyway, that wasn't what I was going to say. I'm here because Abene asked me to come. She says you should move back to her tent—back in with us."

I looked up at her, startled.

Izara had wrapped her hand around her shell pendant. Her knuckles gleamed white with pressure.

The bundle sat before me, partly disassembled, the herbs scattered across it. I lifted my arms, twisted, and stretched. My joints made a satisfying pop. I didn't know I was going to speak until I heard my own voice, low and a little rough. "She wants me back?"

"Nahia, you know her. She told me to say you should move back with us. She didn't say anything more." Izara fidgeted, tapping her fingers against each other, one after another. *Tap-tap-tap-tap-tap.*

I looked in the direction of the central fire. I couldn't see it, but I knew the gatherers were assembling there now, making ready for the day's foraging. I heard Gotzon and Kiria, their childish voices cascading higher and higher.

The confused tumult of emotions from last night was back. I was angry. Why should I go back now? She only wanted the rest of the band to think I supported her, and I didn't. Still, a lonely piece of me whispered: *My mother wants me back. She wants me back. I'm not just the disappointment, the wavering one, the water who couldn't become stone.*

But I'd have to keep my mouth shut if I went to her, wouldn't I? Otherwise, she'd cast me out again. "Did she say anything else?"

Izara shrugged, grimacing. "It's Abene, Nahia. Of course she didn't say anything more."

I looked away from her, letting my gaze wander to the east side of camp. The unmated hunters set their tents that way.

"Zari... what do you think I should do?"

Izara didn't meet my eyes. She shrugged again, her shoulders moving up and down jerkily. "I don't know. Look, why don't you think about it? I'll tell Abene you wanted to consider, and she'll send me back tonight to persuade you, and we can talk about it some more then." She pushed against her knees and stood up, shaking her legs out. "I'll think about it, too," she promised.

I smiled at her, but the smile felt weak and insincere. I didn't want her to think I was angry with her, so I added, "Thank you for coming. I *will* think about it. And I will ask Eneko, too."

Izara smiled back at me, her smile stronger and sunnier than mine, but a little forced. *What isn't she telling me?* "That's a good idea." She leaned down and hugged me. I tried to relax, not to be stiff, but it was awkward. Izara straightened up and smiled at me again, a better smile this time, and she walked back toward the central fire.

I returned to the protection bundle once she was out of sight. Most of the herbs were in good supply. The ones I would need to replenish were common, easily found between here and the cove. I wouldn't even have to venture off the main path. I rolled the bundle back up and tucked it inside the tent with the rest of Eneko's shamanic gear.

I found the herbs for the protection bundle easily, along the side of the path, as I'd anticipated. I barely noticed the forest. I was thinking.

I could keep quiet and return to Abene's. I'd have to pretend I didn't believe in the danger the strangers posed anymore; even more difficult, I'd have to pretend I didn't know Abene had been lying to us when she insisted there was no danger. And I would be in danger myself, of being taken.

There was more than that, too.

In Abene's tent, I'd have to be with people all the time. I would lose all the beautiful hours alone, hours in the woods or by the sea, just watching. I'd lose the study of plants, the singing. I thought back to my life before I became a shaman's apprentice, and it now seemed narrow and colorless and empty.

But what could I do, if I *didn't* move back to Abene's tent? When Eneko was gone, I would be all alone. I'd have no allies and nowhere to go. How could I defend myself from Kerbasi?

I need to talk to Eneko. Now. I won't let tears stop me, or anything else. If he's not there, I'll start the fire, and wait, and when he comes back—then I'll ask him for his plans. His plans, and his counsel.

It was early for me to return to camp. I hadn't visioned; the gatherers were still digging roots around me. I went back anyway, taking the shorter route, the one I'd avoided this past week. The path on which I'd encountered Kerbasi and Omer.

It was time I learned to walk on my own again, without fear.

When I reached the tent, our fire was already lit. There was a large pile of paraphernalia laid out on a hide next to the hearth. Eneko sat next to the pile, cross-legged, staring at the assorted equipment and frowning.

Some of the tools were familiar, but many I had never seen before. A small wooden box, intricately carved; a bone flute; an oil lamp; a buckskin apron; a quiver.

He looked up as I approached. "Nahia," he said. "We must talk."

I stopped short. Wasn't that supposed to be what *I* said? And when had he ever suggested talking before?

"Um," I said. *I will not be afraid*, I told myself, but my racing pulse belied the thought.

He looked at me expectantly and, I thought suddenly, nervously. I sat across from him, and the flames leapt between us, now and again obscuring the lower part of his face.

"I am leaving early tomorrow morning," he said.

My stomach was heavy, as if I'd swallowed a rock whole. "Leaving," I repeated. I had known that. But I hadn't known how it would really feel until he said the words aloud.

"I cannot compel you, of course, but I think you should come with me."

For a moment, time stuttered. Nothing moved—not me, not Eneko, not anything in the world around us. Even the fire seemed to pause.

And then the moment was over, and I could move again. I could raise my hands to my mouth.

Go with Eneko?

I had not even let myself consider such a future. I was excited, and I was terrified. My mind unfolded with new possibilities, like a crumpled hide being shaken out. I could go on learning with him! I could travel—see the mountains, and who knew what else!

And I would still be with him.

But live band-less? Abandon Izara, Abene, Gotzon, and all the Sea People to fracture, or starvation, or slavery?

Am I a traitor, willing to abandon my band at the first sign of trouble? I stared at Eneko, my heart singing, my mind whirling, unable to speak, uncertain.

He said, "You know what is coming as well as I do. You know the best the band can hope for is fracture. And I am not at all certain you will be safe, even before the band dissolves."

I looked away.

"Nahia." Eneko leaned forward. "You are not yet a qualified shaman, but you are not truly part of the Sea People anymore, either. Our power, as shamans, comes from our detachment, but this distance from others also makes us vulnerable. We see too much. We know too much. You understand this already."

I raised my eyes to his. "Eneko, I'm not a shaman. I've tried, but I'm not."

His face lost its usual placidity entirely. His black eyes were hopeful, tender—full of an emotion I couldn't read. "Go on."

I swallowed my anxiety and continued. "I have loved learning with you, but I am not a seer. I haven't had a vision, or anything like it. The boats that I could picture in my mind—that was nothing. I don't know where it came from. As for seeing things, or knowing them—maybe I do, but not because I hear the voice of the spirits. I just think things through. And then I can't keep my mouth shut."

Eneko smiled at me—not in his usual distant way, but at *me*. "Nahia, what do you think a shaman really is?"

This was not the question I had been expecting. "Um. Someone who . . . I don't know, Eneko! Doesn't the fact I don't know prove I'm not one?"

"All I have ever done is 'think things through,' as you said."

The fire snapped between us, sending sparks up into the air.

"To hear the voice of the spirits—it is rare, and it takes time to know what you are hearing. Visions, too, are tricky things. Sometimes a vision is a big experience, yes. Other times, it's as you say: just something that comes out. An intuition. An insight. I think you are too quick to say you do not have this gift." I heard the trees whispering overhead, a counterpoint to the crackling blaze. "But even if you don't, visioning is not all there is to being a shaman. You need to believe me, and believe in yourself. If nothing else, you heard the warning from the land. You knew it was time for the Sea People to leave this place, maybe forever. Why do you know this when no one else does? You may not be destined to have a life like mine. But no matter what had happened, you would not have been content as an ordinary woman of the bands. Your path—it lies elsewhere."

He stopped. The fire crackled. A hoopoe bird called, *hoop-hoop-hoop*, and then subsided.

There was too much in what he said for me to think about it all then. I focused on the last bit. *My path lies elsewhere*. I wanted to believe it was true, but I knew what Abene would say: *What makes you think you are special, girl? You're no different from the rest of us.*

Eneko was right that I had always been a misfit. But how could I be otherwise? I was the band's next headwoman, set apart. And even if Izara was now first daughter in my stead, didn't I still have a responsibility to the Sea People? One that still set me apart?

But if I said so to Eneko, would he take it as a rejection of him?

I said instead, "I can't leave Izara."

"Does Izara want you to stay?"

I stared at him. Did he know Abene wanted me back? And did he know Izara had been carefully neutral about it?

What would happen to my sister if I left? Could I abandon her to the danger that stalked the Sea People? Could I leave Gotzon, already struggling, to the suffering that surely awaited him, either from starvation or at the hands of these outlanders?

And then, clarity:

What can I do to stop it?

Nothing.

Abene will stay until everyone is dead, whether I am here or not.

What about Udane? She knew about the hunters' fight on the beach. And surely, she would take Eneko's warning seriously. If she and Izara joined together . . . maybe together they could convince Abene to relent. Abene might listen to them, given time.

She would never listen to me.

No one would. They didn't *want* to.

Eneko was watching me. "Why don't you ask your sister when she comes back?"

"How did you know she was coming back?" I asked, startled.

He smiled, and said, "I'll return in a little while." And then he disappeared into the trees, leaving me staring blankly at the pile of shamanic equipment.

It was much later when Izara appeared.

I was too agitated to greet her properly, but she didn't seem disturbed. She sat down next to me, leaning her head against my shoulder and looking into the fire.

After a long time, I said, "Zari, I need to know something. What do you know about the strangers?"

She lifted her head, her brow wrinkling. "What do you mean, what do I know about the strangers? I know what everyone knows." She cocked her head to the side. "Do you mean, am I scared of them?"

"Yes, that, but also—"

"I'm not worried," Izara said, interrupting me. "As long as we keep the territory, we'll be fine. There are always new people passing through, just like our mother says. These will be no different. They will come, and they will leave again. We'll still be here, as it always has been. You need to think about yourself instead, Nahi." She paused. "Now. What do you want me to tell Abene? Will you come home?"

I stared at the ground. This conversation had gone all wrong—had gone down a different path somehow. *But if Izara doesn't believe the strangers are a threat, then she won't care that Abene is pretending not to think so, either.*

Izara was waiting for me to respond, but I didn't know what to say to her. I picked up a stick and poked at the earth.

"Eneko wants me to go with him when he leaves." I didn't look at her, but I heard her sharp intake of breath. The fire was dying. I fetched another log from the woodpile, carefully placed it on top, and returned to my seat.

"Well. Are you going to go with him?" She laughed, suddenly. "You know what this means!"

I had no idea what she was talking about. "What? It means he wants me to go with him."

"Oh, Nahia, how can you be such a child? He wants to be your lover." She laughed again. "I've seen the way you look at him, too. And why not? He's so handsome! Those eyes . . . Are you prepared? You know the stories about shamans!" She elbowed me, not gently.

"That's ridiculous, Izara!" My face was burning. I hoped Eneko wasn't anywhere nearby to have heard her. But could she be right? Maybe Eneko was interested in me only as a source of *bizi*. Maybe the life force he could gain from me was why he accepted me.

No. I trusted him. I wouldn't think about it. *This is just Izara being Izara.*

Her laughter shifted to concern. "What's the problem? Don't tell me you aren't interested. I won't believe you."

I didn't look at her. "Do you really think he'd use me that way?"

"Oh, those old stories about *bizi*," hooted Izara. "You're half a shaman yourself, aren't you? Couldn't you be taking his *bizi* just as well?"

Kerbasi's taunts echoed through my mind. *I won't think about Kerbasi. I won't.* "Eneko is my teacher," I said again, firmly.

"Fine, don't believe me." Izara subdued her mirth, with visible effort.

"Do you want to go with him? I wouldn't wish to leave the Sea People, but I'm not you."

I chewed on the inside of my cheek.

"I do want to go. I want to see other places." It sounded so feeble. There was more to it than that. There was Eneko, who had become my closest friend, save Izara; there was my anger at Abene's betrayal, of me and of the band, burning inside of me; and alongside the anger was the fear. "But I don't want to leave the Sea People. No matter what happens with the strangers, you know times haven't been good." I paused again. Why was this so difficult to say? "I don't want to lose you."

Izara sighed and put an arm around me. "I don't want to lose you, either," she said softly. "But you should worry about *yourself*, not about me. If Eneko is really leaving, I don't know what's left for you here." She hesitated. "And then there's Kerbasi..."

I shook my head again, clearing it of ugly memories.

Izara hugged me tighter. "I guess," she said, "that I think you should go."

My world was spinning. "If I go—Izara, listen to me, you *must* listen to me. I spoke to Udane about the hunters' fight after I spoke to you. Please, when things with the hunters get worse—and they will, I know they will—*talk to her*. She can help. I'm scared for you, Zari."

Izara had drawn back skeptically again, but after a moment she said, slightly formally, "All right, that is good to know." She stood. "When are you leaving?"

I stood, too. "Early tomorrow morning, Eneko said."

Izara wrapped her arms around me again. "I love you, sister," she said, into my ear.

"And I love you." My face was wet. "I'll come back, sometime."

She laughed and brushed away my tears. "When you are old and gray, maybe!" she teased. "Or when you and Eneko have a lover's quarrel?"

"Zari!" I protested.

"Promise not to fret about me, Nahi," said Izara. "Or any of us."

I felt so empty. "Hug Gotzon for me," I said. "Say goodbye to everyone." There was nothing else I could say, nothing else I could do. I was abandoning my band, running away—no words could make it anything other than the betrayal it was.

But what choice do I have? Abene betrayed me first.

Izara straightened herself, shaking her curls so they fell behind her shoulders, and took my hands in hers. "Travel well, sister," she said, squeezing. "Luck go with you."

Then she dropped my hands and left.

I watched her go. There was a hole in my stomach. With every step Izara took away from me, the hole grew larger. What if it never left me? Who was I, without my sister? Who would I be in the mountains, on my own? I wanted to run after her, to tell her I'd changed my mind.

Then I saw Abene's glare from last night's fire in my mind's eye.

I had made my decision. I was leaving with Eneko, and the sooner I put questions and regrets out of my mind, the better. I brushed my hands against my leggings. I needed to pack. If we were leaving in the morning, we had much to do before then.

But the hollow place inside that was Izara, walking away from me, remained.

ELEVEN

It was fully dark when we left, more night than morning.

When I'd gone to bed the evening before, I had wondered how I'd know to wake up. I half hoped Eneko might leave me behind. But I woke in the blackness that precedes the dawn as suddenly and as surely as if someone had touched my shoulder, and I knew the time had come. I was full of anticipation, excitement—and shame, too.

I am going to see the mountains. I am going to continue my training.

I am leaving the Sea People behind.

I heard Eneko stirring on the other side of the hide partition. I rose swiftly, driving my thoughts away with movement, joining him in front of the tent. He didn't speak, and neither did I. The shamanic paraphernalia was neatly piled next to the cold hearth. Eneko wrapped his bedroll around it, making a tight bundle, then bound that bundle up in a leather cloak, and finally tucked the whole thing into one of the large gathering baskets. I did the same, rolling my clothing and bedding up and pushing the whole lumpy mess into my basket. It didn't fit as neatly as Eneko's bundle did.

As I straightened up, something caught my eye on the ground next to the tent entrance. I bent down to pick it up.

It was Izara's shell pendant.

I stood, holding it in the palm of my hand. Had Izara accidentally dropped it, somehow, last night? No, the leather tie on which it hung was still intact. And I had swept the hearth area before I had gone to sleep. If she'd lost it, I would have seen it then.

This was my sister's gift to me.

I slipped it around my neck and wrapped my hand around the pendant for a moment, as Izara so often did. The edges of the shell pressed against the skin of my palm, their bite reassuring. When I let go, the shell fell into the hollow at the base of my neck, nestling next to the shaman's pendant.

We began the difficult process of striking the tent silently in the dark. It took some time, but we were able to do it quietly, and apparently without waking anyone. We left most of the tent furnishings, along with the tent poles, stacked next to the ashes of the fire. Someone would make use of them.

Once everything was dismantled, I stood looking out over the camp. I could feel Eneko next to me, radiating heat in the cool pre-dawn air. Other than the sound of his breathing, it was perfectly dark and still. I could see a few bright stars.

The leather pouch, the *tsairi*'s gift heavy within it, tingled against my leg.

I hoisted the gathering basket that held my personal items onto my back, then the second basket with our herbs, food, and basic supplies. The long leather straps hung over my shoulders, so the two baskets lay side by side behind me. Eneko picked up his basket and his bow. I tried to look at him, seeking reassurance, but his face was shadowed, and I could not read his expression. He nodded; then he set off along the path that began behind the tent—our former home, now—at the northwest edge of the camp.

My heart was beating fast. I hesitated a moment, looking over the camp again. I couldn't see the tents, or the central fire, not at this hour, and there was no noise, either. I could have been completely alone, far from any other person, with only the spirits for company. I let my eyes linger in the direction of Abene's tent, where my mother and sister were surely sleeping soundly.

I have no choice. I really have no choice.

Forgive me.

I drew in a deep breath, and I followed Eneko toward the mountains.

The sun soon rose, but it was dark and shady in the forest. The trees were tall and close together, so thick that although I could feel we were climbing, gaining in elevation, I couldn't see where we were going. A dart of joy pierced me as we plunged into deeper forest. It was as if the trees themselves were singing to me, singing one of the morning protection songs.

I hummed along.

I had never traveled much, even within our territory—just the usual circuit of winter camp to summer camp, summer camp to fall camp. The hunters ventured farther than the gatherers always, but especially during the autumn hunts, when they traveled into the mountains to take ibex and *orei*, red deer. Sometimes a few of the gatherers went with them on these journeys, to help with the processing and to collect the plants that could only be found at higher elevations, but I had never gone—Abene always insisted I stay home, with her. Izara had, a few times. After she had returned from her first trip, I'd asked her what it was like, but she had only shrugged and said, "It was different."

By the time the sun was partway up the sky, we had left the Sea People's winter territory behind, heading due north. I was already breathing hard; the early summer humidity enveloped me. Eneko was swift, and I struggled to keep up.

Midmorning, we entered a small clearing with a stream running across it. Here, finally, he slipped his basket off his back. I let the baskets slide off my back, too, and tumbled to the ground beside them. My ears were full of my own heartbeat, and my head spun. I sat as still as I could, and after a little while, the rushing sensation receded.

I noticed Eneko standing beside me. He handed me a water bag, filled with water from the stream, and I drank deeply. "Thank you."

"This was a hard morning's walk," Eneko said. "I wanted to put camp well behind us before anyone was awake. Thank you for keeping up."

I nodded. "We can go slower for the rest of the day?"

He smiled, really smiled, his eyes crinkling around the corners, and my stomach dipped, as if I'd stumbled into an unexpected hollow in the path. "We can," he said. "And we can rest here for a little while." He brushed the top of my head with his fingertips. A tingling sensation spread all the way down my spine. I suppressed a shiver.

"Sleep if you like," he offered, settling himself down with his back against a fallen log.

I stretched out along the ground, looking up into the sky, with the trees framing the edges of my vision. I focused on my breathing for a little while, and noticed my mind was beautifully clear and quiet.

I had never been here before, but it wasn't so unlike home: the same oaks, the same flowers, the same grasses. And yet it *was* unlike home. It was new, somehow. I lay there, lazily watching the clouds drift by overhead, Izara's shell pendant nestling in the curve of my throat. I understood now why Izara had only been able to say, "It was different."

What will happen to her?

I quashed the thought. I didn't want to think about Izara anymore, or about any of the Sea People. I couldn't. There was a whole new world in front of me.

Slowly, I untied the pendant from my neck and carefully tucked it into the little leather pouch, alongside the fragment of hardened clay. And then I lay back down and closed my eyes to rest.

We left the outer fringes of Abene's territory that afternoon, entering the no-man's-land between the Sea People and the Acorn Gatherers. We visited with the Acorn Gatherers sometimes; they were distant kin, but there was a stiffness between our two bands. Udane had told me that when Nene was headwoman, she had quarreled with the then-headwoman of the Acorn Gatherers over the boundary. Some coldness remained, and now there was a stretch of land where no one went.

I knew as soon as we'd entered this stretch, for suddenly there was game everywhere. Rabbits scurried behind brush; roe deer bounded away, startled. In the afternoon, we even came upon a wild cherry bush, covered with bright red fruit. I stopped to harvest as much as I could carry while Eneko went on to make camp. When I'd filled a bag to the brim, I followed his trail to a small clearing in the woods, where the canopy was so thick overhead that little grew beneath.

The sky was almost dark now. He had stretched out our bedding side by side in the center of the clearing and was building a fire. Two pieces of flint sat beside him on the ground; he'd evidently made a spark, for there was a tiny flame in the kindling. He blew at it, gently coaxing the flame to life. I put the bag of fruit on the ground and sat beside it, watching.

Overhead the wood was full of shadows. There was an owl in a tree at the edge of the glade, the large owl we call *arhontzl*, its hoot resonating through the space. I had only ever heard the *arhontzl*'s call in the most inland part of the Sea People's territory, where we travel when the leaves begin to turn. The sound of it took me to autumn—the taste of blackberries exploding across my tongue, the anxiety of harvesting enough food to get us through the winter.

But I didn't have to worry about food just now. The growing season stretched before me. I let my worries drift away. The fire finally caught, sending flames up into the air. Eneko leaned back on his heels and wiped his hands on his leggings.

"Eneko," I said, "where are we going?"

He looked at me, his eyebrows arched in surprise; and then he laughed. "I'm sorry, I forgot I hadn't told you. We are going to what I think of as my home."

"Where you grew up?" I asked, interested. I had never thought of him as a child before.

He laughed again and shook his head. "Oh, no," he said. "I was born on the other side of the mountains, a long, long journey from here—I left when I was still a small boy. No, I found this place after I earned my tattoo, and it is where I always return. It is a mountain valley. There is plenty of food, and a good stream, and also a good place to stay; I have made some improvements to it, through the years. Though we will likely need to make more repairs before winter. Is that all right?" he added, suddenly concerned.

"Of course," I said. Heat rose in my cheeks. I thought of Izara, saying "*He wants to be your lover!*" and my pulse quickened. I hoped it was dark enough he couldn't see me blushing. I asked quickly, to cover my confusion, "Is that where you were before you came to us?"

His smile gleamed white in the firelight. "No. I received my tattoo very young, and it took me years to decide I would continue in this life. In those days, I stayed sometimes with the mountain bands, sometimes in my valley. I came to the coast only when I knew I was serious about being a shaman. And once I arrived, I moved often from band to band, staying a month with this one, a month with another, until I found the Sea People."

He'd bounced from band to band before he came to us? Why did he stay so long with the Sea People, then? I couldn't ask him that. "Is it far to this valley?"

"It will take some weeks of travel, yes." His voice sounded amused.

We were quiet, watching the fire.

"Are you worried about the Acorn Gatherers?" I asked Eneko. "They've been squabbling with us over this stretch of land for years. There might be trouble, if anyone sees the fire."

"No," Eneko said, and touched his shaman's tattoo, the single band that ringed his powerful upper arm. He flashed another smile at me, his dark eyes bright. My breath went suddenly shallow, and again it was as if I were falling. *Stop it*, I told myself, but my body seemed to have ideas of its own.

I looked at his very nice arm instead, watching the light play across the tattoo. Of course he wasn't afraid. We weren't part of the Sea People anymore. We were travelers—and Eneko was sacred.

But I? I had the shaman's pendant, yes, but no tattoo. It would take years of study, presumably, before I might earn one. If I ever did.

Bandless, motherless, sisterless... what kind of woman was I now?

I listened to the calling of the *arhontzl* in the forest. It was soothing, as if it were reassuring me that someday I would know.

TWELVE

That night I slept soundly, more soundly than I would have thought possible. The sun was well up when I opened my eyes, and Eneko was sitting across from me, eating rootcakes.

"You should have woken me," I said, struggling out of the sleeping furs.

He shrugged. "There was no need. Yesterday was a difficult day."

That afternoon, we climbed the steep hill that marked the transition to the Acorn Gatherers' territory proper. I ached with exertion and with nervousness. We were in a foreign land now.

The descent was nearly as tricky as the climb. It was late in the day when we reached the valley floor on the other side. We stopped to drink at a small creek, the water shockingly cold.

I was bent over the creek when I heard a shuffling.

It was not one of the Acorn Gatherers. It was not a person at all, but a boar—the largest one I had ever seen. There was a depression in the leaves where he had been resting, but now he was upright, and he was looking at me. His dark summer coat stood up in a ridge along his back; his eyes were hot, his tusks long.

I froze. Boar were dangerous when startled. Aitor, Oroitz—every gruesome injury from a goring I had ever seen flashed through my mind.

And this boar was so near. I looked quickly around: there were trees everywhere, but none with branches low enough for climbing.

The boar lowered his head. He was going to charge.

There was a swift movement behind me, followed by a whistling past my ear. An arrow appeared from nowhere and lodged itself deep in the boar's eye. He teetered for a moment, then fell to the side.

I turned around, slowly, but there was only Eneko, bow in hand. He looked pleased with himself.

When I spoke, my voice was too high. "I—I didn't know you could shoot."

He raised an eyebrow. "You know I have a bow."

It was true, I did know. I had seen it when I was living in his tent, and as we were leaving, and every day since. It hung across his back, next to his basket. But I had never thought of him as a hunter. I had never known him to hunt. I guess I thought the bow was ceremonial.

He laughed at me, as if reading my mind. "Do you think I transform into a bear to feed myself? Of course I hunt." He walked over to the boar and removed the shaft.

I don't know why I was so surprised. Eneko hadn't hunted with the Sea People—no shaman I could remember had. They were simply entitled to a share of the band's food in exchange for ceremonies. But they had to live somehow when they were on their own. Why hadn't I thought of that? And knowing how to shoot meant they could protect themselves, too. From boar . . . and from people.

If Eneko could use a bow and arrow—then I, if I were a shaman's apprentice—

"Can I learn?" The words were out of my mouth before I'd even considered them.

His smile brightened. "Of course," he said. "We will look for the wood we need to make you a bow as we walk."

"You can make weapons?" I thought, but did not say, *My own bow*? My skin had goosepimpled with excitement. At home, women did not shoot. But I was no longer at home. Nothing constrained me here.

"I can," he said. "Where did you think I got this from?" He was laughing again.

"I don't know," I said. "It could have been a gift, no?"

I laughed, too, but there was a sadness in my laughter: the memory of Kerbasi's hand connecting with my cheek, that long-ago day when Izara and I had found the arrow shafts. I put it from my mind. Kerbasi was far away, now, and would be farther with every day we traveled. He could not stop me. Not from this. Not from anything.

Eneko was watching me. "Let us stop for the day. I will butcher this boar, and while I do so, you will practice visioning." He pointed at the stream. "Follow it until you find a good place."

Later that night, after feasting on fresh boar meat, we sang the protection chant—yet another variation, this one for traveling, he explained. But it did not take long. "For just the two of us," Eneko told me, "we may rely on the night chant only. We will not have to rise early tomorrow to sing. So, if you are not too sleepy, it is time to share with you some stories, I think. You have never heard the story of Bari-Unko, I think?"

"No," I said.

"You knew the story of your band's origins; you told it every time there was a visitor to your people. All bands have these origin stories, and we shamans have a story as well. Our story is that of Bari-Unko, the first shaman. Bari-Unko was a creature of the forest; he was the son of a forest spirit and of Xasi, the mighty hunter."

I had been poking the fire with a stick to make sparks shoot into the air, but at these words my head snapped up. "He was part *tsairi*?"

The firelight played across Eneko's face. Was he smiling? Perhaps not, for his voice was solemn as he said, "*Tsairiu*... that is a word the people of the bands have for those of us who take spirits into ourselves. Who venture into other worlds and can direct the energies there, can bring those powers here, to the mundane world. So yes, I suppose one could call Bari-Unko a *tsairi*. Me, I call him a powerful shaman. Born of a spirit and man, he could hear both the forest and the people. The people of the bands hear only other people; the spirits hear only spirits. Shamans hear both, *are* both. They are the forest, and the forest is them."

Eneko kept on talking, but my mind had stopped, was running over his words again and again. My love for the forest, the exhilaration of being in the wilds: was *this* the voice of the spirits?

I'd never thought of such a thing.

That was the first day of what came to be a pattern.

When I woke, Eneko was always already awake. We struck camp quickly and walked north. As we journeyed higher and higher, Eneko showed me plants I didn't know, teaching me their names and qualities.

When we stopped in the early afternoon, he would send me to practice visioning. At night we sang, and then he would tell me stories. The stories were always of shamans—including, to my surprise, women shamans.

Some were the stories about Benare that I knew from childhood. But Eneko had new stories about her as well, ones I had never heard before. Benare could take the form of animals, he told me—could fly through the air as a hawk or run through the forest as a wolf. And there were tales of other women, too: Lierne, Zabale, Elana.

I cherished those names.

Eneko said women shamans were often the most powerful of all, that women's ability to talk to spirits and people both was stronger. I was skeptical of this—surely, he was just trying to boost my confidence. I could sing the ceremonies, but I was as much a failure at visioning as ever. And I wasn't powerful: I knew I was no better protected against an incident like the one with Kerbasi and Omer than I had been before.

One thing, at least, would change that. We'd found the *hagi*, the wood Eneko needed to make me a bow. He showed me how to split it, remove the bark, and thin it, and now I carried the work in progress on my back, next to my baskets. Eneko thought it would be dry enough to finish by the time we reached the mountains. Until then, he said, I could learn with his bow.

"Look," Eneko beckoned to me.

It was our fifth day of travel. We were still in the Acorn Gatherers' territory, though barely. He was bent over a stand of plants with feathery leaves. When I knelt beside him, he said, "Look well, but do not touch.

We call this plant *tzancho*. In late summer, it makes beautiful big blue flowers, but even the leaves are hard to miss, no? This is a dangerous plant. All parts of it are extremely poisonous; some use it to make a toxin for their arrows. But it can be used in ceremonies, too, and one day I will show you how. Never touch it without protecting your hands, for even a brush may make you ill." He smiled at me, his face brightening.

Eneko smiled a lot these days. I was not yet used to it. Had I ever thought him remote and hard to read? But he had been, I knew. Now he was open and lighthearted, almost always. I was amazed at the change in him. When we were with the Sea People, I had thought of him as much older than I was, almost one of the elders, even though I'd known he wasn't. Before I became his apprentice, I was afraid of him; and after, when he had been my teacher, I found him kind and wise, but reserved.

Now, though he was my teacher still, he was first and foremost my friend. It was as if he'd left a huge burden behind when we quit Abene's band.

This new Eneko sang songs, told stories, teased me. And I could tease him back—if I didn't find myself suddenly awkward and tongue-tied. It was his perfect smile that did it, every time, an expression so full of delight that it never failed to knock me off balance. It touched me in some deep-down unfamiliar place. This feeling had struck me a few times in winter camp, but it was nothing like the longings that assailed me now. Sometimes I found myself tingly and nervous—just like when I used to give a speech or greet strangers. Other times my body would feel suddenly liquid, and I wanted nothing more than to touch him. It was confusing, it was exhilarating, it was terrifying.

I fought against falling into his beauty. *He is taboo. He would make love to me only to fuel his magic. Do I want to lose myself that way?*

But I'm learning to be a shaman myself, like Izara said. Maybe I have my own power now. Maybe I don't have to be frightened.

I repeated the word: "*Tzancho*." My voice sounded strange to my own ears, like I was speaking from underwater. "I have not seen it before."

"It only grows at higher elevations. Which means we are well on our way now." Standing, he dusted his hands against each other. I, too, lurched back to my feet, and we continued along the path as I tried to bring my errant body under control.

That night, with the fire burning brightly, Eneko spread our mats on the ground, but then did nothing else. Instead, he leaned against a tree, his face frozen in a stony mask.

My heart sank. This had happened several times when we were still with the Sea People. It always frightened me when he withdrew this way. *Have I overstepped some boundary? If I woke one morning and he were gone, what would I do?*

But I was braver now, emboldened by the days of travel and by our growing closeness. *I will not be afraid. I will talk to him.*

I said, as I might have said to Izara or Gotzon, "Eneko, are you all right?"

He turned his head, as if with great effort. I saw his eyes were bloodshot. "It is nothing," he said, closing his lids. "A headache. I will lie down."

"Can I do anything?" I offered. "Willow bark?"

"No," he said. "Nothing helps with these. I will be better in the morning."

He went to bed after that, crawling into his furs. I stayed up, feeding the fire, and thinking, *How often have I seen Eneko withdrawn and assumed it was my fault? I've been self-centered. It's time I truly learned to be a friend to him, as he has been to me.*

I sang the protection chant alone that night, keeping my voice low so as not to wake him.

THIRTEEN

When I opened my eyes the next morning, Eneko was sitting beside the fire, alert and awake. I pushed myself to a sitting position. "You are well?" I asked.

"As you see," he said. "These headaches rarely survive the night. Come, let us make a start."

As we walked into the forest, I was assailed by an unexpected sense of recognition. The trees were nearly all oaks, here, their branches thick with oakmoss. Its sharp, sweet scent teased my memory—a summer meeting, years ago; tension and excitement wound together like a braided string; Izara's voice, flush with excitement, as she told me about her first lover.

"Eneko," I said, "are we near the Acorn Gatherers' summer territory?"

He assented. "We should seek them out. It would be good to learn what news they have heard. All right?" he added, looking back over his shoulder at me.

I nodded yes, and we continued, looking for signs of an encampment as we went. But I was uneasy. My mind was full of that summer meeting. There had been three bands that year: the Sea People, the Acorn Gatherers, and the Salamander People. When a hunter of the Salamander People had first come to us with an invitation, insisting that Luntze, the headwoman of the Acorn Gatherers, would be pleased for the Sea People to come, it had set off a debate. Abene had not wanted to go, but Udane and Oroitz had talked her into it.

"We have not had a summer meeting in several years. And the sisters from Lili's line are of an age to be mated. How will they find mates without summer meeting?" Udane had argued.

"To reject the invitation will make her think we are weak," Oroitz had said. "If we go, the hunters will take part in the ceremonial fights, and the women in the races. Everyone will see our strength. You know Kerbasi has fighting skill. He will surely be the men's champion, should he have the opportunity."

So Abene had relented, but it had been horribly tense. Abene and Luntze had been ostentatious in pretending to ignore each other. Worse, Abene insisted that I stay close by her side. I had no opportunity to talk with the girls from the other bands, the high point of such gatherings. Instead, I had spent nearly all my time at the central fire, listening as Abene talked to Garbi and the other elders from the Salamander People. Kerbasi had indeed been victorious, but he had broken and bloodied the nose of the best fighter of the Acorn Gatherers, and the Acorn Gatherers had protested; drawing blood was prohibited. Kerbasi claimed it was an accident, but no one believed him, even though the Acorn Gatherers formally accepted his apology. Abene was torn between fury at Kerbasi and pride at the Sea People's show of strength.

And then there was Izara. Izara and her first lover, a hunter named Herri. Because he was one of the Acorn Gatherers, Abene couldn't know about it, which meant that I was frequently covering for her absence.

I hadn't liked Herri—I thought he was arrogant, though undeniably good-looking, with sharp cheekbones and broad shoulders—but Izara couldn't stop talking about him. I spent hours listening to her.

The scent of the oakmoss brought it back as if it were yesterday.

I knew Eneko was right, that it would be good to hear their news, but I did not really want to visit with the Acorn Gatherers. As the day wore on and we found no trace of any camp, my uneasiness about visiting with them was joined by an uneasiness about not finding them. If they were not in their summer territory, where might they be?

In the afternoon we stopped for a break, sitting propped against a downed tree. "Eneko," I said, then stopped. I didn't want to give voice to my fear.

He looked at me, waiting.

"Do you think—well, do we need to be worried about the strangers here?"

He tapped his fingers against each other as he considered. After a moment, he said, "We are well inland now, so I had thought not. Are you hearing a warning?"

I started. "A warning? No, I'm just—surprised we have found no trace of the Acorn Gatherers, that is all."

"Are you sure you have sensed nothing?" Eneko asked. His eyes were fixed on me in a way that made me nervous.

I swallowed. "I have heard no warning," I said, "truly. I am anxious, but that is not a warning."

Eneko didn't speak for a moment. "I take you at your word. But I think tonight we will sleep in shifts and keep watch. Just in case."

⁂

All afternoon, my nervousness grew. We walked late, then later. Dusk was falling and I was wondering if we were going to stop for the night at all when Eneko halted, suddenly, and put his hand on my shoulder.

It took a moment, but then I heard what he did: male voices, talking. A burst of laughter. The smell of a fire, and meat roasting.

Eneko asked softly, "Can you understand them?"

I listened closely. At first, I heard only indistinct conversation in a staccato rhythm, but then the buzz resolved into words. "... The girl had a nice ass, but her mate was a prick about sharing," one of them said.

"I can," I whispered.

He nodded. "Your hearing is better than mine. If they speak our language, they are of the bands, not the strangers. How many do you think they are?"

"Maybe three. No more."

Eneko squeezed my shoulder before letting go. "Good," he said, "we hear the same thing. Probably hunters, no? Maybe from the Acorn Gatherers, maybe not." He paused, indecisive.

"Are we going to join them?" I asked. "I thought you wanted news."

Eneko's face went still and impassive, an expression I had not seen for some days. "Hunters on the road can be dangerous."

At that moment, there was an eruption of barking. "Whoa!" one of the voices shouted. "Someone's here! Get your bows!"

Eneko sighed. "And so the question of whether we visit is now answered." He raised his voice, shouting, "*Ahai*! We are travelers!"

A pause, and then raucous laughter and some rustling. Another voice, this one deeper, called out, "Well then, travelers, why are you hanging around in the woods in the dark? Come join us!"

"We are on our way," Eneko called back, and we stepped toward the fire.

There were three of them, as I had thought, sitting around the fire. A black dog squirmed violently under the arm of one of the men, clearly wanting nothing more than to leap upon us. A second dog, this one white with large brown patches, cringed back against another's leg. The second dog whined as we approached but made no move toward us.

All three men were young. Their bows were scattered behind them, along with what looked like a water bag, none too full. They scrambled to their feet as we entered their sight, looking first at Eneko, then at me. "Oh-ho!" said one of them as his eyes fell on my face. He was shorter than the others. I flushed. The second man was very tall. He wavered on his feet as he stared at us. The third had sharp cheekbones, which caught the light of the fire and gave him a dangerous look at odds with the blankness in his eyes.

"Herri!" I cried before I thought.

"Curses," said the tall one. "A girl finally shows up at our fire, but of course she winds up being one of your conquests, Herri."

Herri looked puzzled. "Do I—oh, it's Izara's sister!" He turned to his friends. "She's one of the Sea People." Then, to me, "Is Izara with you?"

I stared at him. Why would Izara be with me? "No," I said cautiously. All three of them burst into laughter at my response, slapping each other on the arms. The black dog started leaping and barking. The spotted dog eyed Eneko and me warily, as if we were the ones causing his master to behave this way.

Eneko caught my eye, but I didn't understand what he was trying to communicate. The three hunters were still chuckling, but they sat again. Eneko rearranged his face into a mild expression, and then he, too, took a seat, saying, "I am Eneko, lately shaman of the Sea People. Nahia is my apprentice, and I am taking her for further training. May we share your fire? We have food."

This set the three hunters off laughing again. The round one said, "A shaman's apprentice? He has his own source of *bizi* with him, eh?" Herri laughed so hard at this that he fell over backward, landing on his bow.

I sat close beside Eneko, as far away from the three of them as possible. My face was red with embarrassment, but I also felt anger ignite inside me. Eneko thought we might get information from these three fools?

They quieted as Eneko handed around some of our dried ibex. Between chewing and some usual travelers' conversation, their attention was on him now, not on me. I kept my eyes averted, hoping it would stay that way, and listened to their talk.

It transpired that they were all hunters of the Acorn Gatherers, and they were—in fact—traveling to the Sea People. "We heard Abene's band was looking for more hunters," said the short one, whose name was Hovi. "And the Acorn Gatherers have been struggling. Too many people joining, as bands near the strangers break up. You've heard about the strangers? I see you have. Anyway, we decided to set out. Even Herri here, his own mama told him he should go."

Herri flushed angrily. "Luntze doesn't control me. I could have left years ago. The time wasn't right, that was all."

"Yeah, of course, Herri."

Herri was *Luntze's son*? Had Izara known that? Abene would have been *furious.*

Eneko asked, "You are not concerned about the strangers, then? If you are journeying to the Sea People, you walk in their direction as well."

"Nah," said Pio, the tall one. "I'm not afraid of any man. It is the refugees that bother me, the people from the coastal bands. They come inland looking for a place, and then there's trouble. Hey, do you want some of this?"

He handed Eneko the hide bag. Eneko sniffed it, and a look of recognition passed over his face "Where did you get this?" he asked, as he lifted the basket to his lips. I didn't see him swallow, but he held it there for a moment, then passed it to Pio.

"Bee tree," said Pio. "Earlier today. Thought we'd celebrate a little!" He offered the bag to me. "Here, enjoy."

"No, thank you," I said, keeping my eyes down.

"Ah, come on, give it a try. It'll make you friendlier." Pio had moved closer to me, little by little. He was now sitting almost beside me, but there was nowhere for me to go. The spotted dog sniffed suspiciously at my foot.

Eneko seemed to understand my discomfort. He pushed himself to his feet, saying, "Well, thank you for your welcome, hunters. We'll be taking our leave now." He reached out a hand to me.

I took it, but Pio grabbed me from the other side, yanking me back down. "They think they're too good for us, *hoo*! When we shared our honey wine with them!"

I jerked away, pulling myself up to standing, but something in my movement must have startled the spotted dog, because he sank his teeth into my ankle. I cried out.

The dog let go. There were a confused few moments where Herri shouted at Pio and Hovi, and Pio shouted at the dog, and Hovi said, over and over, "It's not my fault!"

The punctures the dog's teeth had made were deep and bleeding freely. I felt a rage blazing inside, hot as blue flame, and I heard myself shout, "**Tell me why I should not call a curse on you!**"

I had never known my own voice to be so loud or so fierce.

Even I believed what I had said.

The men fell instantly silent. Pio opened his mouth, then closed it again. He looked at Herri. The dogs whined.

Herri stammered, "Truly, we—I—apologize. We meant no offense. My friend has had a little too much to drink, that is all. We all have."

"We will be going now," Eneko said quietly. "You will not hinder us, and you will not set your dogs on us. If you try, I promise that someone will perish."

I stood beside him, hot-cheeked, glaring, trying to pretend that my blood-soaked ankle was not throbbing.

Herri said, "Of course, we will not hinder you. Again, I am sorry for any offense! We wish you well on your travels!"

Eneko gave them one last look, then turned and left. I followed, managing not to hobble. The only noise behind us was the crackling of the kindling.

Once we were far enough away so as not to be seen or heard, Eneko gripped my hand, hard, pulling me alongside him. He whispered, "I am sorry to make you walk on that ankle. Do you think you can go on? I want to put some distance between us."

"I can walk," I said.

By the time we stopped, much later, my ankle was aching, and I was relieved to be off it. Eneko lit a fire, then looked at the bite. He pulled out the medicine bundle and hesitated. "I do not know what is best for this," he said, sounding worried.

"*Zainbela*," I said. I did not question how I knew; the knowledge rose from some unthinking place within me. "I think there is some there? It is dried, but it will still help."

Eneko nodded, though he flashed me an unreadable look. He pulled the herb from the medicine bundle, chewed it, and then slathered the plaster over the punctures. "That will have to do for now. Does it hurt?"

The polite part of me wanted to say no, I was fine... but I was tired of the polite part of me. See where she had gotten me this evening! "It does," I admitted. "But it is not too bad. Do we have willow bark?"

He shook his head. "You need something stronger." He rifled through his bag until he found a small reed bundle with paste inside. He mimed dipping his finger into it, then handed the bundle to me. "Here. Use your finger, but take just a small amount. Swallow it. It will help."

I did as he said, licking a bit of the gritty black paste off my finger. It had a peculiar taste, nutty and fruity at once. "What is it?"

"*Mixtol*," he said. "I will show you how to make it, sometime. Not many know how, for this is very potent and also dangerous. Take too much, and it will kill; take too often, and you will crave it more and more, and that will kill you just as surely. But *mixtol* can relieve pain like no other medicine. And it will let one sleep in cases where pain might otherwise not allow it." He sat back on his heels. "Nahia, I am sorry."

"For what? It wasn't your fault, Eneko." The words were curiously hard to speak. The *mixtol* was fast acting—or perhaps I was just tired. Either way, I felt like I was floating.

"It was, though. You have not traveled before. I have." He sighed. "That honey they were drinking, it had fermented. That was part of why they acted as they did, but not all of it. I know how young men behave while on the road. I should have thought... I should not have put you in that position."

"You didn't put me in any position," I mumbled. "They heard us in the brush—we had to show ourselves." Maybe it was the *mixtol* affecting me as much as any honey wine, but suddenly, the whole encounter struck me as funny. "I would have been bitten by their ugly dog either way," I said, beginning to laugh. Those three fools—how obnoxious they were, how cocky! How silent they had fallen when I threatened to curse them! What buffoons! What stupid swine!

After a moment, Eneko chuckled, too. *We are no different from they*, I thought, and then I could not stop laughing, though my stomach hurt and tears streamed from my eyes.

When the fit had passed, I lay back on my mat, pulling the furs up around me.

"You sleep," Eneko said. "I will keep watch all night."

I wanted to tell him that wasn't necessary, but those weren't the words that came out of my mouth. Instead, I said, "Thank you, *maiti*," and fell deeply asleep.

There is a storm out on the sea.

I am standing on the beach in the Cove of Rocks, watching the horizon. It is night, but I can see the crashing waves, illuminated by flashes of light as the storm moves closer. The wind whips my hair, and rain stings my arms. My skin prickles with danger and the storm's energy.

I should go back to camp, warn the Sea People. But I cannot move.

A hand tucks into mine, and I turn my head.

An old woman, gray-white hair hanging to her waist, stands beside me. Her hair is straight and impossibly still despite the wind. I cannot see her face—I crane my neck, but the closer I look the more indistinct her features are. She tugs at my hand, trying to draw me away from the gale, but my feet will not budge.

"Benare?" I whisper.

The old woman turns her face to the sky and opens her mouth. Thunder erupts, echoing all around me. Lightning splits the horizon.

And then we are running down the beach. She moves with the speed of a much younger woman, pulling me after her, and suddenly we are *flying*, up through the spitting raindrops, up through the clouds, into a clear, star-pricked sky.

Forest rolls away in all directions beneath us. I breathe deeply, pine-scented air filling my lungs as my curls stream behind me.

In an instant, it is over.

I am laying on a fur. A fire burns brightly in the night. On the other side of the blaze a figure sits, watching me: Eneko. I see him from outside of myself. His gaze is bright with green eyeshine, like the lynx . . .

FOURTEEN

I was groggy the next morning, as if my head were full of clouds, but my ankle was better. It was slightly swollen still, and Eneko insisted that I sit with my foot up as he brought water from the stream and fresh *zainbela* leaves. I felt shy lying there as he washed the punctures, chewed fresh leaves, and wrapped new paste around the wound with a rabbit fur. He tied it all in place with a strip of leather, and only then did he permit me to put weight on it. He watched anxiously as I stepped tentatively around the small clearing.

"Does it give you any pain at all?" he asked. "We can rest here for another day. More than one, if you need."

I could walk, and I did not want to lie around. "I am fine! No pain!"

Eneko looked concerned—I don't think he fully believed me—but he nodded and strapped on not just his baskets, but mine, even the drying stick of *hagi*.

And so we left, moving west again, and always uphill.

Before long, we came across the remains of a landslide, the path rising before us littered with rocks and mud. To my side, the earth fell away in a precipitous drop. I kept my eyes on the ground, picking carefully through the rubble, cautious of my ankle. It was only when I reached the top of the broken trail that I looked up. When I did, I gasped.

Valley upon valley stretched before us, each range of hills higher than the next. And beyond them—white-tipped mountains!

"We draw closer," said Eneko. But he did not look at the view; he looked at me.

Ultimately, we had to stop early. I didn't want to—I wanted to keep going—but mid-afternoon I stumbled. Eneko was quickly by my side. "It is paining you, isn't it," he said. It was not a question. "We will stop. See the meadow, just ahead? Can you walk that far?"

"I can walk," I said, annoyed. "I *have* been walking."

"That does not mean you *should* be walking. Dog bites are dangerous."

"I know they are." I didn't want to stop, and I really didn't want to be the cause of our stopping.

"I would be glad to rest," said Eneko, loudly and conversationally, as if to another person. "One of us did not have any sleep last night, after all."

I felt my mouth tugging into a smile.

After we made camp, I had my first practice session with his bow and arrows. Eneko warned me that I needed two healthy legs to shoot properly, but I was impatient and convinced him to let me try. My first lesson, in fact, was almost entirely about balance: where to position my legs, how to hold the bow, how to hold my shoulders as I drew.

"Check your feet," he warned each time I went to draw. And then, when I had ascertained that my feet were aligned beneath my shoulders and planted firmly to the ground, and had finally drawn the string: "Check your elbow." He helped me, adjusting my legs, guiding my shoulders. I was overly aware of his fingers at first, but he was matter-of-fact about it and soon my self-consciousness faded.

The sun was lowering when he finally allowed me to try a shot. "Just one for today," he said, "so you get the feel of it. You will be sore tomorrow as it is." He glanced about, then pointed at a stump twenty paces away. It had a strange shape, peaked, similar to the fur hoods the hunters wore in winter.

I didn't stop to think. I took the arrow he proffered and nocked it, leaning it against my right cheek. I fixed the target in my eye and let fly.

The shaft sailed true, hitting the stump at the peak. A shower of wood exploded.

Eneko whooped, and I laughed in amazement. It felt so natural, so *easy*. "I want to try again!"

"Not tonight." He took the bow from me and put his free arm around my shoulders, giving me a squeeze. "This is the right time to stop, when you have taken your first shot with such success. It's a good omen. You will practice again tomorrow, and every day that follows, but for now, let your body rest."

I knew he was right—my ankle throbbed, and now my shoulder ached too, with the unaccustomed effort of drawing the string. His embrace was warm, and I melted into it for a moment.

In the days that followed, as we came ever closer to that line of white-tipped mountains, we walked through a land so different from my coastal home that it staggered me. The air was clear and sweet, the sky near, the woods thick; there were oaks and pines, but also trees that were completely unfamiliar. Despite the differences, the forest still sang to me. If anything, its pull was stronger here.

I had felt a connection to the forest my whole life, and I had always thought it was land-sense, something inherited through the headwoman's line. But if it was land-sense, why did I have it here, so far from home?

Perhaps I did hear spirits. Perhaps it was nothing to fear.

FIFTEEN

It was midsummer, the days at their longest, when we arrived at Eneko's home.

As he said, it was a mountain valley. To one side there was a cave, a slide of rocks forming a pathway up to its mouth. The cave faced southeast, overlooking a field full of wildflowers. This field sloped steeply down at its southern edge, and at the base of that slope, the forest began. A stream ran along the eastern side of Eneko's valley, and to the west and north, the land rose. A mountain peak towered overhead.

I stood in the middle of the meadow, turning in a slow circle, taking it all in. The air was light and pure—not salty, as at home. The red and white wildflowers glowed bright in the afternoon sun. This was a secret world, hidden and protected.

Eneko seemed anxious. "It has been a long time since I have been here," he said, "and work needs to be done to make it ready for winter. But do you think it will suit you?"

He wants me to like it, I thought.

I was pleased and embarrassed, and I could not meet his eyes. "It is beautiful here," I said softly. I looked up at the mountain's crown.

“Nahia,” he said. His voice was filled with tenderness, and with something else, too, something I couldn’t name. “Will you stay here with me?”

My ears were full of my own heartbeat. I felt liquid, like a mountain stream tumbling down the mountainside, but also shy.

Do I want to be Eneko’s lover? Is that what these feelings mean? What will happen if . . . ?

I looked at him. Our eyes met and my breath caught.

I was tired of thinking, tired of asking myself *what if.* I trusted him. I wanted him.

I slipped my hand into his and leaned against him, holding his gaze. His eyes were deep and brown and soft. My pulse was racing. I was not sure what should come next. I had Izara’s stories, and those of other women, but no experience of my own.

Eneko leaned down toward me, hesitated. “Are you certain?”

“I am,” I whispered.

And then he kissed me. His lips were cool and soft at the same time, searching. My own lips parted, as if of their own accord, and I felt his tongue slip between them. There was a pressure mounting within me, a *wanting* I had never known before.

I pushed myself against him, and his arms enfolded me. One of his hands slipped beneath my tunic, caressing my back, reaching beneath my leggings to pull my body firmly against his. I wrapped my arms around his neck, pulled him closer, *closer*, with an urgency I didn’t understand.

And then I didn’t have to think at all.

SIXTEEN

Light flickered at the edges of my eyelids.

I rolled over, burrowing my face into the sleeping furs, but still the sun warmed the back of my head. The pelts were soft against my cheek, and hot, with a slight tang of woodsmoke from last night's fire. A bird trilled, faintly but sweetly, and another answered. After a moment, I rolled over and opened my eyes, blinking up at the roof of the cave.

Aside from the birds, it was quiet. I stretched my leg across the bed to touch Eneko, but his side of the mat was cold. That's right—he had said he would go hunting this morning. I remembered waking, barely, to the feel of his lips on my temple as he left. It had been dark then, and I had fallen effortlessly back into dreams.

I stretched. From this angle, all I could see was a sliver of azure sky, punctuated by a bright sunwell up in the east. Before I had come to this valley, I had never slept past daybreak unless I was ill. In Abene's tent, I woke early to start the fire and prepare the morning meal; in Eneko's, I rose early to chant.

But here, Eneko told me to sleep as long as I liked. "Sing whenever you arise," he had said, stroking my hair. It was our first morning together in the valley. “There is no need for dawn songs here. Our songs are for us alone now.”

And so I learned I liked sleeping late. I was hesitant at first, but soon enough my reluctance passed, and I luxuriated in the extra hours of slumber. Eneko always rose first and was often gone when I woke; but more often, he was sitting by the cave entrance, watching me.

The day was well started now if the sun was reaching the sleeping area. I rose and wandered to the mouth of the cave. The days were shortening; we had passed midsummer and were hurtling toward fall. Morning was cooler than it had been even two weeks ago. I breathed deeply as I looked across the valley and began to sing. “*Sun rising in the east, awaken us.... We and all our relatives, awaken us.... Sun rising in the east, this singer... I and all my relatives, protect us....*”

The meadow stretched out before me. The flowers were different now than they had been when we arrived, purple and gold instead of red, but the forest was still a deep thick green, cool and inviting. The air was crisp, almost sparkling.

Winter was sure to come to this high valley earlier and harder than it did on the coast. Eneko and I had collected and stored some food, but not nearly enough to get us through. I should have gone hunting with him, but though I loved archery, loved the feel of my arms and shoulders strong as I pulled the bow, loved watching the arrows go where I directed them, I still preferred foraging to killing.

And so foraging I would go. I slung my gathering basket over my shoulders—then grabbed my bow and arrows, too, just in case. I tucked my flint knife into my belt so it would be in easy reach, and set out.

Since we had arrived at the cave, I'd been busy learning the new terrain and new plants. The late summer mushroom season was starting, and the tricks I knew for finding fungi by the sea seemed to work just as well here. I searched the wooded hollows, places where mist lingered into the afternoon, searching under downed trees and low bushes. I was rewarded with an abundance I'd never imagined, more than I could harvest.

Unfamiliar as this new land was, the voice of the forest was still present. I listened to it, following its pull in new directions, letting it teach me about this place. This alpine territory was achingly beautiful. The trees often give way to sudden vistas, and I traveled up and down our mountainside, seeing, feeling, on fire with awareness.

The sun was high and hot in the sky when I stumbled onto something new—a serviceberry bush! And, behind it, in a wall of limestone, the yawning black mouth of a cave.

My stomach growled. The bush promised a snack, and the cave relief from the sun. I ate serviceberries until my hands were sticky, and then I slipped inside.

The darkness was a shock after the brightness of the day. Even when my eyes adjusted, it was difficult to see, but I could tell it was a large cavern, extending far back. There was something alluring about those depths. Following an impulse I didn't understand, I picked up a stray pine branch that was lying at the cave mouth. I used my fire-starting drill to make a spark that lit it.

Something was drawing me in.

Holding the lit branch before me, I made my way deeper into the cave. All was quiet, except for a slow *drip drip drip* of water. It was eerie, yet also comforting: the plopping water, the blackness beyond my small circle of light, the cave's close embrace. I walked deeper. Soon, I was so far in that the light from the entrance was a distant dot, no more than a point to orient myself.

There was a pool back here, a small round body of water. I leaned my torch against the wall and used my hands to bring water to my mouth. It slid down my throat, cold and earthy in taste. The walls drew closer around me, looming shadows that I sensed more than saw.

It felt like I could hear the earth speak, if only I listened hard enough.

As I moved to sit down, something fell from me. I scrabbled around to find it. Dirt—rocks—and then there it was: the hardened clay I had found that day in the forest last winter. The hardened clay. The *tsairi*'s gift. It must have dropped from my pouch as I bent.

I stood there, holding it in my hand. An image arose...

Izara stood before me, just as she was the night before I left the Sea People. She shook her curls so they settled behind her shoulders, and took my hands in hers. Luck go with you, sister, she said.

And then she dropped my hands and walked away.

My heart twisted with the sudden sharp pain of missing my sister.

Where was Izara now? Were the Sea People still clinging to the shore, hoping to fend off the strangers? The ache of missing her was joined by a stabbing guilt. How long had it been since I had thought of her? Of any of them?

And what could I have done for them by staying?

I felt cold. The old Nahia would never have believed she could leave band and family so easily.

I tried to tell them what was coming, I argued with myself. *No one would listen to me.*

I should have tried harder.

These thoughts would not serve me! I had made my choice, for good or ill, and dwelling on what might have happened was foolish. I tucked the *tsairi*'s gift back into its pouch and grabbed the torch, lifting it into the air. Its light caught the rock, illuminating the cavern, and that is when I saw it: a painting of an *orei*, a red deer, its towering antlers spread across the wall behind the pool.

My knees gave way.

I lifted the torch again, more slowly this time. Yes, it really was there. It looked at me and I at it.

I have a message for you, it seemed to say.

But though I sat for some time, I could not hear it.

I returned home, my basket heavy with mushrooms, herbs, and fruits. The slope leading to our home was steep, and I climbed slowly. Eneko's bow was leaning against the cave mouth, I saw when I was halfway up, and I hurried the rest of the way.

The fire was cold and dark. Eneko was slumped against the cave wall, his face drained of color and his eyes closed. *A headache, and a bad one.* As he'd warned me, no remedies ever helped; once the headache arrived, he spent the rest of the evening curled up in pain. Usually, the headaches came on hot days—like today—when we were tired and overheated. The next morning, the pain would be gone, and he would be his usual self.

I tiptoed past, hoping not to disturb him. His eyes opened briefly as I slipped by, then closed again.

I quickly shrugged my basket off my shoulders and set about restarting the fire. I put the mushrooms aside to dry and piled the greens, to be cooked for our evening meal. Then I sat, looking out across the valley, into the forest on the other side. The pine trees swayed in the breeze, their needles rustling. It was as though they were breathing.

If you are going to be a shaman, you should be able to heal a headache. Even one of Eneko's headaches.

There was a new plant I had found this morning; I'd brought it home intending to show it to him. It looked much like a plant from the coast called *mendix*. *Mendix* was a strong tonic for swelling or inflammation. Overheating and swelling went together, I knew; maybe this new plant, if it was like *mendix*, would be good for Eneko's headache.

I found the plant. It was hairy, with long stems, leaves in pairs, and starlike flowers. I plucked a leaf and placed it on my tongue, waiting for the warning tingle that would tell me it might be poisonous. None came. It even tasted like *mendix*. Satisfied, I chopped the leaves and flowers roughly, then poured some water into a cooking basket and added the sliced plant. Once the cooking stones were heated, I added them as well.

When the infusion was ready, I took it to Eneko. His head was tilted back against the cave wall, his face shiny with sweat. I knelt beside him.

"Eneko," I said. "I have something for you. An infusion."

"No," he said, not opening his eyes. "If I rest, it will pass."

"I beg you," I pressed. "Give it a try."

He grunted and pulled himself upright, accepting the cup. Gingerly, he took a sip. His eyes widened and then he drank the infusion quickly, shuddering as he swallowed it down.

Soon after, he crawled into bed and slept. He slept deep and hard, barely moving, through most of the afternoon. I sat at the front of the cave, watching the trees, listening to the wind in the pines. Time softened, melting. The sky deepened into a richer blue, and the first star came out.

Eventually, I heard Eneko stirring. He came up behind me and sat, one leg to either side of me, and wrapped his arms around my waist. His lips brushed the side of my neck. I leaned back, resting against him.

"How was the hunting?" I asked.

"It was good, until the headache. I took an ibex."

I looked toward the lone tree that stood before the cave and saw the ibex hanging from its branches. *How did I miss that?* "Wonderful," I said, snuggling into him.

"Was it *harritz*, in that infusion?" he asked. "Did I show you that plant?"

"I don't know what it was," I admitted.

"Show me."

I pushed myself to my feet and padded back to the basket, retrieving one of the stalks. I knelt before Eneko so our eyes were level and held the stalk out between us.

He took it in his hands and examined it closely. "Yes," he said, "this is *harritz*. You say you didn't know it—why did you make an infusion of it?"

"It looked like *mendix*," I said. "I thought..." What could I say? *I'd thought I'd try an experiment?*

Eneko was shaking his head, and—unbelievably—smiling. "I don't know how you do it," he said. "*Harritz* and *mendix* are similar, yes, but *harritz* is much stronger." He gazed at the *harritz*, the smile fading. "This changes things," he said, as if to himself.

A shadow crossed his face, so quickly I almost didn't see it. For a brief moment, I was frightened—I had never seen this mood. *Do I* truly *know him?*

How did I come to be living in this remote place, far from my people? What have I become? Am I now tsairi*—a wild girl who can abandon her family for an unknown man?*

And then the moment passed, and Eneko was Eneko again—teacher, friend, lover.

Maybe he saw the confusion on my face. He put the plant to the side and took my hands in his. "It was good thinking. And I am grateful for it. *Harritz* is the only plant I know that works on my headaches, but it is hard to find. I should have taught it to you." He laughed. "But I suppose I have now learned I didn't need to."

His smile faded, and he gazed into my eyes, lovingly, sadly, searchingly. It was as if he could look right through me, as if he could see everything I thought, every feeling I had. I wanted to look away. What was he seeing as he looked at me?

But I did not drop my eyes. Instead, I gazed back, wondering if I could ever learn to see into him as he did me.

There were too many disturbing thoughts haunting me today. I would not give them space.

I slipped my hands beneath his clothing to trace the muscle along his back. His hand slid under my tunic in turn, across the skin of my waist, drawing me closer to him.

Our lips met. I pulled back, leant my forehead against his so I could look into his eyes. Then I wriggled out of my tunic, out of my leggings. The warmth of his body, the touch of his hand—I wanted more, always. I lay backward, pulling him down on top of me.

And then I was submerged in love, immersed in it, and there was no longer any space for fear or doubt.

SEVENTEEN

Eneko and I were practicing archery at the western end of the valley, aiming at a lone birch tree. We kept moving farther and farther back; I was learning to shoot at a longer distance. I hit the target, a whorl in the center of the tree, and went to retrieve the arrow. Suddenly, there was a noise from the margin of the woods—a cracking branch. I spun around, bow at the ready, before I realized I didn't have anything to shoot.

A figure stood at the edge of the forest, watching us.

A man? He was wiry, with long, ropy muscles, and he stood in an easy stance that signaled power, or maybe danger. His face was clean shaven and his hair long and gray, hanging loose around a brown and angular face that was lined as an ancient oak. Around his neck hung a set of necklaces made of animal teeth, as if he had been swallowed by a succession of increasingly large animals, and his left arm was tattooed from the wrist up. It looked almost like a sleeve.

A master shaman.

Eneko had gone still at the unexpected noise, but as I watched, he relaxed, and his face lit up in that heart-stopping smile. This time, though, it wasn't for me. "Hodei!" he shouted, and ran toward the figure. Hodei raised an arm in response. They embraced, holding on to each other for a long moment. Though they were the same height, Eneko looked small and compact next to Hodei's sinewy strength.

I slowly made my way toward the two of them. Hodei, the shaman who had been with the Salamander People! Eneko was gesturing at me to hurry, and I broke into a jog.

"Nahia," Eneko said, "You have not met Hodei before, but you know of her."

Hodei bowed to me, and suddenly I saw what I had missed.

"But you are a woman!" I blurted out.

"I am glad to finally meet you, Nahia." Hodei laughed. Eneko was chuckling, too. "I've heard much of you." Two cold gray eyes raked over me, hard as granite.

I bowed back, feeling exposed. *What has she heard?* Eneko was looking at me expectantly. Was I supposed to formally welcome Hodei, as if I were the headwoman of this little camp of two?

"I welcome you, Hodei," I said, extending my hands decorously. I saw the corners of Eneko's mouth turn up, and heat rose in my face. Hodei was amused, too, even as she placed her hands in mine.

I looked at my feet. *Why do I always get these things wrong?*

But after my overly formal greeting, it wasn't so bad. We cooked some of Eneko's ibex to welcome our visitor. Hodei told us of her journey, which had been long and indirect. "I wanted to see how the world is changing," she said. "And it is changing. I do not know if you would recognize the coastal lands anymore. Much of the forest is gone, and most of the bands are no more. There are unaffiliated hunters roaming throughout the country, some solitary, some in groups, moving inland as they search for a home. These are dangerous times."

The Sea People. I swallowed hard.

Hodei's goal was to pass over the mountains to the western sea. "I was born there," she told me, "though it is many years since I called that land home." I looked at her in wonder. I'd been brought up on hair-raising tales of the western sea: it was said to contain towering waves and many-tentacled monsters—like our *olagi*, only larger—that grabbed unsuspecting people and pulled them into the water.

She laughed at my expression. "The western water is real enough. And it does contain many strange creatures. It is as different from the sea you know as the roe deer is from the *orei*. But I left there years ago, and in the time since I've seen much stranger places . . . some of them indescribable. Still, I shall try. Have you heard of *belexka*, the fish people? They are part human, part fish, and from time to time they come ashore in hopes of luring one of us home with them."

I was unsettled by this eccentric person—unsettled and drawn, both. Hodei's stories of the places she'd seen called to me, but at the same time, I wasn't sure I believed them. Or rather, I didn't trust that Hodei told the whole truth. Something about her reminded me of Anai, the shaman of my childhood, the one with whom Abene had quarreled. Hodei was charming, but like Anai, she was detached and elusive. Almost unlike a person at all.

Was this what I would become? Was it what I already was?

No. Eneko is not like that. And I'll be with Eneko.

But *would* I be with Eneko? Women shamans might be rare, but shamans with mates were unheard of.

I pushed the nagging thoughts aside. "Will you stop traveling when you are home?"

Hodei laughed, big and deep. "No. I don't think I'll ever stop traveling."

We made a hide screen for Hodei, and a private space for her at the rear of the cave. There was plenty of room, and she clearly meant to stay for some time. I thought I would resent her, this visitor who broke up the life Eneko and I had made for ourselves. But I quickly grew used to having her around. I wasn't comfortable with her, exactly, but she was exciting. And she took a special interest in me.

She, Eneko, and I hunted together in the early mornings, at her insistence. Hodei commented on my growing skill with the bow and arrow, and Eneko told her, proudly, that I had never hunted at all before we left the coast, that I had demanded to learn, that I was on my way to being the best archer he had ever known. I protested, embarrassed, but perhaps it was true. I liked the feeling of self-sufficiency that came with a bow.

But that was the mornings. Most of the time, Hodei worked with me on what she called *azkerta*. This turned out to be another name for visioning. She explained it in a different way than Eneko had, and I found her explanation made the process easier for me to grasp.

"The idea," Hodei said to me, "is to enter an open state, a meditative state. You can do this any number of ways, but what is important for *azkerta* is that you enter this state with a purpose, so the spirits can reveal to you the root of a situation, the cause of a problem. And then also, the solution." Her eyes bore into mine.

"Like what is making a person sick?" I asked.

"That is one purpose. But there are other reasons, too—what is making a grove of trees die, or a person behave in a way that causes problems. When all seems lost, *azkerta* can reveal a path—or several."

Hodei set me to practice while gazing at the bark of a tree, rather than water. I asked her why, and she laughed. "For different shamans," she said, "the best focus is different. New teachers will teach using what works for them, and Eneko has always had an affinity for water. You may find the spirits speak to you best through boles, or the stars, or some other way. But the technique is always the same. You should practice with as many different subjects as you can."

And, to my surprise, it was easier now. Maybe the months of practice had helped me more than I realized. I still didn't see other worlds—I always knew where I was, and I only saw what was in front of me here, in this world—but when I thought of *azkerta* as a kind of thinking, rather than looking for a vision, it was easy to slip into meditation and learn what I needed to. This was what I did the day I made the *harritz* infusion for Eneko's headache, I realized. I hadn't understood what I was doing, but it was *azkerta*. It wasn't at all like the stories of visions I'd grown up with, any more than my forest-craving had been what I'd expected spirits to sound like. I remembered Eneko telling me visions were sometimes things that "just came out." Visions, like the spirits, weren't what I'd thought they were.

Hodei said I was doing very well with *azkerta*, with the same appraising stare she'd raked me over with the first day.

She taught me much. She told me animal spirits often brought messages, as they were interested in the human world. "Be alert for such messages," she told me. "A friend in the spirit world can help you when you most need it."

I thought of the rabbit that I'd freed from the trap. "Are these animal messengers true spirits, or are they *tsairiu*?"

She paused for a moment. "*Tsairiu*—this is a word people use to mean many things. It is complicated. A *tsairi* can be a shapeshifter, but it can also be a shaman of great power, who hears one animal-spirit clearest, and speaks for that spirit. It may be an animal that others fear. Take—oh, take a bear, for instance. When a bear appears to a seer, it has a message. Usually such a message is not good news. But bears are also powerful protectors, and they can offer weighty guidance. There are shamans who have the bear spirit lodged in them—*tsairiu*, as you say—who can communicate with them. Benare was one."

"But Benare—I was taught she was evil!"

Hodei shrugged. "Evil, who can say what this word means? It is a word the bands use for things that frighten them. Bears are strong, sometimes dangerous. Is that evil?" She paused, and then began to speak again; but she had changed the subject, and was speaking strictly of the mundane world. "Hunters, in their fear, may wish to kill one, but this is unwise. If a bear *is* killed—this can be deadly for the living, because the bear spirit is so powerful, and in its rage at dying it will bring you misfortune. Someday, you will learn the ceremony for this, in case it should be needed, but it is better to avoid such a circumstance."

In the evenings, Hodei joined us in the protection chants. She taught me new songs, songs for healing, for visioning, for greeting the spirits of the mountains. Eneko groaned with the effort of remembering chants for ceremonies he said he'd long forgotten. We passed the nights singing, watching the stars, waiting for dawn. As summer passed, the night became darker, the stars sharper.

At night, singing, I was so filled with happiness I could almost touch it, taste it, become it. I felt as vast and beautiful as the sky surrounding me.

One evening, as Eneko laid out the herbs we used for the protection chant, Hodei interrupted him. "Use this," she said, passing him a small wooden box. He took and opened it, sniffing. A sharp, pungent smell, not unpleasant, pervaded the air. He looked back at Hodei, his eyes wide. She nodded at him. Eneko closed the box and set it at his side.

We began the chants, but the songs were unsettled and restless. The harmonies were shaky, the atmosphere tense, and this made me tense as well. We'd been singing together ever since Hodei had come to us, and we'd never had this problem before. What was wrong?

We finished the first round, and Hodei raised her hand, fingers spread.

Eneko reached for the box. He held it carefully, stroking it. His long fingers moved across the lid, slowly, delicately. The back of my neck prickled. Something about the box, about the way Eneko handled it, unnerved me. Hodei, beside me, was not reassuring. In the firelit cave, with her shining eyes and piles of unbrushed hair, she looked fully inhuman—almost like one of the *isuge*, the spirits who bring the summer storms. I looked back to Eneko, trying to catch his eye. His face, too, was remote and alien. He murmured something under his breath, unfamiliar words spoken in a quick staccato rhythm. As I watched, he lifted the lid and the sharp smell blew out again.

I was seized with dread. It's nothing, I told myself, but I didn't believe it. My heart was in my throat, my breath shallow.

With a sudden violent gesture, Eneko reached his hand into the box, and scattered a handful of the contents over our fire. The flames leapt, and the cave filled with smoke. The pungent smell was overpowering. I coughed, choking on the thick, heavy scent. Hodei's hand pressed down on my shoulder.

"Relax," she said. "And breathe."

I took a deep breath, then another. My throat caught on the first inhale, and I coughed again, but the second was smooth, as if I'd been born to breathe smoke and not air.

I was in the *orei*'s cave, the one I'd found while gathering, before Hodei came.

I had no torch this time, but the cave was illuminated, the walls shining. I was kneeling before the pool of water, my hands crossed over my chest, and reflected in the water I saw myself, sitting with Eneko and Hodei around the fire, all of us chanting. But before me, on either side of me, rose the cave walls, as I remembered them. Behind me was the *orei* on the wall.

Or was it? The air was chill against my back, chill and damp, as if I were sitting in fog. I felt a pressure behind me, a sense of something reaching toward me, grasping.

I rose to my feet and turned.

The cave was gone.

I was walking through the forest near the Sea People's winter camp. I knew it instantly, though I'd never been there in the summer. The night was warm and heavy and dark, but I could see as clearly as if it were day. Every trunk, every leaf, was outlined in light. The sea, not far away, made a rushing sound.

My feet moved noiselessly through the leaf-litter. The trees sighed overhead. Fog stole in and surrounded me, obscuring my vision with tendrils of ghostly white. I sensed nocturnal creatures moving around me.

There was a bear. I could smell it, and I heard it, too. It shuffled through the leaves beside me. Above me an *arhontzl* chittered, warningly. But I was not frightened

There was a light in the forest, far ahead. As I walked toward it, I realized it was the central fire, and I walked faster, soon reaching winter camp. The mist was heavier here, and the world eerily empty. The tents were overgrown, tattered, starting to fall apart. Udane's had a gash in its side.

I ran toward the central fire, pausing only when I reached the edge of the clearing.

Sitting there were Izara and Abene. My heart soared to see my sister, and then plummeted as I looked more closely.

They were thin, too thin: collarbones and knees protruding. Their heads were bent toward each other. They were talking, but I could not hear them. Abene's face was drawn, defeated. Izara took Abene's hands in hers and whispered something urgently.

I opened my mouth to call out to them, but no sound emerged. I tried to walk toward them, but I could not move any closer. I could only stand there, watching.

Behind me, the sound of a human foot breaking a fallen branch. I turned and saw Kerbasi. My eyes shot to the shadows behind him: yes, Omer was there, too, lurking.

Kerbasi was laughing. "So you couldn't stay away from us, eh, Nahia? We knew you'd be back."

The fog was coming thicker now, obscuring the forest, obscuring his face, obscuring everything except his hand, reaching toward me.

The *arhontzl* chittered. The bear growled.

Eneko said, "Nahia."

It was like plunging into ice-cold water. I jerked, and I was back in the mundane world.

My throat was hoarse, as if I'd been shouting. The fire was burning, but my sweat-soaked skin was cold and clammy. My heart raced.

There was no Kerbasi here, no winter camp, no threat. The smell of the herb Eneko had thrown on the fire, so heavy in the air before, had dissipated. Our cave now smelled of the ordinary, comforting scent of burning pine. I didn't see the small wooden box at all.

My eyes smarted, and my head was heavy. I couldn't quite remember what had happened. Had we left the cave? Or had I fallen asleep?

Eneko was staring at me, his mouth slightly open. I glanced at Hodei. She was looking at me with interest.

"What did I do?" I asked. "What did I say?" My voice was little more than a whisper.

"Nothing, nothing," Hodei said. "You surprised us, that is all." Her tone did not match her words; her voice was cold, and the words hung over me like icicles.

I shrank into myself. I started shivering, my teeth chattering.

"Eneko," Hodei said. Even the name, as she spoke it, was sharp. Eneko shook himself and spoke the usual closing words of the protection chant. When he finished, he sat next to me, put his arm around me. I huddled against him. He was warm, so warm. My skin had dried, but I was still cold.

"I think it best we sleep now," said Hodei. The ice that had been in her voice was gone, melted away as if it had never been. She sounded simply thoughtful. "I have much to consider." She stood and bowed, first to me, then to Eneko. "Good night."

I expected her to go to her space in the back of the cave, but instead she walked out into the valley, disappearing into the darkness.

I gazed at Eneko. He shrugged at me, then took my hand. "Come," he said. "Let's go to bed."

EIGHTEEN

The next morning, I woke to Eneko's arms around me. I jolted away without thinking, Kerbasi in my mind. But then I smelled the mountain air, saw the sunlight, felt Eneko's tender presence. I rolled over to kiss him, but he withdrew to a sitting position.

"Are you feeling all right?" He was looking at me, concerned.

"I think so," I answered, my throat scratchy. My dreams had faded; I could not recapture them. They were mixed up with last night's vision, a shadowy, oppressive mass at odds with the daylight. "Yes, I'm fine. Truly." I sat up as well, pushing the hair from my face, and made again to kiss him.

This time he didn't withdraw, but the kiss, though deep, was brief. He rested his forehead against mine, looking into my eyes. "I am worried for you, Nahia," he whispered. "I don't know what you saw last night—no, do not speak of it. Your vision is for you alone. The *ikuspe*—that is the herb in the box last night—you shouldn't talk about what it shows you, or what any other plant-gift might show you. That experience is private, a way for the spirits to speak with you. You will have to learn for yourself what they were saying." He drew a breath. "But what the *ikuspe* told me—it told me that I must share a foreboding with you. I worry. I sense a darkness hanging over you, and I worry."

I drew back, folding my arms across my belly. The vision that burdened me—how could Eneko know of it? How could the *ikuspe* tell him what I was seeing, what I was feeling?

He reached out, caressed my face. "I do not wish to frighten you. What I learn when I take *ikuspe*—it is more felt than known, never precise. It is like being underwater and navigating there. All I can say is I feel danger lurking around you, and something trying to draw you away." He managed a melancholy smile. "You will know what is right. Just listen, and think."

It occurred to me to wonder if Eneko had sent for Hodei.

His words about the *ikuspe* and what he saw when he took it were the closest to a teaching he had offered since she came. Hodei had become my teacher instead. It seemed too perfect, too obvious, to be anything but deliberate. I remembered Eneko saying, *This changes things*, the day I had made him the infusion of *harritz*.

But...how could Eneko have sent for her? There had been no one for him to send. Was this something else he could do through the *ikuspe*?

I tried to put the thought from my mind, but it kept coming back to me. Along with the image of Izara's too-thin face.

I had been nervous to see Hodei again. But when I met her, it was as if there had been no trance, as if nothing unusual had ever happened. She asked me nothing about my vision and said nothing about what she might have experienced in turn. Eneko had said we weren't to talk about visions, and maybe that was why. Hodei behaved as she always had: remote, inscrutable, arch.

She did give me new instructions, however. She sent me to practice *azkerta*, as usual, but she gave me two new items to take with me. One was a familiar-looking little reed bundle, which she brought out from her basket full of herbs. I looked at it, and then at her, and asked, "*Mixtol*?"

Hodei raised her eyebrows. "You know *mixtol*?"

I explained about the hunters in the forest, and the dog bite.

She nodded. "Be careful with *mixtol,* always. Eneko told you of its dangers. I tell you as well: it must be used sparingly and treated with respect. This here is not *mixtol*, but it must also be treated with respect. It is prepared as a paste as *mixtol* is, which is why we use this type of carrier. We call it *aubli*. As with the *mixtol,* take the tiniest amount. One small bit, from your finger, before you begin your practice. And for the second . . ." She reached up and plucked a hair from her head, a single long gray strand. She placed it in my hand, wrapping my fingers around it. "Take this with you, when you go out to practice today. When you come back, tell me what you have learned."

"What I have learned," I repeated. What did she mean?

"What I said," she said, answering my unasked question. She gave me a little half-smile. "Go on now."

There was clearly no additional explanation forthcoming, so I took myself, the reed bundle, and the strand of hair to a piece of forest that had become my preferred *azkerta* spot. It was on the edge of a meadow, where a set of fallen trees formed a squared space in which I could sit and direct my attention to wood, or to earth, or to whatever focus I was trying. Today, I had brought a bark cup, which I filled at a stream along the way. I was thinking of last night and the quiet pool in the *orei*'s cave. I had an idea that still water might work better for me than running water. Certainly in the *ikuspe*-fueled vision it had.

I sat between the logs, placing the cup on the ground before me. After a moment's thought, I dropped Hodei's hair into the water. I dipped my finger into the reed bundle, took a small amount of the *aubli*, and licked my finger clean. And then I settled myself.

The aubli was bitter on my tongue, and its taste lingered. I swallowed, several times, trying to force it down. And then the bitterness faded.

I was once again in the *orei*'s cave, facing the pool of water, hands crossed over my chest. Once again, I felt the pressure behind me, the shadows grasping at me: they were clearer this time, like vines crawling around my legs and arms.

The pool's surface did not reflect my image; instead it showed me Hodei, alone. She was sitting before a tree, as if practicing *azkerta*; but aside from her and the tree, I could see no other living thing. It was as if she and the tree were suspended in a cloud.

My task was to tell her what I had learned. So I stepped into the pool.

I knew that in life, the pool could not be deeper than a few handspans, but my foot did not touch any bottom. Instead, the water closed over my head, and I found myself moving through a haze.

Hodei sat beside the tree. She was dressed in her full regalia: not just tunic and leggings, not just a shaman's pendant, but the many necklaces of strung teeth—wolf, *orei,* boar—and a horned headdress.

When I drew near, she looked up and smiled at me. There was something satisfied in her smile, something knowing.

Hodei lifted her hand: in it was an antler shed from a roebuck. Its three points glistened in the strange half-light. She threw it ahead of her, where it vanished into the grayness.

"Bring it back to me," she said.

And then she was gone. In her place stood a roebuck with just one antler. He barked and bounded off into the vapor.

I stared blankly into the grayness, feeling more and more uneasy. With Hodei gone, the shadow returned, its tendrils clinging to me and intensifying their grip. My legs and arms were enveloped, and I could not follow where the roebuck had gone. So I turned to face the dark, ignoring the dread in my chest.

Before me, again, was the Sea People's winter camp.

Again, I could see though it was dark; again, fog drifted through the trees; again, the bear was close beside me, but I could not see her. The *arhontzl* chittered overhead. I walked through the woods toward the fire, where, again, Izara and Abene sat, their bodies bony. Behind them I could see the collapsing tents, the overgrown and empty campsite.

I could make no sound, nor could I touch them. I watched as tears formed in Abene's eyes. Had I ever seen my mother cry?

Never. Not when Aitor died; not even when our little sister was born dead. Izara took Abene's hand in hers, cradling it tenderly, as if Abene were the child.

Again, a cracking branch behind me. Again, I turned to find Kerbasi, laughing, hand extended; and Omer, lurking in the shadows.

Something in me cracked, an echo of that cracking branch. In that moment, I knew myself in a new way: large, fierce. *Angry*. I met Kerbasi's eyes. I lowered my head, glaring. His hand faltered, fell to his side.

I heard the growl of the bear. I could see her now, on all fours beside me, ears pinned back. My hand reached up to rest on her back, her fur thick under my fingertips.

I saw the sudden fear in the men's eyes.

"**Go**," I said to the bear.

And then they were running: Omer and Kerbasi, yelling as they tore through the forest; the bear huffing, intent, close on their trail. They disappeared from view, hidden by the fog.

I heard a scream, loud and high and full of terror.

And then my head broke through the water of the pool.

I was sitting in the forest, in my *azkerta* spot, drenched in sweat, shaking. The cup had fallen over and the water spilled out.

It was a long time before I was able to move.

I fell asleep. It was just a nightmare, I told myself. One born of my guilt, of my fear, of the leftover *ikuspe* in my body. But it had seemed horribly real.

It *couldn't* be real. Hodei could not turn into a roebuck; bears did not come and go at my command. I was human. I was not *tsairi*, and neither was she.

I don't know how long I sat there before I rose to my feet, brushed myself off, and started back to the cave. I moved slowly as I walked from the forest into the meadow. My foot caught on something. I crouched to look.

A roe deer's shed antler, its three points catching the afternoon light.

My palms went slick. But I picked it up and took it with me.

Hodei was waiting for me outside the cave, leaning against the stone with her eyes closed. "And what do you have for me?" she asked, holding out her hand.

I placed the antler there.

She smiled. It was a different smile than her usual half-mocking look; there was pride there, and something more.

"I thought so." She went inside, antler in hand, pausing only to say, "Well done."

I stared after her with a sinking sensation in my belly.

NINETEEN

The next morning, Eneko and I went out alone. We invited Hodei, but she laughed and said no, she had much to do on her own. There was something carefully offhand in her voice. I looked closely at her when she said it, but she just smiled and raised her eyebrows as if daring me to inquire further. I dropped my gaze. I did not want to think about yesterday's lesson.

"I am glad to have some time alone with you, *maiti*," Eneko said. "I will show you how to make fishhooks."

We walked, hand in hand but not speaking. The silence wasn't comfortable. I thought perhaps he knew something about my vision from yesterday, but how could he know? Could Hodei have told him about the antler? If she had, what exactly would she have told him?

We followed the stream as it wound down the mountainside. We reached a deep pool in a field of boulders, shielded from the summer sun by cork oaks. Eneko scrambled onto one of the rocks, a wide, flat one, and beckoned me to follow. He reached into his basket and pulled out an ibex bone—one of the toe bones, I thought—then a knife, larger than mine, with a handle made of ash, and a small grinding stone.

"You have fished before, yes?" he asked me.

"Only with a trap." Fishing with line and hook was a hunter's activity.

He nodded. "This method is easier if you are traveling." He used the knife to carve a thin slice from the middle of the bone. "The hardest part of making the hook is this. The bone must be the correct thickness, and it is easy to break. Once you have your cut, it is simply a matter of shaping the hook, so the ends are pointed." He handed me the bone and knife. "You try."

He was right; it was hard. My first attempt resulted in a pile of bone splinters. But eventually I managed to cut a piece I could use. I took the grinding stone and began to shape the bone shard's ends. Eneko had already finished his hook. He'd attached it to a straight branch with a fine cord made from plant fiber and had cast it into the stream.

The sun warmed my back as I bent over the fishhook. Concentration drove my worries into the back of my mind; there was no room for any thoughts but those of the tool before me. I hummed to myself as I sharpened the ends.

"Nahia," Eneko said suddenly, and I looked up. His face was serious, his eyes sad. My earlier worries came rushing back, all at once. "Are you sure you want to do this?"

"Do what?" I asked, confused.

He didn't answer right away. I remembered, with a sudden clarity, his words from yesterday morning. *I sense a darkness hanging over you, and I worry.* What if he knew about my visions, not from Hodei, but from his own?

I felt the bear's fur under my hand, heard myself saying "**Go**..." I felt the twining darkness reaching for me, tendrils wrapping around my arms and legs.

What if I, myself, was the darkness Eneko sensed?

He placed his hands gently on my cheeks, his thumb stroking the soft skin under my eye. I was comforted by his touch, but not the words that followed.

"To be able to enter a vision is a great gift... but it is also dangerous. Especially when one is new to seeing. Sometimes, spirits... they have their own mind, and they will try to bend you to their will."

I swallowed. Eneko's words were too close, too sure. He must know every detail of what I'd seen and done. And if he did, what must he think of me?

A spirit hadn't demanded anything of me—not that I'd understood, anyway. None had bent me to their will. But there was so much darkness in my visions.

Eneko had told me once that *tsairi* was just a name the bands gave to people who took spirits into themselves. He'd implied that he did this himself. But Eneko would never let darkness invade him, nor a vicious spirit influence him. But I...

I swallowed.

The shadow-vines that ensnared me. The brown bear I'd set on Kerbasi and Omer. Had I wanted to do that, or had the bear spirit? Were the vines a darkness within me, an evil that set me apart from others?

The bear, the shadows... they were just visions.

But the antler was incontrovertible proof that my visions were not "just." They had implications for the mundane world. What did the sinuous darkness in my visions say about me?

"You should know, no matter what those spirits say to you, no matter what Hodei says to you," Eneko continued, his voice low, "no matter what I say to you, you do not have to do anything you do not want to do."

I wet my lips. "I don't understand."

"I know," Eneko said. His dark gaze was desolate. "But I don't know how else to tell you what I mean."

There was a pressure behind my eyes. *There is no reason for me to cry. No reason, and I won't.*

I forced the tears back. Eneko was still looking at me. I smiled and kissed him, wrapping my arms around his neck, tugging him toward me. After a moment, he pulled his head back a handsbreadth. "You are so dear to me, *maiti*," he said. "Dearer than you can ever know." And then he lowered himself beside me, drawing me close. And the darkness within me was blotted out by his light, at least for a time.

That night, the *ikuspe* powder did not make an appearance, and I finally began to relax. I would be free of visions.

Once we began the first song, our voices settled easily into a strong true harmony. All my concerns evaporated with the song, as fully as if they'd never existed.

My body was tingly, extraordinarily alive. My skin prickled with awareness, as if a storm were coming, and I were part of it. The fire, the trees, the sky, the stars—Eneko and Hodei and I were bound into this world. I felt life flowing through me, and I knew: *I am part of the meadow, the oaks, the moonlight, the flowers, the mountains. I am part of everything.*

The chant ended. I waited for Eneko or Hodei to speak the closing words, but the silence stretched out. The fire crackled, and the air did as well.

And then, they began a different chant, one I didn't recognize. There was an urgency to the melody, a driving rhythm, but I didn't understand most of the words.

Eneko moved closer to me, not breaking the song, and gestured for me to remove my tunic. I hesitated. Hodei was rummaging in a leather bag I hadn't noticed earlier. My heart sped up. Eneko tapped at my arm, insistently. His tattoo, the single band on his upper arm that marked him as an initiated shaman, stood out black in the firelight.

Hodei turned back to us, a pouch in one hand and a long, slender bone tool, polished to a sharp point, in the other. I had never seen a tool quite like it—it was similar to an awl, but much longer, and its point much finer. I found myself staring at her tattooed arm, bands ornamenting it from shoulder to wrist in a shadow sleeve. The bands were of different designs, some with embellishments, others curving in intricate patterns. But the band at the top was plain, identical to Eneko's.

Eneko and Hodei stopped chanting. The silence was charged and heavy.

"Nahia," said Hodei, "you have attained the knowledge of a shaman. You are ready to join us in your own right—if you will."

My heart beat faster than ever. I looked from Eneko to Hodei and back again.

I can say no. That's what Eneko was trying to tell me.

If I say no, I can step away from the darkness in me.

But refuse this? Give up the chanting, the azkerta, *this sense of connection with the world? I don't even want to give up the visions; I'm happier now than I've ever been before.*

Surely, such happiness is a sign that I am doing right?

I can be a shaman and human, too. Eneko is human, fully human.

Eneko and Hodei were waiting. I pushed back my fears.

"I am ready," I said, and removed my tunic.

Hodei smiled as she settled herself on my right side. "This will hurt," she warned me. "It will take some time. And you will need to take close care of the mark for some weeks, while it heals." She smiled again. "But I am glad you made this choice."

"If it hurts too much, if you need Hodei to stop while you rest, she will," Eneko said, concerned.

"Of course," Hodei said. "But I do not think she will need me to stop. She is shaman-born. The spirits watch over their own. *You* know that."

Hodei dipped the bone tool into the bag. When she withdrew it, its point was covered with a black pigment. "And so," she said, as she applied the point to my arm.

Sharp pain, as the point pierced my skin. A moan escaped my lips, and I closed my eyes. Against the black of my eyelids I saw the rabbit-*tsairi* I'd freed from the trap, so long ago now. I heard the growl of the bear, the call of the *arhontzl.* There was no twining darkness, not here, not now.

"Do you need me to stop?" Hodei's voice sounded as if it was coming from far away.

"No," I said, and it was true. "They are with me."

My upper arm was wrapped in moss, shielding the new tattoo. My arm ached, but I felt good, strong, washed clean of troubles. I breathed in the morning air, savoring its sweetness.

I didn't want to wake Eneko; he so rarely slept well. I crawled out of the bedding and padded to the front of the cave. Hodei was already up. She stood as soon as I emerged, smiling as if she'd been waiting for me. "Come," she said, "let your man sleep. We will go hunting."

Hodei said she wanted small game only, things easy to carry. "I must be leaving soon," she said, "if I am to cross the mountains before winter." So we went after rabbits, the fat ones of late season. My sore arm didn't hinder my aim: one, two, three rabbits fell beneath our arrows. As I picked them up, removing the arrows and tossing the carcasses in the basket I carried, I thought of the rabbit in the snare that long-ago day. These fat bunnies looked so different, they might have been a completely different kind of animal. But they were just larger, better fed, healthier. Like me, now.

Hodei, finally sat, beckoning me to join her. She'd taken two cups from her basket and filled them in a stream. She held one out to me.

I put my basket down, handed her the arrows and accepted the cup of water. She placed the arrows in the quiver. "Well shot today," she said. "You aim better than any hunter I have known."

We sat quietly, sipping, watching the sun stretch over the grasses. I was not easy, now that we were quiet. There was something in the way Hodei held herself, something in her silence that told me she had words to give me.

Sure enough, after a time Hodei spoke. "Nahia. How well do you know Eneko?"

I was startled. "W—what do you mean?" I stammered.

Hodei didn't answer my question. She looked at me, her face serious, her gray eyes narrow in her brown face. "Do you understand why shamans live their lives alone?"

My throat was swollen with all the things I didn't know. I shook my head.

"To be a seer is not easy. I think you have grasped this already, yes? Yesterday was just the beginning. There are many trials, so much one must learn. And to learn these things, one must be alone."

"But you learn from a teacher, no?" I asked.

Hodei inclined her head. "Sometimes," she allowed. "But with a teacher one can only go so far. The day comes for every shaman when she must go forward on her own." We were sitting cross-legged, and she reached out and tapped my knee. "I do not know what lies ahead for you. The spirits of your homeland, they cling to you. They are keeping your new protectors from you. These new protectors, they hover around you like a cloud, but they cannot come near. This I have seen."

I pulled away, filled with shame. If she saw so much, she must know about the violence within me. Even if she herself could take animal form, a roebuck is not a bear, and she enacted no vengeance on anyone. We were not the same sort of *tsairi*.

But Hodei was calm. "You have a choice, Nahia. Eneko has told you as much," she said. "You are shaman-born, make no mistake. When we took the *ikuspe*, both he and I saw you in the spirit world. No one who is not a shaman could have made such a journey. When I saw you there, I knew the time had come to test your abilities, and if you succeeded, for you to receive the tattoo. But having the tattoo—it means you are a shaman, yes. You have the gift. But it does not say what sort of shaman you shall be. What you do with the gift is your choice. You can go on learning." She gestured to her own arm, covered in tattoos from wrist to shoulder. "Or you can choose another path."

She stopped then, and waited, as if expecting me to respond.

The morning was bright, but I felt the twining shadow-vines from my visions reaching around my legs and arms again. I saw Izara and Abene, by the fire, surrounded by the abandoned camp. The chittering of the *arhontzl*, the growling of the bear.

Hodei's words had brought clarity. The grasping darkness in my visions—it was not evil. It had purpose. It was the darkness I had left behind me.

The words tumbled out of my mouth. "You were at the coast, Hodei—have you any news of Abene's band, the Sea People?"

Hodei didn't seem surprised by my question, as abrupt as it was. She shrugged. "Only very little news."

"Tell me," I pleaded.

She sighed and shook her head. "I passed through their summer territory. No one was there."

"And that is all you know?"

"There was a bit of gossip in the interior. Some of the hunters from the Sea People sought new bands early in the summer, when there was a fracture. They said your mother chose to keep the gatherers along the coast."

Surely not.

Surely, she and Udane would have led the women and children to one of the interior bands.

Surely. Surely.

Abene and Izara, alone at the fire, tears running down my mother's face.

Hodei was watching me. "There was a story that the Sea People's women had been taken. By the strangers."

I knew it, but I hadn't wanted to know it.

I stared across the stream. It wasn't shock that kept me silent—it was the heavy weight of responsibility, coupled with dread. I knew what the vision of my mother and sister had meant. I had known it the first time I'd seen it, and I'd known it the second. I just hadn't wanted to face it.

With a sudden fierceness I wished I was a proper shaman, like Anai—someone who wouldn't care, someone *detached*. Then I could stay here and keep the beautiful life I'd managed to build.

But I did care.

Izara rescued me once. Now I must rescue her.

I wasn't sure what I could do. I hadn't even been able to defend myself in the past. But I was different now, wasn't I? Something had woken in me. I had the bow. I had a shaman's power. I would find a way.

Hodei was watching me. "You are shaman-born, yes. But if you are determined to involve yourself in the living world, that is your decision." She drained her cup and stood.

TWENTY

Hodei left the next morning. She went early, before the sun was up.

"Are you sure you must go?" I asked, fiddling with the sleeve of my tunic. "You could stay a while longer. I . . . I wish you would."

But Hodei demurred, commenting to Eneko how lucky he was to have such a beautiful and competent partner. I was too distracted even to be embarrassed by this. Hodei embraced him, then turned to me. She took my chin in her hands. Her gaze was intense, but affectionate.

"Remember what I said, Nahia," she told me, her eyes holding mine.

I have already made my choice.

Her mouth quirked up in a smile—I don't know if she heard my thoughts, but I had the sense she had. I squirmed uncomfortably. Hodei laughed and dropped her hands. "Remember," she said to me again, and then she left.

Eneko and I stood together at the mouth of the cave and watched her cross the valley. His arm was around my waist, and I drew comfort from the heat of his body.

Now there would be nothing left for me and Eneko but pain. I would have to tell him I was leaving, and then I would have to go.

He turned my face with his free hand and kissed me, softly. "You liked Hodei?" he asked against my mouth. "She was my first teacher."

I was surprised, but as he said the words it seemed obvious. "I didn't know that!"

Eneko laughed and drew back. "I was a very small boy when Hodei was shaman with my band. I was—oh, maybe a little older than your friend in the Sea People, the little boy with the light hair."

An image of Gotzon, laughing, his head shining in the sunlight, flashed before my eyes. My chest was suddenly tight. *Gotzon, where are you? Are you dead? Or have you somehow managed to survive?*

"I was young, but already skilled at hunting. I was old enough to go with the hunters every day, and I shot well enough that I could almost have earned my place among them. But I preferred to trail after Hodei instead. She was younger then—her hair was still black. I idolized her, worshipped her, the way children will with their older siblings, or their aunts and uncles. Only I never felt so about my older brother, or my uncles, or any of the people of my band."

Eneko paused for a moment. He gazed west, the direction Hodei had gone. I could see the little boy who had trailed after her in his face. "I don't think anyone was surprised when she made me her apprentice, though I was just a small boy."

"But how could she know, that you had the talent, when you were so young?"

"It isn't hard to see when a child has the gift. It makes itself known, one way or another. Someone with the gift—well, she stands out." He winked at me, mischievously. "I knew you had it from the moment I came to the Sea People. It's why I stayed as long as I did."

I stared at him, speechless.

He laughed and twined his fingers with mine. "For me, becoming shaman's apprentice was a joy. It wasn't like it was for you. I knew Hodei already, and I revered her. I spent my days with her, in her teaching, and only left her to sleep in my mother's tent." He paused. "When Hodei departed, she took me with her."

"When you were so young?" I asked, startled. "Or this was later?"

"I was in my eighth year."

I was truly shocked. I tried not to be, but I was. Eneko smiled at me—that intoxicating smile of his—and my heart twisted. "She brought me out this way, to a valley a few days' journey west of here. And we lived in a cave much like this one, and I learned about plants, and chanting, and all the things you have been learning."

"When you were in your *eighth year*?" I asked again. I tried to imagine Gotzon sitting up all night, learning the protection ceremonies. I couldn't picture him sitting still long enough to sort plants, let alone chanting.

Eneko chuckled. "It was maybe not as intense for me as for you! I was a child. I was given time to play. But still, I was busy, and it was years before I began to wonder about my band, why I had left them, and what I was doing in a valley with only one other person. And when I did start to wonder, when I did finally think of it, I was angry. So I ran away."

"Returning to my band was not a simple matter. I am from the mountains and I was used to hard journeys, but still—it was a very long walk. And I was not quite sure I knew where I was going. It took me the better part of a season to find them. They were happy to see me, even after the time that had passed. My mother cried, to see how big I had grown." He sighed. "It didn't last. I stayed with them only a month—maybe not even so much—before I left. The difference between me and them was too great. It was then I first knew myself as someone *other*. I understood that I saw the world differently than most people. And I knew I could not stay."

"Where did you go?" I asked.

"I made my way back to Hodei. I walked through the winter—it was foolish, but I was very young. And I learned much from such a harsh trip." Eneko's face was shadowed now. He picked up a stick from the pile of kindling and held it. Anyone else, I thought, would jiggle it, or break it, or poke the earth with it. Not Eneko. He let it rest, cradling it in his hand. "When I returned, things were different. We were not yet equals, but I was no longer a child. I knew my worth. And I knew what I needed to learn."

"You know, don't you," I said.

He gave me a long, perceptive look.

"But it isn't the same," I said. "You know it isn't the same, don't you? Your story and mine? I *must* leave. I have to. My visions—they show me Izara, over and over. It is the Sight that is sending me back."

Eneko didn't speak, didn't move a muscle.

I cleared my throat. Why was this so hard to say? "You—you could come with me," I finally managed.

His mouth curved a little, but his eyes were sad. I knew before he spoke. "No, Nahia. You know I cannot. I am a shaman; I do not interfere with the lives of the bands."

"But—" I started, and fell silent.

There was no judgment in his voice, just simple fact. "As I am sure Hodei told you, you must decide for yourself what path you will take. Only you can know what the spirits are telling you; only you can know which responsibilities are yours. If you feel that this is what you must do, I will not try to stop you." He laid his hand on my arm. "You can always come back—you know that, yes? You can always stay with me, here, or wherever you might find me."

His eyes were wet; so were mine. I let the tears run down my cheeks.

I did not leave that day, nor the next. A week passed before I could make myself go.

But eventually, the morning came when I stood with Eneko before the cave, my bow and my baskets slung across my back. I reached for him, pulling his mouth down to mine. I meant for it to be a simple goodbye kiss. But I did not want to say goodbye, and the kiss deepened, my lips moving searchingly against his. His warmth poured into me, the strength and comfort of summer sunshine.

I moved to slip the bow and baskets from me, but Eneko stepped back, breaking the contact. He turned his head from me.

"Go," he said. He was breathing heavily. "If you truly must go, go now. I promised myself I would not ask you to stay, and I am losing my resolve."

So I left.

I set out across the valley, looking over my shoulder every few paces until he was out of sight.

Leaving him was like being ripped in two. Every step was pain, and I was blind to everything but my own misery. The only thought I could hold on to was *I must keep walking, or I will never leave.*

I retraced the journey Eneko and I had made several months before, and nothing—not hunger, not caution, not anything—penetrated the gloom that surrounded me. I moved through the forest without seeing it, walking until it was too dark to see and then collapsing in the brush. I would sleep until the first rays of dawn woke me, and then I would crawl from my meager hiding place and set out again. I slept little, but mostly soundly.

But one night, I woke fully and completely when it was still dark. I could tell from the stars that dawn was hours away. I was tucked into a stand of brush, my baskets and bow beside me. My breathing was shallow, my veins hot. I was terrified, but I didn't know why.

And then I heard it: the short bark a roe deer makes when startled, followed by the hissing call of a lynx.

I lay still as stone, not breathing, not blinking.

There came another bark, tapering off into a whine. And then chewing and growling, as the big cat devoured its kill.

My heart, which had frozen along with the rest of me, started beating again, a fast wild rhythm. The lynx was so close. It must have been just outside the brush in which I slept.

I lay paralyzed. *How could I be so stupid? How could I be so* stupid*?* When Eneko and I had traveled, we'd made a fire every night. Why hadn't I done the same? If I didn't want to take the time to make a fire, I could at least have climbed a tree. I spent the rest of the night awake, motionless, curled into a ball. As soon as light came, I hurried up and off.

The lynx had jolted me out of my stupor. After that evening, I paid more attention to my surroundings. I no longer trusted the protection of the brush, but slept in trees. Even in the daytime I was nervous and kept my bow and arrows close at hand.

With those, I knew I could defend myself from most animals if I was awake... except for bears. They would be frenzied in this season. I saw one once, from a distance, across a meadow. He was in a thicket of brambles, so engrossed by the berries he didn't see me. I carefully skirted the edges of the clearing.

I worried, too, about encountering people. Hodei had said the land was full of unaffiliated hunters, searching for new bands. I should be able to defend myself against them, too, but still I did not want to meet such men.

As the days passed and I had less and less travel food, I ate less. I didn't want to be troubled with hunting, butchering, and preserving while I was traveling; I wanted to make good time to the coast, and so when the dried meat was gone, I lived off the plants I could forage along the trail. But I couldn't devote much time to gathering—I wanted to arrive at the coast before fall really set in—and in my hurry, I must have made a mistake and taken something poisonous. I spent an entire precious day curled up by a stream, taking as much water as I could but unable to keep anything else down. I felt a little better the following day, and kept moving, but from then on, I seemed to swing constantly between unbearable queasiness and overpowering hunger. I ignored it as best I could, but it slowed me down.

And then, finally, I did encounter a bear.

It was late in the afternoon. My feet were tired, and my mind was muddled with exhaustion. I entered a glade, golden in the late afternoon light, with a stream on the far side. The grasses smelled sweet and were warm as they brushed against my ankles.

A hot drink and cooked food sounded like unimaginable luxury, and yet, I thought, they were easily within my reach. *I will make a fire, and I will heat some water, and I will wash myself. And then I will make myself a warm meal.*

I was in such a hurry I tripped over a chamois carcass—and then I heard a deep growling.

A bear was standing directly in front of me, on her hind legs, her forelimbs in the air.

Her shaggy fur was a beautiful brownish red, standing out like the sun's corona. Her large paws were bloody with the chamois. The bear's musky smell mixed with the odor of carrion. Nausea surged up my throat.

I looked at her. She looked at me. The sun's reflection made her eyes glow yellow.

I knew the worst thing to do was to run. But I was so close to her. And I had interrupted her while she was eating.

I had my bow and arrows. I could shoot her. But I was all alone. I'd have to kill her with a single arrow, and I didn't know if that was even possible. I'd never killed anything so large before.

And of course, this was a bear. I didn't know the right songs, if I killed her.

"*Go*," I'd told the bear in my vision.

The decision came down on me at once, as if sent from elsewhere: No. I couldn't shoot her. A bear had come to my aid in my vision, not so long ago.

I focused my mind.

Bear, will you let me pass?

The bear's yellow eyes glistened in the fading sunlight.

I took one step backward, then another. The bear watched me, but she didn't move. Didn't growl.

I had almost fully retraced my path across the meadow before she turned back to the chamois. When her head swiveled away, I let out my breath, slowly, quietly, and turned toward the trees.

The fading light caught a little pile on the ground before me: a set of bear claws, five of them. They were clean and had clearly been there for some time.

They were Bear's gift to me.

TWENTY-ONE

The land had changed. Some of this was to be expected; when Eneko and I crossed this region on our journey west, it had been spring. The trees were still green, but they were now the dark green of early autumn. The nights were cool, edging to cold, and I saw splashes of color on the slopes higher up.

But the turning of the seasons was not the only difference.

At first, I thought I was imagining it, but the signs became too obvious to ignore. When Eneko and I had passed through these lands before, most of the foothills were unoccupied. Now they were full of traces of people—the forests had been thinned, new trails looped through the trees, and here and there I saw a broken arrowhead discarded in the drifts of leaves. Most telling of all, the forest spirits were muted.

And soon, I encountered not just broken arrowheads and new trails, but people themselves.

I heard them before I saw them. I was walking, my eyes on the ground, when I was startled out of my reverie by a strange sound. At first, I thought it might be birdsong, but it was like no bird I'd ever heard before. And then I realized the sound was made by human voices. I'd grown so unaccustomed to people that I hadn't recognized the noise of men. Quickly, I hid myself in the brush.

The voices came closer and resolved themselves from snatches into a song I recognized, a song sung in deep male tones.

"Lie there... lie there... instead of me..."

It must be a hunting party from a band. No raiders or marauders would sing so freely, and there were too many voices for them to be unaffiliated hunters in search of a home.

I was torn. I didn't want to talk to them. But the foraging had begun to thin, and I was very hungry. If I visited with a band, I would have a warm fire and a good meal this evening—assuming I could convince them to accept me as a guest.

My heart was pounding. Part of a band or no, men on their own could be dangerous. But I had arrows, my bow, and my aim, if they were needed. And I remembered Eneko, on our journey west, gesturing silently to his tattoo when I asked if he wasn't afraid of the Acorn Gatherers.

I, too, have the tattoo now.

I decided to take the chance. I stepped out from behind the trees and into the hunters' path.

There were four men and a boy who looked about Gotzon's age. All five stared at me open-mouthed, as if *tsairi* had materialized before them. Their dogs went still as they saw me, waiting for a word from the hunters to corner me.

I raised my right arm in greeting, letting the sleeve of the tunic fall to reveal the dark band encircling my upper arm.

"A shaman!" The hunters visibly relaxed, their postures loosening, and they raised their arms to return my greeting. One spoke to the dogs, who also eased, tongues lolling.

They were the Ibex People, a band I'd heard stories of back home. Their headwoman was the sister of one of Oroitz's former mates. Her name was Ihintza. When they brought me to her, I saw that she was strikingly beautiful, with strong features and long, dark hair with a reddish tint and a few white threads. She had numerous children, including twins, a boy and a girl, who had been born last spring. Her band seemed to be thriving—I had never seen one so large.

But all was not as it seemed.

"We are too big," Ihintza admitted as we sat alone by the fire that evening. "With the troubles along the coast, we have had many new people join us. But these coastal people—well, you can't blame them, after what they say happened to their bands, but many of them are angry, and they've brought their anger here. Our head of hunters has his hands full, trying to keep the young men under control."

"Have you had trouble?" I asked.

"Oh, no, nothing serious. There has been some infighting among the hunters, that is all. It is handled. But outside our band, it *is* dangerous—there are too many young men wandering the woods alone. And there are many bears this season, hanging around the camp. Wolves, too—not as close, but we have seen signs. There is not enough food for all of us." She gave me a meaningful look.

A shiver ran up my spine. Bears and wolves? *Are they* tsairiu, *here as a warning? Why so many? Spirits usually travel alone.*

Even if they were just ordinary predators, to have so many of them would be peculiar. Bears and wolves usually avoided humans, unless there were large herds of deer or ibex nearby. Ihintza had said the fall hunts had started and the game was not plentiful, so that couldn't be the circumstance here. It was strange.

Ihintza continued, "We cannot stay so large for long."

I knew what she meant. Large bands generally didn't hold together for much longer than a season or two; invariably, some faction would break off. "Will it be an easy split?"

Ihintza sighed. Her face suddenly looked much older. "Well, perhaps. My sister may take one part of the band in the spring and become their head-woman... but she would have to travel far, I think. Territory is becoming hard to find. You must have seen this, in your travels. Worse, we haven't a shaman to help us. And if there is any time we need a shaman's protection, it is now." She eyed me. "Perhaps we can convince you to stay?"

I laughed, and a warm feeling spread across my middle, though it was edged with guilt. It was nice to be wanted, but I hadn't sung the protection songs at all since leaving Eneko. It just seemed too much effort for me alone. I would sing them tonight, I promised myself. It was the least I could do for Ihintza and her people. "Alas, no. I am searching for my mother's band. I must make my way east as quickly as I can."

Ihintza sighed again. "It was too good to be true, your arriving like this. You are seeking your band? They are from the coast?"

I nodded. "The Sea People. Our territory was along the shore of the eastern sea, where the coast is rocky. I don't suppose you have heard anything of them recently? I know they had begun to fracture...." I played with a stick, poking at the earth in front of me. "My mother was headwoman."

Ihintza looked surprised. "But one of our new hunters came from the Sea People! Did you not meet him?"

A pit opened in my belly. I reminded myself to breathe.

Ihintza seemed to notice nothing; she was scanning the crowd. "I don't know where he is," she said, pushing herself to her feet, then extending a hand to help me up, "but you should talk to him. His name is Omer."

Omer was not easy to find. Eventually, Ihintza had to send one of the hunters to track him down. "This is odd," she said. Her brow was wrinkled with concern.

I had spoken barely a word since Ihintza had identified which hunter from the Sea People was among the Ibex People. I was focusing on my breathing. In, out. In, out. But Ihintza's voice pierced through my haze. "Omer—if he knew I was here, if he heard my name—he has reason to avoid me."

"Ah," Ihintza said. She must have heard something in my tone, because she added, "Do you want me to call off the search? I can have someone else speak to him for you, if you wish."

"No," I said. "I want to speak to him myself."

I did, too. Before, I expected myself to be frightened of meeting him, but I found I wasn't: blood rushed through my veins fast and hot. I was eager to speak to him. Eager to look him in the eye, with my tattooed arm, and my bow and arrows beside me.

"Do you want to speak to him alone?" Ihintza asked.

"No," I said, "I very much want you to stay. This is not a lover's quarrel."

I think Ihintza must have understood what I was not saying, because her face settled into a kind of terse anger. "He will be found. I promise you."

Omer was eventually dragged before us by a pair of hunters. His head was averted. The two hunters pushed him into a sitting position, not gently, clearly annoyed by the trouble they had gone through to find him. He sat, head down, waiting. I waited, too.

Finally, Ihintza said, coldly, "Omer, do this woman the courtesy of meeting her eyes. She has questions to ask of you."

Omer looked up, and I gasped.

His right eye was missing. The whole right side of his face was covered with angry red lacerations: foul, ugly, poorly healing.

"He was wounded by a bear before he came to us, so he said. But he can, in fact, speak, when he wishes." Ihintza's tone was tart.

"She knows," said Omer. "She knows it was a bear." His voice was shaking.

"I do know." I felt like I was in a dream. "What happened to Kerbasi?"

He looked away.

"The bear killed him," he whispered.

I don't know if my shock was visible on my face. "**Go**," I'd told the bear. And the bear had followed my command.

I wasn't trying to kill anyone. Not in the living world. I was just trying to protect myself.

Omer looked up at me, then at Ihintza's stern face, then back. "Nahia—*please*! I've been tortured enough. Look at me! I'm mutilated! Don't cost me my place here, too. I know what we did was wrong. But nothing happened to you!"

My breath was fast and hard. I hadn't intended to hurt Omer. I certainly hadn't intended to destroy Kerbasi. I hadn't known what I was doing.

But something *had* happened to me, when he and Kerbasi attacked me. They might not have been able to carry out all that they had planned, but they'd wounded me all the same.

I took a deep breath.

"Whether you keep your place here is Ihintza's decision, not mine," I said. "I only want to know of the Sea People."

Omer shook his head. "I would tell you if I knew anything. You must believe that. But when I left, only the gatherers were still at the coast."

"All the hunters left?" I asked.

"Oroitz stayed, and Bakar," he said. "Bakar would not break *bakai*, so he said. But the rest of us, yes, we left. There was nothing to stay for!" His voice rose. "Truly, you must believe me!"

"Nothing to stay for, but the safety of the rest of them," I said. "Of the gatherers, the elders, the children. Instead, you chose to leave them there, with no protection."

He grimaced. "We would not have been able to do anything, had the strangers come. Haven't you heard? They are many—many! There are so many of them."

I looked at his face, and I didn't know what to feel. He had mocked me. He had tried to violate me. He had dared to call my sister a bitch.

I couldn't feel sorry that he had been mauled, or even that Kerbasi was dead.

But I could not vision again. Not without more training. I didn't know my own power. What if I hurt someone who didn't deserve it?

Ihintza said, "Take him away. But keep him under guard until I have the chance to speak with the head of the hunters." After he was out of sight, she said to me, "Should I exile him?"

I looked away. After a moment I said, "It may be, without his friend, that he is too cowardly to be a danger. And he has paid a price for what he did. I cannot make this decision. But if it were my band..." I stopped there.

"That answers my question," Ihintza said. "We are not in need of hunters at all right now, let alone hunters who do not follow the *bakai*. It will be done." She sighed, pushing her hair out of her face. "About the Sea People...we have other newcomers. It's possible one of them heard something on their journey, so I will inquire for you—better from me, I think, than you. But I should warn you, I have not heard word of any coastal band remaining." She shook her head, slowly. "Everyone seems either to have fled inland...or been taken."

"I know," I said.

"If you cannot find them, or..." Ihintza said. "Well, there is a place for you here, should your travels bring you back this way."

"Thank you." On an impulse, I reached into my basket and pulled out one of the bear claws. She took it from me, turning it over in her hand, and then she looked up at me. Her eyes were wide—with respect, I thought, not fear.

"I thank you for this token," she said solemnly. "And I repeat: there will always be a place for you here."

We were both quiet then, listening to the fire pop, the laughter and conversation among the people. I felt sick. I was suddenly glad that Eneko had not come with me, that I had left him behind in the mountains. I did not want to see his face, upon learning what I had done in the waking world.

After a time, Ihintza said, "Those that have joined us—they say the coast is devastated, with no game to be found. The forest is a fragment of what it was, replaced by blackened wastes of burned stumps. These strangers, they seem to destroy everything before them. Broken land, that's what is left now." She paused for a moment, pressing her lips together, then repeated, "A broken land. And now the disharmony is coming here as well."

TWENTY-TWO

As soon as I entered the country the strangers had taken, I knew it. It wasn't that there was a visible boundary; I didn't stumble into a scorched patch, nor did I see any of the strangers themselves. No, the change was more subtle. For the first time I could remember, I could not hear the forest spirits.

Everything on the surface looked the same: it was the coastal forest where I'd grown up, the same canopied woods. Scattered among the dusty pine trees were bursts of bright yellow from the turning oaks. Rays of sunlight pierced the canopy, struck the patches of yellow, and made the whole forest shine gold.

But despite the forest's brilliance, its voice was gone. Or not quite gone—when I strained, I could hear a weak thrumming. It was just enough to let me know the spirits were not yet completely dead. But they were dying.

As I drew closer to the shore, I found the first visible signs of the strangers. I saw the burned spaces, and stretches where the invaders seemed to have cut every tree right down to the ground, nothing but a low stubble growing around them. It was dead and wrong, a ghost landscape.

Soon after I saw the first burned patches, I spied the strangers themselves.

It was a near miss. It was early, and I was gathering mushrooms. I wasn't fully recovered from my earlier illness, and I was often a bit off in the mornings. I didn't hear them coming until they were almost beside to me, but there was a stand of brush and I was able to duck behind it.

There were two of them, men with dark short hair—it didn't even reach their shoulders—and beards. They were shorter than most men of the bands, and their clothes were like none I had ever seen before. They were wearing some kind of wrap that looked as if it had been woven, like a basket, and their tunics were loose and flexible. They carried bows and arrows, but the style was different than those I had made. When they spoke, it was with deep, guttural sounds, nothing at all like my language, or even Esti's language. They passed quickly, talking.

I stayed hidden long after they disappeared.

After that encounter, I ran.

I journeyed late into the night, eating just enough to keep me going, sleeping for only a few hours. My anxiety pushed me onward, onward, onward.

I reached the Sea People's territory faster than I'd dared hope.

Immediately, I made my way to last year's summer camp. I told myself I didn't expect to find anyone—but still, when I arrived and saw it was an overgrown tangle in the woods, my heart plummeted. No one had been here this year.

They will be at winter camp. I desperately wanted it to be true. *Surely, they are at winter camp.*

And so I raced on.

Yet when I reached it, days later, it was much the same. Heavily overgrown, silent, abandoned.

I walked through camp, slowly, my pulse faster with every step. The spot where Eneko's tent had been was a gigantic snarl of weeds. So were the areas where the hunters without mates had lived. Esti and Oroitz's tent had collapsed into a pile. Udane's tent had a gaping hole in one side.

But the hearths were still visible. People had been here, not so long ago.

There was no fog, no *arhontzl*, no growling bear. It was day, the sun hot and bright beyond the trees. But winter camp was the ruin I had seen in my vision. Eventually, I came to where the central fire had been. Unlike in my vision, there were no flames, no Izara and Abene.

How easy this would be if they were sitting there, waiting for me!

I sat and wondered what to do.

My options were few. I could explore the rest of our territory, hoping to find someone, anyone. But I knew in my heart I would not. I could seek out other bands in the interior, ask after my sister there... but I'd already done that, with no luck.

The strangers must have them.

Just as Hodei had said.

Just as my gift had told me. Just as I had known, in my heart.

Of course, if I drew close to the strangers' encampment, I risked capture myself. I would have to take good care not to be seen. But if I found it—Eneko had said it was not a half day's journey from here—I could make a reconnaissance. See if the Sea People's women were truly there among them. Make a plan.

I set off right away, before thoughts of all the things that might go wrong could slow me down.

The strangers' camp was not hard to find. But it was hard for me to believe it was real, even when it was standing right in front of me.

Nothing could have prepared me for this.

As Eneko had said, it was half a day's walk north. On the way, I began to encounter more burned, blackened clearances. The land was eerily free of birds—of any animals, really—and the trails had become so numerous that they resembled a twisted pile of rope.

Eventually, I came to a massive clearing, its edge far too regular to be natural. I lurked in the forest's edge, and I looked out.

It was late in the day, the shadows lengthening. Maybe fifty steps from where I stood was a wall of wooden stakes, one small break in its length. Through the break, busy figures passed, back and forth, looking at this distance like ants around an anthill. Beyond the wall clustered a collection of structures the likes of which I had never seen before. They were made of wood and stone, and there were many of them—so many that I could not count them.

The sheer number of them took my breath away. So, too, did the number of people. Omer's voice came unbidden to my mind: "*There are so many of them.*"

There was no way for me to sneak into this camp.

I stood, clasping my shaman's pendant. My blood thrummed loud in my ears, and my neck went damp.

I knew what my next step must be.

There was no reason to wait. I took my bow in hand, readjusted my basket so it would not hinder my draw, and strode across the clearing toward the wall.

Amazingly, no one took any notice of me until I passed through the gap in the stakes. Maybe, with so many of them, they did not notice a single interloper.

Inside the stakes, the earth was smooth and well-trodden, pounded down by many feet. My breath was coming quickly. I was struck, too, by a stench the likes of which I had never encountered. It smelled like a tent where there had been illness, except much stronger—the illness of many tents, concentrated.

There were a few old men sitting together outside, passing an unfamiliar vessel back and forth. Herri and his companions, drunk on fermented honey, flashed before my eyes. Were these men intoxicated, too?

One looked up and saw me staring. A smile spread across his face, revealing gaps where several teeth were missing. Then the smile dropped, and I knew he recognized me for what I was: an outsider, a woman of the bands. He began to shout.

I raised my bow quickly, nocking an arrow and aiming at his throat.

He went silent.

Around me, there rose more shouting. I felt, rather than saw, bows drawn, arrows aimed in my direction. I kept my shaft trained on the toothless man.

"*Where is my sister?*" I demanded.

I heard murmuring everywhere. A younger man stepped into my range of vision, closer than the first. He had a bow, that same peculiar style I'd seen when I glimpsed the strangers on my way here, but he did not draw it—just held it warily at his side. He smiled at me disarmingly, revealing a crooked toothrow. He, too, was missing several teeth, for all that he was young. I shrank back, aiming my arrow at him instead.

"My sister!" I shouted again. And then, in frustration: "**Izara!**"

The air between us shimmered.

The young man did not break eye contact with me, but barked something. I heard someone running.

A few moments passed. He and I looked at each other. The strangers around me continued to whisper. The man continued to smile. I tried not to look at his face. I tried not to think.

I could not hold this many off forever, I knew that. Sooner or later, they would rush me, and then what?

Footsteps against the flattened earth. A woman's voice, speaking to the group. I thought she might be rebuking them, but I did not look away from my draw.

And then I heard a voice I knew: "Nahia?"

I looked up. A woman stood there, dressed in those strange, flexible clothes. The late-day sun lit up her wavy hair, turning it brown-orange. On her beautiful face was a look of shock—a look I felt echoing across my own features.

It was Izara.

TWENTY-THREE

I was stunned into stillness.

I had demanded my sister, and now here she was.

Why wasn't I rushing to her, taking her into my arms? What was she doing here, dressed like the strangers, speaking to them, walking among them? I couldn't move, couldn't speak. I stood as frozen as a shaman's figurine, my bow still in hand but no strength in my arms.

Izara had no such difficulties. She rushed to me and knocked the bow aside, pressing me into a tight embrace. I stood rigid.

"Nahia, what are you *doing* here?" she asked. "I am so glad to see you, but oh, I thought you were with Eneko, somewhere far away . . . !"

She stepped back, her hands on my shoulders, and looked into my eyes.

Behind her, the men were talking unintelligibly to each other. She called over her shoulder at them, a stream of liquid syllables exiting her mouth, apparently fluently. One of the men called something back, and the people, amazingly, began to disperse.

Izara turned back to me. I was still holding myself stiffly. I tried to soften.

Shouldn't I be happy to see her? I'd come to find her, after all. Well, I *had* found her. And she was safe, apparently.

What was I doing here, Izara had asked.

What is she *doing here, so at ease, so calm, speaking their tongue?*

Izara was looking at me expectantly. My throat was dry. I swallowed. "I heard of trouble on the coast..." My voice sounded soft, indistinct, like it was coming from far away. "The people of the interior were saying everyone on the coast had run or been taken. I had to find you."

Izara laughed.

"Well, as you can see, I am thriving!" She tugged on a strand of my hair, playfully. "Kiria, Tora, and I—oh, I'll tell you the whole story later, there's no time now—we were caught and brought here. It was a shock at first, but I soon saw that this could be the answer for us—that we could live *here*, in the village! So I convinced my mate—oh, there is so much to tell you! I'm mated now!—I convinced Argi we should go to the Sea People and bring them here. We were only a few elders and gatherers by then." A shadow passed over her face. "It was a hard spring. But now, all is well."

My stomach was churning with emotion: relief, anger, and under it all, a kind of horrified fascination. My mind spat out questions faster than I could ask them. *The Sea People are here? Are they all captives? Are you a captive? Where is our mother? Where is our aunt?*

She was leading me through the structures now, down a narrow, rutted path. I was dazed, almost stumbling as I walked. There were round wooden structures *everywhere*, so close together.

Suddenly, what Izara had said sank in. She was *mated*? *How can she be mated?*

Izara was still talking. "Abene and the others came to join us here. It has solved all our problems. Argi—that's my mate—Argi's people brought with them—well, you'll see, I can't explain it, I have to show you. You'll be *so* surprised. You can't imagine the things they know."

I couldn't imagine many things, apparently.

Izara seemed—impossible as it might be—*happy*. She walked confidently, weaving through the press of round wooden structures as if it were a familiar stand of forest. Perhaps this place *was* like a forest, a bizarre forest where the trees were all exactly the same.

I cleared my throat. "Who is here?"

"Abene, Oroitz, Esti and Gotzon," Izara ticked off, "Bakar, Alaia. And Kiria and Tora and myself, of course."

Gotzon is alive. Gotzon is safe. I had prepared myself for his being dead. "All the hunters left you, truly? All but Bakar and Oroitz?"

"Yes," Izara said, not looking at me.

I thought back over her list of names. "Where is Udane? Did something happen to her?"

"Oh no, she's here." She hesitated for a moment. "Udane and Abene had a falling-out, so our aunt hasn't been around much."

How did this happen? When?

Izara was still talking. "Oh, Nahia, I know this must be strange to you, but Argi's people—they are like us. Good people." She put her arm around me and gave me another hug. "Well, you'll see, now you are back. And you must tell me all about Eneko, too! Was I right? Did you?" She laughed at the expression on my face. "You did, I can tell!"

"Zari!" My face was hot. Izara laughed again, as if this were all normal: sister teasing sister. My anger was growing. I couldn't, I wouldn't, talk to her about Eneko. She would never understand about him. Or what I had done for her.

I left him for you, I thought but did not say. *I left him for you, and you don't even seem to care.*

I left my training for you. I left my teacher. Everything.

We had come to some sort of central gathering area, like the central fire, only much larger, and surrounded closely by more of those wood and stone structures. These were bigger than the others I'd seen, rectangular rather than round. The open space was full of people—all strangers, I thought, for they wore the strangers' clothing. They were stacking bundles of what looked like dried grasses. Several looked up as we approached.

With a shock, I recognized Tora. Her tiny face peered at me in astonishment from under the unmistakable cloud of black hair.

Izara shouted, "Look who has come back to us!"

I shrank, wishing I could disappear. There were so many people, and I had never liked to be the center of attention. Izara's arm around me tightened.

With a sickening twist of my stomach, I thought of the darkness in my visions, reaching for me. I couldn't see it now, but I felt it here, encircling the structures, weaving through the people in the open space.

The people were coursing toward us. There were more than in any band I'd ever seen, more than at the largest of summer meetings. I saw Alaia, heavily pregnant, and I glimpsed Esti's shock of long bright hair.

They really are all here. Izara brought *them? But why?*

I looked at my sister's face, with its fixed, confident smile.

Was this truly Izara? The sister I remembered would never have let herself be captured. And if by some chance she were, she never would have suffered other free people to join her.

Where was my sister?

I was introduced to wave after wave of strangers—in our language, I noticed, although they chattered to each other in the unfamiliar tongue. I was overwhelmed; it was all I could do to acknowledge the introductions.

Aside from Tora, Alaia, and Esti, the people in the central area (the *plaza*, or so Izara said) were not of the Sea People. There were women and girls from other bands, including at least one woman from the north, and there were men of the strangers. There were many more men than women.

My breath shortened as the crush surrounded us. There were too many people here. How could Izara stand it?

After a while, Izara told them all—in our language—that it was enough for the day, they should go home for the evening meal. The people made a strange gesture at her, lifting their hands to their foreheads, then turned to leave. This was odd enough to penetrate my confusion.

Is Izara giving orders here? But I didn't voice the question. I wouldn't have known how to ask it.

Izara brought me to one of the wooden structures, a circular one. There was a firepit in front of it, a small pile of ash enclosed by a ring of stone. I saw an old woman resting there. She leaned back against the wood, her face turned up to the fading sun, her eyes closed. And then, with yet another shock, I recognized her:

The old woman was my mother.

Abene had been crying, in my vision. But here, when she opened her eyes, all semblance of frailty disappeared.

Her gaze was snapping, angry, decidedly not full of tears. I remembered every transgression I'd ever committed, every way in which I'd disappointed her, culminating with the ultimate betrayal: my departure with Eneko.

"So you've come back," Abene said.

"Yes, Abene." Unexpectedly, my anger flared again. *You deceived us. You told us not to worry. You told us this would never happen, but you knew it would.* I felt my face hardening, my eyes narrowing. I met her gaze as I'd never dared to before.

Abene was, apparently, unimpressed. "Hmph," she said, and heaved herself up. She brushed her hands off on her legs and walked off toward the central area. *Plaza*, I supposed.

Izara touched my arm. "Don't worry," she murmured, "she'll come around. You did leave the band against her wishes, after all."

"Did I? She made me his apprentice. In her heart of hearts, she wanted me to go," I said to Izara as I watched after Abene. "And I'm not worried either way."

But my sister wasn't listening. She opened the structure—"We call it a *house*"—and pulled at my arm, leading me inside.

The interior was open, with a floor of compressed earth, cleanly swept. I saw shadowy lumps against the walls that I recognized as bedding. It wasn't all that different from a tent, except it was larger. It was also smokier, which made it seem close despite its size, because there was a hearth inside in addition to the one outside. This inside hearth was banked, but the scattering of charcoal told me it had been used recently.

Izara picked up a round stone bowl from the floor. It was filled with a rancid smelling paste—animal fat, it must be. She crouched by the hearth, then stood and turned back to me. A small flame now burned within the bowl in her hand. I blinked against the sudden light.

Izara held the flame near my face, looking at me critically. "Let's get you cleaned up and properly dressed, and then we can go outside. There's"—she spoke a word I didn't know—"to be ground, and I can tell you how this all came to be while we work."

I stripped off my sweaty leathers, which Izara took away. Soon, I was dressed in a very short top and a short skirt, made of the flexible stuff everyone else was wearing. "It's called *linen*," Izara told me. "They make it from their plants. Isn't it so much more comfortable?" I found it scratchy, and wished I could put my tunic and leggings back on, but Izara was adamant. "You can't wear those old things; you'll stick out like—well. Anyway, they are filthy."

She was right; they were filthy. So I let her garb me like one of the strangers.

I kept my arm hidden from her, so she wouldn't see my tattoo. I don't know why. I should have wanted to show it to her, to talk about what had happened to me. But Izara was so scornful of my old clothes, the sort of clothes both of us used to wear, that I was afraid she would laugh at me.

She led me outside, to a flat open space at the side of the *house*. There were big slabs of polished stone there, the kind of polish that comes from hard grinding. She had a strange basket on her hip, cradling it with one arm as if it were a child. But no, it was not a basket. It was shaped like a basket, but it was solid, heavy.

With yet another twist of my stomach, I recognized it. It was made of hardened clay.

Izara placed the vessel down between us. It was filled with what looked like grass seeds, though they were bigger than any grass seeds I'd seen before.

"What are they?" I asked.

She tossed her hair back impatiently. "It's too complicated to go into right now. I'll show you tomorrow. For now, take this." She handed me a rock, large enough that I had to hold it in two hands. While I was struggling to grasp it, she poured seeds onto one of the slabs. "Now grind."

I picked up the rock and pushed it against the seeds on the enormous grinding-stone. Izara poured seeds into her own slab, and then began her story.

"Things fell apart quickly after you left. The hunters—well, we don't need to talk about that. Without them . . . the rest of us, we didn't know what to do. Udane wanted to travel, find a band to join. But Abene refused. She insisted that her land-sense told her to stay.

"I think there was more to it than that; Abene knew a lot more than she'd been telling us, you know? Since we came here, I've heard many stories from the other women. There is trouble in all the seaside bands, and it has been getting worse for some time. I think Abene knew that, knew there was nowhere to run.

"At any rate: the day I first came here! Tora and Kiria and I went out looking for snails. We were on that pebbly stretch at the Cove of Rocks, yes? We'd been out for only a short while when Tora noticed Kiria was missing and wasn't on the beach. So we went up the cliff, to the lookout, to see if she had gone to the north cove."

I nodded. Getting to the north cove wasn't easy. It involved a lot of scrambling, but for little ones, it was a fun game, and the north cove, with its sandy flat beach, a rewarding destination. Izara and I had run away to the north cove many times as children, escaping a day of chores for what seemed to us a grand adventure.

Izara continued. "Well, that day the cove was full of people. I was so surprised I almost shouted. Tora *did* squeak, but we were far enough away that they didn't hear it. We couldn't see them very well, but it was obvious they weren't band people."

I had stopped grinding. My seeds were pretty well broken up. But Izara was still pounding away, even though her seeds had become a powder, far too fine for eating.

"We thought Kiria might be with the group at the bonfire. We decided to sneak a little closer. So we stood up to go, and—and behind us were three strange men."

There was too much inside me, I could not contain it. Rage, dread, resentment. Kerbasi rose in my mind, extending his hand, laughing. The bear's fur beneath my hand. Omer, as I had last seen him, his right eye gone.

Izara was oblivious to my distress. She was still grinding, still talking. "We tried to run, but of course it didn't work. They tied us up and marched us away—not to the beach, but here, to the village." She must have seen my look of incomprehension. "The village," she repeated, waving her hand about us. "You know, this big camp.

"I was so astonished, that day. We came down that hill to the west. The men were talking about something to each other, and I looked out and saw all this from up there. And I was thinking so hard. Not just about how we were going to get out of this, either. I couldn't help but wonder: How do they build such a big camp? How do they support so many people? How can we do it, too?"

My nausea was back. It rose in me, one wave of sickness after another, like the tide in a storm. I fought to keep it down.

"Well," Izara carried on, "we got to the village, and here was Kiria, and a couple of other girls, too, from bands farther north, and some women and elders also. They put us all together, all tied up, at one end of the village. And I was thinking, how am I going to protect Tora and Kiria, and the other girls? The other girls had been there a little longer, and they pointed out the leader to me. He was one of the men who'd captured me. He was young, but the other men respected him."

She laughed, shrugging. "So when he came over to us, I got to my feet. I chose him as my mate—you should have seen it! I just told him how it would be!"

There was so much in this story that made no sense.

"How did he know what you were saying? Did he . . . speak our language?" I asked slowly.

"No, of course not," Izara said, grinning. "He can speak a little *now*, but how would he have been able to speak it then? But he understood me, all the same. We had a ceremony and everything. I had to work on him for a while, about letting me go where I wanted and such, but we got there. And now we are as you see us."

I stared at her, horrified.

She put her stone down and stood, peering at my work. "Forest and seas, Nahia, what have you been doing? Your grain is barely ground at all! Well, leave it. We have to make the evening meal. I'll tell you the rest later."

Izara flounced into her house, and I stared after her.

She looked the same, despite the new clothes. She sounded the same—the impetuous, boisterous girl who'd been my reflection for my whole life. But it was as if being captured by the strangers had knotted up her spirit; bound it up, just as they had bound her body when they brought her here, so she could not fight. So she would be content to be a prisoner.

Or had her spirit been hobbled before she came to the strangers' camp? Was that why she'd admired them, even while being abducted? *It was a hard spring*, she had said. Had that hard spring broken her will? What *had* happened when the hunters left?

What had I abandoned Izara to, when I left with Eneko?

TWENTY-FOUR

We took the evening meal privately, not with the rest of the group. At first, I thought Izara arranged this for my sake, so I wouldn't be confronted with crowds again when I was so tired, but apparently the strangers ate on their own—always.

Either way, I was grateful not to have to meet new people. It was only Izara, Abene, me... and Argi.

Argi returned late in the day, when the sun was low in the sky. He seemed like all the other strangers to me: dark cropped hair, short for a man, fit. There was nothing to mark him as a leader. He swung through the entranceway eagerly, tossing his bow and arrow to the side. Izara rushed to meet him, jumping up from the fire and pushing her entire body flush against him as she kissed him. I looked away, but not soon enough.

Argi was courteous enough to me, welcoming me to his and Izara's home in words I could understand, though they were heavily accented. He asked about my journey. I answered only briefly; it was all I could do to respond to him at all. *And what have you been doing today? Kidnapping, raping, razing, pillaging?*

Izara would be irritated with any suggestion that Argi had done her harm, so much was clear. The two of them were openly affectionate throughout the evening. With every word they exchanged, every look that passed between them, every casual touch, I felt sicker.

How could Izara be happy with this man? This man who'd stolen her, who'd taken her as a prize? And yet she called herself mated to him. Worse, she'd brought others here, too.

How could she?

How did *she?*

The evening meal was simple: cakes baked of finely ground grains. They were dry and tasteless, and despite my hunger, I could only manage a few bites. I saw Izara looking at me, but she didn't comment when I gave up my attempt at eating. Instead, she asked, "Do you need to visit the *privy*?"

"The what?"

She laughed and stood. "Come on, I'll show you."

I followed Izara into the village. It was still light enough to see. I heard one of the village men, shouting in that strange language, and then the crack of a hand meeting skin and a woman's cry of pain.

I gasped and whirled around. Fights were rare in the band, but when they happened, they involved everyone. Well, almost everyone. But these sounds came from inside a structure, not from a tent. The wooden entranceway to the structure was closed, and somehow that made the fight seem private, not an affair for the rest of us.

I heard the man's voice again, quieter now, but still sharp. I looked at the structure, my heart beating fast, thinking, *I am an outsider here. What do I do?*

Izara had noticed my distress. She looked at me curiously, then said, "Oh, that's Ty and Ana. They fight every night." She kept walking, unconcerned. She called over her shoulder, "Don't worry about it, Nahia."

I followed her, glancing back at the structure from which the cries had come. I was tired, and though I was shaken by the fight, I'd had so many shocks that day that I was numb. I wanted to sleep. Maybe in the morning everything would make more sense.

I could never have imagined the shock still in store for me that night: the "privy."

The "privy," I learned, was a small structure. It was set back with a clear space around it. As we drew nearer, I knew why. I gagged. Did they keep dead animals in there? Or sick people?

Izara stopped gestured at the entrance. "Go on."

My hand was pressed over my nose and mouth. I looked at her, uncomprehendingly.

"Oh, don't be a child."

I still didn't understand what she meant. But she clearly wanted me to enter the stinking structure, and so I did. The stench inside was overpowering, far worse than outside. There was a bench, made of wood, with a hole in it. The smell seemed to be coming from the hole. I looked into it, cautiously.

Nausea overwhelmed me as I realized exactly what the structure was for.

I bolted outside. "You can't be serious," I said to Izara.

She rolled her eyes. "Look," she said, gesturing to the sea of structures behind her. "The village is very large, and we live here all year round. If you need to pass water or waste, use the privy. It keeps the fields clean. When the pit is full, we dig a new one. It's very sensible."

"It's a structure for *excrement*?" My stomach was still uneasy. I put my hand across it, willing it to subside. "The villagers go *inside*?"

Izara narrowed her eyes at me. "*All* of us do," she said. "So do you need to, or not?"

A moment passed. "I'm fine," I said.

We went back to Izara's structure.

We were woken the next dawn by a visitor—or rather, Izara was. I heard the knock and rolled away from the entrance. I would have gone back to sleep, but Izara shook me awake, saying, "Nahia, come meet Maia."

Standing in the entranceway was a woman with unusual coloring. From the north, maybe—she looked a little like Esti, with long, straight, honey-colored hair. In her hand was a vessel, steam rising lazily from the vessel's mouth.

Izara embraced the woman, then turned to me, saying, "Maia, this is my sister Nahia, who has come to stay with us."

Maia smiled at me, her eyes crinkling. "Welcome, sister of Xara."

I nodded at her, rubbing at my eyes to clear the sleep from them. I'd traveled for weeks without sleeping; why should it be so hard to wake now?

"Maia brings us breakfast every morning," Izara explained.

The woman handed me the vessel, then squeezed my shoulder, gently. I managed not to draw away. This woman seemed friendly enough and I didn't want to offend her.

The vessel held a thick hot liquid. I sniffed. It smelled unfamiliar, rich and heavy. The nausea that had become my ever-present companion surged up my throat. I was becoming resigned to never feeling well again.

Maia spoke carefully, using band language. “Now I bring for you also, Nahia. Katcha. Good to eat in morning. You will like.” She squeezed my shoulder again, then gave Izara a hug before melting back into the sea of people that wandered the path between the structures.

The vessel was warm in my hand. Without thinking, I wrapped my other hand around it, too, cradling it between my palms. The heat was comforting at least. *They must cook the clay in a very hot fire for the container not to dissolve when full of liquid.* I looked closer and saw there were streaks of soot on its side: it was warm not only because the katcha was warm, but because it had been placed directly in the fire to cook the food within.

At the outside hearth, Izara tried to build the fire up, but the fire was smoking and hissing. Of course it was: all the wood in her pile was green. I stayed silent, watching. I could hear Argi and Abene stirring in the darkness inside the home.

Izara poured the katcha into wooden bowls. “Sit,” she said, handing one to me.

Katcha turned out to be more of those seeds, again ground very fine, but this time cooked with water into a soft and textureless paste. We made a similar food in the band for the elderly or the ill, but this was much smoother—slimy, almost gelatinous. It slid over my tongue unappetizingly. The taste, too, was strange—bland—but it stuck in the back of my throat as if I'd swallowed soapwort.

“What kind of seeds are these?” I asked cautiously.

She smiled at me mysteriously. "Finish eating and I'll show you."

"I'm done."

"Really? There's plenty more."

I put the bowl aside and stood up. Izara shrugged and led me down the path between the houses. "Katcha is made from barley."

"Barley?"

"It's one of the plants Argi's people brought with them. Oh, Nahia, it seems such a small thing, but it is huge. It was the day we had the mating ceremony, soon after I arrived, that I realized..."

We were walking past what seemed acres and acres of the little wooden houses, all alike. As we passed, the people made the same gesture at Izara that they had yesterday. At me, they stared with unrestrained curiosity, not bothering to hide their interest.

My skin prickled. I could feel myself blushing furiously.

There was a flash of pale yellow and brown as two small figures darted toward us. With a shock, I recognized Gotzon and Kiria. They hugged me with such enthusiasm I nearly fell over. "Nahia!" they shrieked in unison. I hugged them back dazedly. They were both taller and rounder than I remembered them. Before I could say anything more, they were gone again, racing each other down the path between the structures, giggling.

Is Gotzon, too, happy here? Oh, spirits of forest and sea, help me. He can't grow up here. He can't.

Izara chuckled. "Some things don't change, eh?"

I smiled back, weakly. Something was bothering me, something other than Gotzon. After a moment, I realized what it was.

For all the people here, all the structures, there were no children. The strangers seemed barren as a limestone cliff—almost all men, so few women, and all their children ours.

Izara led me toward the break in the stake wall that ringed the village. I stared at it, thinking, *It looks like a corral the hunters would build for a game drive.*

Well, that's what it was, wasn't it? A corral for stolen women and children. How could Izara see this as anything but what it was?

Izara was talking about Argi again.

"The afternoon after our mating ceremony, Argi took me and Tora and Kiria for a walk around the village. Kiria and Tora were living in our house then; it was before the band came to the village, and of course Argi didn't speak our language yet. So we were playing a language game. Kiria would touch this or that, and Argi would tell her the word for it in his language, and then I'd tell him it in ours."

We were walking through the clearing surrounding the camp, and Izara was still talking.

"Argi took us to a large building, larger than the other structures. Of course, we didn't know what it was, so Kiria touched it and Argi told us it was a barn. And then he led us around it, and behind it, in a fenced area, there were these animals. Remember when Eneko was talking about the hairy deer? As soon as I saw them, I thought, *This is what Eneko was talking about.* 'Sheep,' Argi told us. He said something more, but of course I didn't understand it."

"I was trying hard not to react, or to show him how astonished I was. But he must have been able to tell I didn't know what was going on, because he pulled me over to the fence and stuck my hand through it. And one of the sheep came up and nuzzled my hand. It was completely tame, like a dog! It was as if it thought I was its mother."

Her voice was full of admiration. "And that's when I realized what they were doing. Nahia, they *raise* those animals—sheep, and there are others, too, goats and cows and pigs—and so they are *never without meat.* Think of it! They *always* have food. The danger of starvation is gone. Isn't it the most amazing thing?"

"But Zari," I said, focusing on the practical rather than the spiritual, "how do they keep them fed? You know in bad years, we haven't been able to keep even the dogs alive."

She smiled again, gesturing to our surroundings.

During our walk, we'd left the village, passed through a small stand of trees, and entered another clearing. Here, as I'd seen on my journey east, the forest had been stripped all the way down to the ground. Even the stumps had been dug out and carted away; the ground had been leveled. At the edges, where the open space met the forest, there was a ring of charred stubble, with an occasional burst of color from a stray wildflower.

The middle of the clearing was filled with tall golden grasses, waving in the breeze.

They should have been pretty—pleasant, even . . . but I was overcome with a feeling of dissonance, of some fundamental *wrongness*. I stared at the grasses. I was missing something, I knew. I looked from the blackened edge to the brilliant center, again and again, trying to understand.

One of the strangers appeared behind the grasses, and I jumped. The man raised an unfamiliar curved tool and swiftly drew it through the golden stalks. They fell to the ground in a lifeless heap.

I jerked back; it was so unexpected, so violent. The clearing was full of people, I realized, bent into the grass. And the people were all carrying those cutting tools. *Swish, swish* went the tools, and another pile of grass would fall.

And I finally understood why the clearing looked wrong: *The grasses were all the same.*

No true meadow would be so monotonous. No, this one had been made by the strangers. They had killed the forest and were growing their own plants in the space that had previously been the realm of the spirits.

Were they sick, or crazy? If the weather was bad, or a root disease struck, they would lose everything. Not to mention all their meals must taste the same. No wonder the food had been so bland.

Izara's hand snuck into mine. "We have plenty to feed the animals, you see. This is a field," she said warmly, "and it is where we plant the crops. Barley, which we make into *katcha*, is one of them. There are others: wheat, lentils—oh, and flax; we don't have any of that this year, but flax is made into linen." She squeezed my fingers. "Don't you see, Nahia, *we can never starve.* Remember how you always used to worry? Well, now no one has to."

There were so many things wrong with this; where could I even begin? "Izara, there is plenty to eat in the interior. They are *killing the forest* to make food, rather than moving to where it already exists. How? Why? This is madness! The spirits are suffering!"

Even as I spoke, I realized: *She doesn't see that it is madness. Izara is mad too.*

Izara's face had been shining with pride and happiness, but at my words, it darkened. "I should have known, Nahia. I don't know why everything has to be a bad idea just because *you* didn't think of it."

Izara put me to work, not in the first *field* we visited, but in another, where there were no other people. In this field, the strangers' plants were green, only partially grown, with no visible seedheads.

"What we will do is called weeding," she said, pointing at one of the green shoots. "This plant is barley, but it's still young."

I nodded.

"We only want barley in this field," she continued, "so what we need to do is go down these rows and take out any plant that isn't barley. Like this one." She reached into the row and pulled out a small green shoot, dropping it on the ground.

"But that's *artozi*!"

"I know, Nahia," Izara said, irritated. "It's not barley, so we don't want it growing here."

"But *artozi* is good for lots of things. Medicine—"

"But it's not barley," she interrupted. "So if you see it, take it out."

I took a deep breath, struggling to contain my shock. "You want me to kill useful plants?"

Izara sat back on her heels and pushed her hair out of her face. "Yes."

I stood up, shaking my head. There was a stand of trees between this field and the next, but it was only a thin barrier. I could see the tall golden grasses, could hear the *swish-swish* as the tools cut through them.

I heard my own voice, as faint as if I were speaking through a pile of furs. "What if the plants don't grow?" it said. "What if there is bad weather, or the animals eat them?"

Izara stood too. "I know it's a new way of thinking. But you can do it. Come on." She patted me, condescendingly.

I shook my head again. She was wrong, I knew she was wrong. I stood staring across the field.

If I was to rescue Izara from . . . from *this* . . . I needed to understand what was going on. So we knelt beside each other and began to work. As I pulled the *artozi* from the ground, I thanked it.

And then I reached out to my sister's spirit: *Help me to know how to save you.*

TWENTY-FIVE

I tried to *weed*, as Izara called it, but I just couldn't do it. I couldn't leave useful plants to wither in the sun. So instead, I collected them, carrying them in my arms since my pouch had been relegated to storage along with my familiar comfortable clothing. I would bring them home to eat. Green shoots are not the best, but at least they wouldn't go to waste. Izara scolded me, telling me it was pointless, that we had food, but I ignored her.

One of the village women seized Izara as soon as we reached the house, gabbling insistently in a half-and-half mixture of the strangers' language and ours. I took the opportunity to duck inside. No one was there; I could steal a small moment of privacy.

I piled the shoots alongside the basic foodstuffs Izara kept—vessels full of seeds, a bag of dried meat. As I rose, the shaman's pendant caught against the scratchy tunic Izara had forced on me. I wrapped my hand around it.

What the strangers were doing—clearing the forest, killing or abducting all of us who lived within it—it was wrong. More than wrong. It was a violation of the world so profound, I couldn't wrap my head around it.

I could see, though, why Izara had been swayed. The last few years of hunger, emptiness, and constant worry about food had been brutal.

That could drive anyone to say yes to anything. And Izara had never felt about the forest as I had. She couldn't hear the spirits.

But how she could subject herself to a life with the people who had abducted her? That was something else.

I had to act. But I didn't know what to do, or how much I could do. Could I fight the strangers in some way? Or was the only resistance possible to lead what remained of the Sea People away?

I knew what Hodei would tell me. She would tell me to practice *azkerta*. But the last time I had practiced *azkerta*, someone had died. I still did not understand how it had happened.

If I tried *azkerta* now, how could I be sure my fury would strike the strangers and not the Sea People? Not Izara? I could be sure of nothing, because I could not even control what I was doing. No, *azkerta* was closed to me.

Eneko . . . what would he tell me now?

Just thinking about him—imagining him here, beside me, leaning against the wooden wall of the house—made my heart twist painfully with longing. But he would never come here. *A shaman does not interfere with the lives of the bands.*

But what if it is *more* than the lives of the bands? What if the spirits themselves are at stake?

I was going to interfere. I had to interfere. I could not let this stand.

But this was too big for me on my own. I needed allies. And that, I decided, was where I would begin.

Alaia was close to her time. I knew this from the gossip between Izara and Abene; apparently her ankles had become so swollen that she was not able to work. I set out the next morning with *gotsa*, a green helpful for swelling, but mild enough not to disturb her coming child. It took me some time to find the home where she and Bakar lived, dogs barking at me as I walked. I would not have recognized the white and fluffy beasts as dogs but for their bark; they were much larger than any dog I had ever seen.

I passed a group of older men, sitting, and I kept my eyes averted. Izara had told me that, indeed, they enjoyed fermented barley. "Don't they have to work, too?" I had asked. Izara had rolled her eyes at me and huffed, but it had been a serious question. Izara and the other women in the village seemed to be working all the time, from first light until after dark. Why did these men not have to join them?

Eventually, I came to a house with gathering baskets leaned up against its walls. I knew it must be Alaia's or Udane's, for no one else would have these.

"*Ahai*," I called through the doorway, and walked in.

The structure was dark and smelled of sweat. There was a shape on the side opposite the hearth from me, a shape that moved and pulled itself to a sitting position as I entered.

"Who—Nahia?" The familiar voice was heavy with sleep.

"I am sorry to disturb you," I told Alaia. "I've brought you some *gotsa*."

"Oh, thank you!" Alaia cried. "I have been wishing for *gotsa*—I am so swollen I can barely move—but I can't get it myself in this state, and there has been no one I can ask. Come, let us sit outside, out of this close space. I have been wanting to talk to you."

I retreated, waiting for Alaia beside the outside hearth. In a few moments, she joined me, huffing with the effort of movement. She hugged me, then sank gratefully to a seated position, accepting the *gotsa* with a sigh.

"It is only a little," I said ruefully. "Is there truly no one else who would bring it for you?"

Alaia's mouth twisted. "Udane would, but I have not seen her, not to speak to, for some time. And everyone else—they are always busy. It is *harvest*." The foreign word sounded like a profanity on her tongue. "There is so much work to be done, they tell me. As if I am letting everyone down simply by being with child."

I was shocked. "Surely not everyone? Not Bakar?"

"No, not Bakar. He is beside himself, trying to help, but he does not know one plant from another, and he is not a woman."

I had heard enough of Izara's "there's work to do" to understand the pressure Alaia felt.

"I don't understand what has happened to Izara," I said. I don't know why I felt I had to apologize for my sister; a lifetime together, maybe. "Truly, Alaia, if there's anything for which you have need, please tell me. I am happy to pick *gotsa* all day, or whatever plants you wish!"

Alaia laughed. "Thank you, little sister," she said. The old nickname, from the days when Izara and I had followed her as if she were our elder sister in truth, warmed me. "It will not be long until my carrying is over. But if it does not come soon enough, I may be taking you up on that offer."

I hesitated, but there was nothing to stop me, so I plunged ahead. "Alaia, are you happy here?"

Her mouth bent again. "Who could be happy here, eating slurry, watching as our land is razed? I am here because I had no choice. Izara led Argi and his people to us, and they herded us away. *Tck!* With a child on the way, and the world as it is, where else could I go?" She shifted restlessly. "I'm grateful Bakar came with me. I didn't expect he would. He could have run."

"What about Esti?" I asked. "What did she say?"

Alaia shrugged. "What does Esti ever say? Oroitz follows Abene. Abene came willingly, so Oroitz and Esti came willingly. And here we all are, with no way of leaving. There's no escaping the stockade now."

She stopped and sighed. "I'm sorry, Nahia. I don't mean to complain about your sister, or your mother. My tiredness is getting the better of me. I haven't slept, not really, for days. It is just hard to think about what there is for me—for us—here." Her hand was on her belly. "I don't know what the world will hold for this little one. I almost wish she weren't coming."

"Hush," I said, for there is no worse omen for a birth than to say such a thing. But I understood what she meant, and I couldn't argue.

Alaia looked at me. "You were far away. Why did you come back?"

I didn't know how to answer her. "I knew Izara was in trouble," I finally said, looking at the ground. "But I didn't understand the kind of trouble she was in. And now I don't know what to do."

We sat in silence for a time. "It may be that you can do nothing. I want to tell you: you should leave, while you still can. I don't want to see you in the situation I am now in. Although . . . I know how you must feel. You see, I have been wondering what has become of my sister, Lorea." Lorea was one of the women Abene had mated to other bands. "I have no way to find her. I can only trust her new band has traveled inland and is safe. If she were here, as Izara is, and she did not want to leave, as Izara does not... I am not sure I would be able to abandon her. So I understand."

I put my arms around her. "I know you do, older sister."

Alaia freed herself from my arms and gently turned my face to hers. "Two things I will say. First, you should speak to Udane. She, too, sees the madness here. She may not be able to help you with Izara... but then again, she may."

I nodded. I had been thinking the same.

"And for the second, I have a request," Alaia said. "When my time comes, will you be with me? To have you there—it will give me strength, I think. And my child, too."

I kissed her. "Of course, I will be there," I promised.

I'd felt unwell ever since I'd arrived at the village.

As the days passed, I did not improve. I couldn't become accustomed to the powdery grain, the viscid pastes, the soapy flavors. I was constantly nauseated and spent far too much time in the privy. Naturally, this made me even sicker.

It was worst early in the day. Every morning, Maia, the woman from the north, would bring the katcha. Every morning, the heavy bland smell of boiled barley would turn my stomach over. I tried to eat it, but I never managed more than a bite or two. Izara would watch me, foot tapping, which did not help.

"Forest and seas, Nahia," she chided once, "it's *food*. Eat it and be thankful."

"I'm trying," I'd muttered, near gagging. "It's just... different."

Where Izara was impatient, Argi was concerned. One afternoon, he brought a basket of mushrooms and chestnuts home for me, cleaned and ready to cook. I fell upon them greedily; I was too hungry, too glad to have them, to ask where he got them. But Izara had no hesitation. She raised an eyebrow at him, asking, "Udane?"

Argi looked ashamed, I thought, but he nodded. Izara's face darkened.

Abene raised a hand, dismissively. "My sister will do what she wants. If she refuses to harvest, she refuses. It is your challenge now. Ask the land for guidance."

Izara glared at Abene, her face reddening. I could hear her thinking, *land-sense, what is it? Just a lot of superstition!*

I looked back and forth between the two of them. I had never heard Abene refer to Izara's having any land-sense before. It was me she'd pressured about listening to the earth, right up until she'd stripped me of my rank.

But the truth slowly dawned on me. Izara—and Abene, too—thought Izara was headwoman here.

Maybe she was, as much as anyone could be. I thought of the constant parade of women through Izara's house, the deferential gesture the villagers all made to her.

Abene's persistent silence suddenly made sense—she'd handed her role over to Izara.

Udane appeared the next day, as if summoned by that conversation, her foraging basket overflowing with *real* food, *gathered* food. I was elated. Unlike Abene, who had become elderly in the time I'd been gone, Udane seemed much the same—although she, too, now wore linen.

She was loudly pleased to see me—"I should have come to visit sooner, I know, but I have been busy," followed by a poisonous glare at Izara—and generous with the nuts and roots she'd gathered. "No one could live off the rubbish these people eat."

I snuck a glance at my sister. She was shifting ceramic vessels in the storage pit in the back of the house. Her mouth turned down sulkily, but she didn't say anything.

Udane, it emerged, did not work in the fields; she spent her days foraging instead. "Pah," she said, "I won't waste my time with that barley stuff. No taste. No body."

At this, Izara could not keep quiet. "You'll be glad enough for the *stuff* come next spring, when there's nothing in the woods."

Udane dismissed this with a flick of her hand. "I'll be eating shellfish in spring. There's enough for one old woman."

When she insisted I walk her back to her structure, my sister immediately jumped up. "I'll come with you," she said, removing the jar of grain she'd been stirring from the glowing charcoal at the edge of the fire. But just then Maia arrived, and Izara surrendered. "Don't be long," she called after us. "There's—"

"Work to do," I muttered along with her, but under my breath. Udane looked sideways at me and smirked.

As soon as we were out of Izara's line of sight, she grabbed my wrist, pulling my head down toward hers. "We have little time," she said in an undertone. "Listen to me. Will you take the headwoman role and lead our people inland?"

I pulled away from her, rubbing my arm. I could taste the horrid katcha I'd eaten that morning in the back of my throat. "What do you mean, take the headwoman role?"

I thought I'd kept my voice low, but one of the passing villagers looked at me curiously. "*Shh*," Udane snapped, pulling me close to her again, more gently this time. "I mean what I say. We cannot leave without a strong woman to guide us. What band would take us in? A few elders, a couple of unproven girls! Especially now, with so many seeking refuge. But you are headwoman-born. With you, we have a chance. You can make a path for us."

I stared at Udane. "Who is planning to leave? Who among you? When?"

"I do not yet have answers to those questions," said Udane. "Before you came, I could not see how we would escape. They need us to work their barley. But now... now, I can plan..."

A group of men, all strangers, passed close by, and Udane fell silent. One of the men smiled at us.

My aunt was not wrong. I *could* lead the remaining Sea People inland—I knew exactly where to take them. Ihintza would welcome me, and I did not think bringing the remaining women of the Sea People would alter that welcome. Indeed, the Ibex People had too many men.

"I must know who desires to leave," I whispered.

"I will find out, if you will agree," Udane whispered back. "I think most everyone, except perhaps Izara. And if Izara stays, so will Abene." She spat. "My sister, your mother—she betrayed us, you understand that? She knew this could happen, yet always denied it. And your sister has betrayed us the same, taking up with that *irrotzi*."

"I can't leave Izara here!" I protested.

"Hush!" said Udane. "Don't speak to her of this. She will only work to stop us."

"Surely, if we got her away from Argi, she would agree to come!" I insisted. "Surely she wouldn't want to stay here on her own!"

Udane shook her head, but she didn't argue with me. "I will talk with the others, see what they say. Speak nothing of this for now, Nahia."

We'd reached Udane's structure. Tora stood before the entrance, looking anxiously down the path. Her expression lightened as she saw us.

Udane pulled me in toward her again and breathed in my ear, "Think this through. I will find a way for us to talk freely sometime soon. We have some time; we must wait for Alaia's baby to be born." Then she straightened again and said, loud enough for Tora to hear, "Get back quickly now. There's *work* for you to do."

For the first time since I had arrived in the village, I felt a spring of hope inside me. I did not want to be headwoman of the Sea People. I did not want to lead. I had left that behind me when I went with Eneko. But if I could convince Izara to come away, to live as our people were meant to, I would do it. I only had to be headwoman long enough to take my old band to Ihintza.

If I could convince Izara.

After a few days, though, my hope began to fade. Izara was so sure of the superiority of the strangers' ways, I did not see how I could sway her. She loved the katcha, and the linen, and even the sheep—to say nothing of her new status.

And I began to think that I, too, would never be able to escape now. The waiting wore me down, so that there was less and less left of me, just the ever-present nausea, the endless grinding of grain, and the endless walls of the palisade.

TWENTY-SIX

I opened my eyes and found myself alone in Izara's house.

I pushed myself up on one hand, blinking to clear my vision, and looked around the empty hearth. This had never happened before. Normally I woke with Izara to accept the day's ration of katcha from Maia. But this morning her and Argi's bed was empty, the furs pushed back in a pile. Abene's was the same. Nothing was tidied; it was as if everyone had woken and silently left together, responding to some signal I couldn't see or hear.

Pale light trickled in through the cracks in the walls. It was still very early. I dressed and went outside.

Izara and Argi were sitting by the outside hearth. She was laying back against him, her head on his chest, his arms around her and his lips on her cheek. I was embarrassed, and angry—this was the man who had abducted her, dragged her here! But at the same time, looking at the two of them, I had a sharp, stabbing ache of loneliness, of longing for Eneko.

I could go back to the mountains. I could leave all this behind.

But I couldn't, of course. Even if I could abandon Izara, how could I abandon Udane, or the rest of them?

Argi looked up and saw me. He smiled. "Good, I must go to tend the animals. You will stay with Xara?"

It took me a minute to realize he meant Izara. Her face had been turned from me, but as Argi spoke she glanced up, and I saw how tired she looked. I nodded.

"What happened?" I asked, once Argi was gone.

Izara pushed her hair back, her face drawn and her eyes bloodshot. Had she been crying? Izara never cried. "Oh, it's good news, really. Alaia had her baby—a little girl."

"*What?*" I said. "Why didn't you call me!?"

"There wasn't time," Izara said dismissively. "Besides, since when do you attend childbirth?"

"Alaia *asked* me to be there!" I cried. "I told her I would be. It never occurred to me you wouldn't wake me!"

Izara sighed. "I'm sorry," she said, a little stiffly. "I told you, there wasn't time. And really, there was no need for you to be there. What would you have done?"

"I happen to know something about medicine," I said, equally stiffly. "I have been studying—"

"Oh, *studying*," said Izara. "Is that what you were doing with Eneko?"

"I *was* studying," I said, stung. "I learned so well that—"

I stopped. I had never told Izara about my time away, never let her see the tattoo. I didn't want to tell her now. I didn't want to talk to her at all, in fact. The anger inside me was burning hard. I struggled to control my breathing.

Somehow, Izara and I were further apart than we had been when I was in the mountains.

She stood up. "Come on. Maia was busy last night, too, but she'll have made katcha by now. Let's take our bowls over to her house."

Maia welcomed us. We sat around the outside fire, and Izara and Maia talked. I let my mind wander; it was too much effort for me to follow what they were saying. Maia's language was closer to ours than to the strangers', but it wasn't the same. She and Izara spoke a mixture, and used some of the strangers' words, too. I wrapped my hands around my bowl, seeking comfort from its heat, and rested my eyes on the western hills. Beyond those hills lay the mountains. And in the mountains was Eneko.

I can't think about him. I have to stay here.

Izara finished her meal quickly, and she stood to go. I started to rise, too, but Izara pushed me back down again. "No, no, you sit. Finish your katcha. I am going to the barns; I'll be back in a little while. Maia will look after you."

I had hoped, with Izara elsewhere, that I could go find Udane, but Maia sat next to me, silent and unmoving. Didn't she have work to do, too? I thought perhaps I should be uncomfortable, but I was beyond discomfort at that point: *everything* was uncomfortable, and I didn't care anymore. I pushed the viscous mass of katcha around with my eating stick.

Maia said, "I do not bring katcha for all in village. At first, was for Argi only, for he helps—how do you say, helped?—me. Then Xara come, and she, too, helps me, and she helps other women here. So I bring katcha for Xara and Argi, both."

I turned to look at her, really look at her, for the first time. Her long face was solemn, her blue eyes bright.

"You are from the bands to the north?" I asked. Her coloring was darker than Esti's, but her accent was similar.

Maia nodded. "From the north, and the east, far from here."

"But your people, they are band people? Like ours?"

"Yes," she said. Her voice was very soft, her face expressionless.

"You were taken. But you could leave here now. No one guards *you*, do they? You could travel back to your people. Why are you still here?"

Maia drew her hair behind her ears. "I cannot travel back to my band, no. I will tell you. These people..." she gestured to the structures.

"The strangers? The villagers?" I said.

"Yes, these strangers. Some—not these, but others—come to start village in my band's territory. They are all men. We try to hide, but they clear forests, nothing left for us to eat. They know we are there. And then they find us, find our camp. They kill the men and elder people, take the girls. They take me." She was silent a moment. "My whole band is gone now. Everyone dead, or in those men's village. Argi's people, they stop by that village on their way to here, and Argi takes me with them. Is better here, so I am happy."

"But Maia," I said, "they are the same people. How can you be happy?"

Maia squinted at me. "No, they are not the same. These men different, better, not like the first village. They only kill when they must! They do not kill elders, or children. And then, your sister comes." She smiled at me. "When Xara comes, these men, she does not let them scare her. She stands up, tells them she will be with Argi, they must listen to her. And they do listen to her. Now, we women, we have headwoman." She stood up. "This is why I bring katcha. For Argi, and then for Xara—and now for you, sister of Xara."

She made a gesture at me, not unlike the one I'd seen the people in the field make to Izara, and then disappeared into her house.

I went to Alaia's to greet her baby daughter, and I made my apologies. Izara hadn't woken me, I told her. Izara was with me, and she rolled her eyes as I said it, but she did not protest. Alaia had squeezed my hand, said she understood. There was a smile in her eyes when they met mine—a secret smile, one that made me think she had been talking to Udane, that she knew our plans.

Surely, Udane would find me soon so we could make that plan into something more than a few words exchanged while walking through the village. Now that Alaia's daughter had arrived, it was time to move.

I had made no progress in swaying Izara, though, or even in finding the space to have a genuine conversation. She was always busy, and what conversation we did have verged on the hostile. In hopes of encouraging some peace between us, of finding a way we could talk, *really* talk, I acquiesced to her demands that I help with the village's work.

At this season, work began early in the morning and continued until darkness threatened. The villagers had begun the tedious work of drying the grasses. Every day, those who worked the fields brought large bundles of grass stalks to the plaza. Women took the grasses from the bundles and spread them out, letting them dry, before flailing them to release the seeds. Izara often went to talk to these women, taking me with her. She stood in the middle of the plaza, giving instructions. I dawdled beside her, peripheral, not really paying attention.

One day, our visit was interrupted by a shout from the village gate. We all turned.

Argi and a group of men were marching in together, a large, dark figure on their shoulders. I squinted, trying to get a better look—and then closed my eyes in horror.

It was a bear.

A big bear, and it was dead.

The men lifted the huge, inert shape high into the air, shouting, then laid it on the ground in the center of the plaza to a resounding cheer. Izara whooped in celebration, too.

My stomach was sour, and my mouth tasted like dry leaves.

Even before I became an apprentice, I'd known that bears should never be killed except in dire need. The killing of a bear meant a shaman was needed. There were songs to sing, rites that must be performed. I had known this even before Hodei spoken of it, back in the mountains, though I hadn't known *why* a shaman was necessary. Izara knew it too.

But now I knew more.

My hand on the bear's back, its fur beneath my fingers.

"Go."

I looked at the men in the plaza, skinning the bear. Argi stood over them, laughing. Some of the villagers were passing around cups of fermented barley, cheering as they drank.

I felt the fire in my belly, never far these days, flare high, higher, *higher*.

Izara saw I was upset. "Bears eat the pigs; we have to kill them, or we'd have nothing. It's the same with wolves. They steal the sheep, so they need to go."

I was afraid I would cry, but my eyes stayed dry.

One more mystery was solved, though I didn't see what good it did to know. The predators Ihintza had mentioned, thick in the forest around the Ibex People—they had left the coast *because* of the strangers.

I did not know the ceremonies for the death of a bear, but Bear had protected me before. I owed her something.

Did I owe her vengeance? Should these men be punished?

My thoughts turned, again, to *azkerta*. But was it right to call on Bear to avenge her own death? No, I could not vision for that. *I* had to do something, deliver *some* punishment, even if it was small.

My dried herbs were still in the gathering basket I'd brought with me from the mountains. When I got back to Izara's structure that afternoon, I pulled out the hide bundle that held them. One of the pouches contained ground *elorri*.

When no one was looking, as we were handing the food round at evening meal, I slipped the powder into Argi's bowl.

TWENTY-SEVEN

The *elorri* brought the expected results. In the night, I heard Argi groaning with pain, then footsteps as he fled the house. Izara dashed after him. I was glad of the dark that hid my smile. It was too small a penalty, and I knew it, but it was *something* for the bear. Not enough. But something.

Argi and Izara returned an hour before dawn. They crawled back to bed, and so, most unusually, were not up with the sun. I wondered if they would be able to participate in the village's work that day at all. Izara would, probably, but Argi might need a day or two to recover. Abene, too, was slow to rise that day; maybe Argi's moaning had kept her awake. Maia had not yet arrived with the katcha.

I was alone outside, blinking blearily, trying to wake up, when Udane arrived. She had gathering baskets slung over her shoulder, and she said to me, as if she had been expecting me there, "I am going foraging today. Would you like to come?"

I glanced over my shoulder into the house. It was quiet within, my foraging baskets sitting in the storage pit next to where Izara and Argi slept. "I don't have a basket with me."

"I thought you might not. I brought this extra one."

So I went with her, feeling dizzy with the freedom.

We moved through the village quietly. There was fog drifting along the paths, intermingling with the smoke from morning fires. Once we passed the outer walls, both fog and smoke dispersed.

Soundlessly, we began climbing the big hill outside the village. Trees rose up on either side of us. My mood soared. I'd been in the village for weeks now, looking over the walls, longingly, to this western hill. And yet I'd never climbed it.

I wanted to rush up the slope, to plunge into the forest, but I myself held back. We'd only clambered up part way when I noticed that Udane's breathing was labored. I looked back at her. Her face was flushed and strained, her gait uneven. She had always been slow, but it couldn't have been this bad before?

There was a level area about three-quarters of the way up, and we stopped there. She leaned on her walking stick, wheezing. I stood next to her, patting her back, relishing the silence and the smoke-free air. The dawn mist had blown away, and I could see the sea, a beautiful bright blue, in the distance.

I haven't been to the ocean since I came back. And when I lead my people inland, I may never see it again.

I'll go, every day, for the rest of my time here. I'll go even if I have to wrestle Izara.

I let my eyes wander from the sea back toward the foot of the hill. The large clearing, with the village at its center, sat immediately below the little shelf where Udane and I stood. There was a ring of forest around the clearing, but it was full of gaping holes, some black from recent burning, some fields full of barley or other grasses. A little way to the north there was a smoldering patch, the start of another clearing, this one too large to be a field. Another village? Surely they wouldn't build a second so near to the first, would they? There would soon be no forest at all left, if they did.

Suddenly I doubled over, as if someone had struck me in the belly.

The forest was in pain. I felt it. The village, sitting in the midst of this barren, beaten land, was an open sore.

I had known they were clearing, had seen them at it. I'd even walked through razed patches on my journey. But the destruction was much more obvious when seen from above. *So much* had been cleared.

I didn't know I was going to speak until I heard my voice. "How could they do it?" I whispered. "To stay in one place, they will sacrifice everything else? The old ways, the spirits, all other life? There is food in the interior. They do not need to do this."

"These strangers, they respect nothing," Udane spat. "They came to our shores, but in their minds, they are still at home, I think. They have their own ways, their own laws."

My heart ached for my homeland, for all the beings that had made it up, so many of which were now gone. I was filled with hopelessness. How could I, how could *anyone*, avenge this?

The best I had done was give Argi the flux. It was like spitting into the wind.

The scale of this destruction was so massive, the transformation so profound. And there were so many villagers. No one person could have stopped them. Even if all the people of the bands had joined together, I did not think we could have stopped them.

Udane's hand sought mine. "When I first came to this place, I was in despair. I could see no way out. But then you returned. With a proper headwoman, we have a chance. And by removing so many from their *village*, perhaps it will fail."

"If we do leave... I think I know where we might go." I told her quickly of the Ibex People, and Ihintza's invitation to me. "I'm sure she will accept us. They have too many men and need women. But I don't feel right leaving Izara and Abene here." I paused. "What if Alaia were to lead the remaining Sea People to Ihintza's band? I think... when faced with everyone's leaving... Izara might come to her senses. I could wait for that, then bring her and Abene to join you."

And after, I could go back to Eneko, I silently added. *If I knew you all were safe, I could return to where I belong.*

Udane was shaking her head. "We need a leader," she said. "Alaia is a good girl, but she is from Lili's line, not the headwoman's line. And she has a newborn. You, Nahia, carry your grandmother Nene's blood, as well as Dania's. You were born to lead. My sister was wrong to punish you when you spoke out. Speaking out is what a headwoman must do. It was a sign of what you are." She squeezed my hand. I looked up, meeting her eyes, then quickly looked away again. There was so much need there, such longing. It made me nervous. "I know, it will be difficult. But I trust in you, Nahia. You are headwoman-born. All you have to do is choose it."

The words were an echo of something someone else had told me once.

Udane cradled my hand between hers. Her touch was gentle, despite her rough skin. "It is meant. Your return here, when we had all given you up as lost—it is a sign. Surely you, trained as a shaman, can see that?"

She paused, and I realized she was looking at my upper arm, where my tattoo was now exposed. Without thinking, I'd pushed the arms of my tunic up as we climbed the hill. I drew my hand away from her and tugged my sleeve down. "I put aside my training to come here."

Udane ignored me. She went on, softly, almost to herself. "Carrying a child, our mother-leader, our hope."

A child?

There was a rushing sensation in my ears. *Carrying a child?* I grasped for something, anything that might make sense.

Surely I would have noticed if I were carrying a child. Surely Udane must be mistaken.

Or would I? I'd been busy since I left Eneko. I'd been traveling hard. I'd been in the village, trying to untangle things, mired in gloom. *Would* I have noticed the signs? I thought back over the last months.

I'd been sick.

I hadn't had my monthly bleeding.

This can't be true. It can't.

But it was. Udane was right; all the signs were there. I'd ignored them. I'd thought I was just sick with shock.

How could I have been so dense? I hadn't even thought of it as a possibility. Shamans don't have children. Sex was only for *bizi.*

But it hadn't been about *bizi* when Eneko and I were together. I'd thought it was simpler than that. Well, it *was* simpler than that, wasn't it? I had fallen in love. And now I was pregnant.

I was pregnant. I was pregnant, and alone, and living among strangers. And now I was being asked to take responsibility for my band, to lead them on a path fraught with risk, from the captivity of the stockade to the freedom of the uplands.

This is too much. I cannot bear all this.

I dragged myself back to the present. Udane was looking at me expectantly. I struggled to find something to say.

"Nahia, I know you want to help your sister, but I am begging you. If you do not take this on, we will lose everything we are." She let her walking stick fall to the ground, then took me in her arms. "*You* are our way back."

I thought I'd escaped being first daughter. But I hadn't.

The old duty had been with me all the time. It had bound me in my visions. It had gripped me when Hodei told me the rumors about the Sea People. And when Udane had first spoken to me about leading the band, it had tightened its hold almost to the point of breathlessness. It was firming up, hardening, becoming once again the invisible, inevitable burden I had known from my earliest childhood.

Not even a season ago, I'd been in the valley with Eneko and Hodei. I'd been amazed by my own happiness and by my own abilities. In a flash of memory, I saw the night I had earned my tattoo.

The world had been so large and full of possibility that night. It had shrunk smaller and smaller ever since.

If I did as Udane asked, if I became headwoman, my world would shrink still further. I would never escape the burden of the band's expectations again. I would never be able to return to the peaks, to Eneko, to my shaman's training. I would never again pass a night chanting for protection; I would never master the Sight, the visions that drew me even as they frightened me.

I would lose all of it.

"They won't let us go easily, you know that. I need to know your plan," I said slowly. "And Izara . . . Izara will fight to keep everyone here."

I don't want *to be a headwoman. I never have.*

But these are my people, and they need me. I must accept this burden.

Udane gazed into my eyes. Her nails cut into my flesh. "I trust you, Nahia. You will succeed." She released me. "Let us talk more as we forage."

TWENTY-EIGHT

It was late in the afternoon when we returned to the village. Our baskets were laden with mushrooms and nuts and the last of the season's fruits. As we approached, the wooden palisade rose before us. From a distance, those walls looked weak and flimsy, an inconsequential barrier that could easily be breached, but as we drew closer, they grew larger and more solid, until finally, close up, one could see how formidable they were.

There was a figure waiting for us outside the break in the wall, a figure with shining hair that caught the light. The figure's hands were on her hips.

Izara. I didn't have to hear her voice to know that she was angry.

"What did you do to Argi?" she demanded, as soon as Udane and I were in hearing distance.

I started. I'd forgotten about the *elorri*. "What do you mean?" I asked, trying to sound innocent.

Izara's eyes narrowed. "He was sick all night. Very sick. Too sick."

"Little wonder. The slop these strangers eat would sicken a dog," Udane sniffed.

"This is between me and Nahia!" Izara snapped. She was trembling, her foot jiggling. She did not shift her gaze from me. "Why were you gone when I got up?"

Udane was clearly hesitant to leave us alone. Her eyes ranged between us, and she tapped my hand, gently, to let me know she would stay if I wished it. Almost I asked her to; almost I told Izara that she and I could talk after Udane and I had processed our day's take. I needed time to think. So much had changed in just a few hours.

But there was no use in delaying this confrontation. Sooner or later, it would come; and in one sense, it would be better to get it over with. I sighed. "Udane, can you take my basket?"

I helped Udane strap the second basket on her back, watched her disappear into the maze of structures. It took her a long while. I knew Izara wouldn't speak until Udane was out of sight, and the pause gave me time to gather my thoughts.

Udane's plan, explained to me on the hill, was straightforward: Formally challenge Izara's leadership, and install me as replacement. Then I would lead the group to Ihintza's Ibex People. According to Udane, all the remaining Sea People (other than Izara and Abene) would follow. She thought some of the other women stolen from the bands might join us, too.

In my aunt's view, it would be simple... but I knew it wouldn't be. Izara wouldn't let us go without a fight. And I didn't think Argi would let us go without a fight, either. They were many more than we were. We would have to be very smart about this. Perhaps a formal challenge was a mistake—perhaps all should be done by stealth. I wasn't sure yet.

Everything could be resolved if only I could make Izara *see*, if only I could break through her bizarre new thinking. Then *she* could lead Udane and the others to the Ibex People. Izara was from Dania's line as much as I was—better, she *wanted* to be headwoman.

Udane had disappeared. I turned back to my sister. The look on her face made me cringe. I didn't regret giving Argi the *elorri*, but I wished I hadn't done it last night.

"Argi was sick until daybreak," Izara said. "A mysterious sickness that struck *only him*, no one else. And then, just as mysteriously, it passed."

"I am sorry to hear of it," I said. "It sounds like the sickness that comes from bad food. You should have called me. I might have had something that could help."

Izara let a breath out. I could see she was wondering if she had been wrong; if perhaps Argi's illness had been unrelated to me. I felt a twinge of guilt for misleading her.

But she had another arrow in her quiver. She gestured at me to walk with her away from the village, through the gates and back toward the hill Udane and I had just descended. "What are you and Udane up to?" she demanded.

I swallowed. "What do you mean?"

"Oh, forest and seas, Nahia! The two of you, sneaking off together, whispering, criticizing me, not doing any work..." Izara stopped abruptly. The hard words were like pebbles dropped into water. *Thump, thump, thump*, and then silence.

I stared at her, but I did not speak. She stood tall and rigid, her lips pinched into a line. She looked like Abene.

Eventually, Izara blew a loud breath out. Her body collapsed, softening, as if it had been the breath that kept her so stiff. She looked over her shoulder at the village, then turned back to me and said, very quietly,

"Udane has been working against our village—our *people*. She has threatened me. I think maybe you know that."

I ran a hand through my hair. "Izara, you've practically refused to talk about Udane—or anyone else—since I arrived. How am I supposed to know what is going on?"

"I will tell you now, then! Udane has been slacking since she got here!" Izara exploded. "She sneaks out to look for *mushrooms* instead of working in the fields. You know that. Of course you know that! She brought you some, because you were too picky to eat what we had. Where did you think she got them?" She tapped her fingers against each other, one after another.

I looked at the ground for a moment. *Don't become angry*, I told myself. *Don't let her make you angry.*

"She never helps! And then last night, Tora told me Udane and Oroitz were conspiring together—conspiring to steal the the Sea People and take them away." She made a furious sound. "She's greedy for power! She's jealous of me!"

"But—" I began, then stopped.

Tora had told Izara?

Udane had assured me that all the Sea People were committed to leaving. But Udane's own daughter, apparently, was not. If Udane was wrong about Tora, how much could I trust her assurance that the remaining Sea People would embrace my leadership? Had Tora told Izara about *my* role in Udane's plan?

Surely not; Izara would have come right out and said so. "If they want to leave," I said, "why don't you just let them?"

"They *can't* leave, Nahia!" Izara shrieked. "You know what happens when a band fractures. It's no different here! If people leave, we'll go hungry. The fields will go unharvested and rot. All my work will be for nothing!"

I could feel my mouth twisting. "I thought you were impervious to hunger now. 'We won't ever starve this way'—isn't that what you said?"

"That's only true if everyone does their share. We need enough people to get everything done. You've seen it: we are always busy! That's the way it works!" Izara's voice was building in pitch again. "Why do you think Argi wanted the Sea People? It's because *he needs the hands*. Other strangers, when they raid to get enough people to do the work, they kill the ones that aren't strong—but Argi isn't like that. He keeps the old people and the little children. He wants everyone to be happy here, and he wants people to *want* the benefits. Even you!" She covered her face with her hands. "You've been impossible ever since you arrived, refusing to speak to him, and still he brings you food, tries to make you comfortable!"

"There are some here who do not want these benefits. Are they free to leave, or not?"

Izara crossed her arms over her chest. "You *have* been listening to Udane. That's why I don't like your sneaking off with her! Maybe you should get your information from *me*, not from a jealous old crone who doesn't know what she's talking about!"

"Izara, if you are not ashamed of what you have done, if you are not ashamed of this village, then you would not be ashamed to have me speak with Udane. Perhaps you should think about that."

"*Ashamed?*" Izara's voice spiraled up, cracking on the word. "I would be ashamed *why*? For saving the band from starvation? For holding the land that has been ours since Dania's days?"

And with that, I lost every semblance of calm I'd had.

"*Saving the band?*" I mimicked Izara's voice. "*Holding the land?* How have you saved the Sea People from anything? You are destroying them, not saving them! And you are not honoring the land, you are killing it! If you have land-sense, then you should know you can't change everything about the coast and say you are honoring it!"

Izara's lower lip quivered. "How would you know? You don't have any land-sense. And Abene says—"

"You know why we do not take plants or animals without giving thanks. I know you know, for you were taught the same as I was! If the land cannot support us, we must leave! We can't make it suffer for our presence."

Izara was almost shouting now. "This land is all we have! This land is all we are! You weren't there. Our *own hunters* turned on us. In the face of death, we had to find a new way, and my choice allowed us to stay in our territory. I *am* saving the Sea People!"

My hands were tight at my sides. "Here you are, enslaved by those who raze the forest, who replace the animals with their own, who kidnap women, and you celebrate it. You are so twisted, you can't even see what you have become."

"Enslaved? I am no slave. And neither are the Sea People. It is *our band* who has become the village. It is I who have become headwoman!"

"Have you? Or does Argi let you play at it, because he likes your body?" As soon as the words were out of my mouth, I knew I had gone too far.

There was an abrupt silence.

Izara was motionless, but I saw her eyes move. They traveled slowly down my body, coming to rest on my midsection.

I drew my breath in. "Izara," I began, "I shouldn't have—"

She came to life. "Don't say anything else to me." Her gaze was fiery, her voice low. "You've had your say. You think you would be a better leader than I? You, who abandoned us? How dare you judge me? You were out having fun with your shaman. *Studying*, or so you say. You come waltzing back once you're *haurxi*," she gestured at my belly, "thinking you are the great savior mother, and a great seer, too. But you're just a beggar. You complain and stir up trouble, but you contribute nothing. All you do is take."

My stomach slammed up against my ribs, almost as if I was falling. My heart pounded erratically, and there was a rushing sound in my ears. But my voice was calm and cold as I said, "I left because you told me to."

I saw Izara flinch. My blood raced.

After a moment, she said, "So you want to be the headwoman now."

"I don't *want* to. But I'll do what I must for the women who have asked for my help."

Her gaze was fire; I saw no spark of love there. "I'd like to see you try."

She turned her back on me and went back to the village.

I stood and watched her go. My hands rested on my midsection. The evening air was thick and oppressive; there must be a storm coming, out on the sea. The forest stood behind me, I knew, but I could not sense it at all.

I should feel something. Anger, fear, shame, anticipation? Something, anyway.

But all I felt was numb.

My mind was whirling. Izara's face, twisted in anger, as she said, "*All you do is take*"; Udane, pleading, "*you are our way back*"; Hodei saying, "*What you wish to be—only you can know.*" The forest's voice, so muted here. My hand on the bear's fur. Omer's injured, eyeless face as he said, "*There were so many of them.*" And through it all, my own body, swelling beneath my hands, swelling with a baby.

I was coming apart. There was too much inside me for one person to contain. I could not see any way forward.

Azkerta can reveal a path when all seems lost. So Hodei had told me.

I did not want to do it. Last time I sank into a vision, I had unleashed forces that I neither intended nor understood. But all *did* seem lost. My sister was captive and couldn't see it; the women of the Sea People cried out for a leader; I was carrying a child... and yet all I wanted was to return to my valley in the mountains. The world was being destroyed by men, men who stole and raped and killed, but who managed to convince at least some of the women they stole of the rightness of their ways.

I had to take the risk. I did not see what else I could do.

TWENTY-NINE

The walk to the beach was steep and twisting, hard to find by moonlight. I had to tread carefully. When the path leveled out, I stopped for a moment, catching my breath.

Before me, the cove was flat and sandy, an expanse of sand bounded by cliffs. The bluffs cast shadows and made the shoreline a jumble of darkness, but the moonlight reflecting off the waves illuminated a large boulder at the edge of the water. I picked my way across the beach and sat on it, placing my small reed bundle beside me.

The evening meal had been a tense affair. Izara and I had avoided speaking to or even looking at each other. Argi was still in bed, recovering. Abene had tried, at first, to chat with Izara, but Izara had responded in monosyllables. Eventually, Abene gave up and took her bowl outside, where she ate alone. I had choked down a few mouthfuls quickly, then rummaged among my medicines to find the *aubli*.

And then I'd left. Izara did not ask where I was going.

I sat on the boulder, looking out at the sea, and my fear sat next to me, as present as the reed bundle. The moon was large in the eastern sky. The sound of the waves was deep and soothing. Slowly, I was lulled into calm, like a crying baby rocked to sleep against its will.

Then a voice called my name.

I was fully awake, all at once. I leapt off the rock, scanning the shore. A figure, glowing pale in the moonlight, was at the other end of the strand, moving slowly toward me.

For a moment, I was breathless. But then I saw the pale glow was only long, loose, yellow hair. It was Esti. She made not a whisper of noise as she came; she might have been a ghost. When she had crossed the beach, she sat down on the sand next to where I stood.

And greetings to you, too, Esti. But I didn't say the words aloud. I sat on the sand at her side. My terror was gone, replaced by annoyance. I wanted to be alone; was that so much to ask?

It occurred to me to be grateful that I had not taken the *aubli* before she arrived.

I decided to ignore her, to stare over the sea without speaking, but the peace I'd found earlier had fled. *Why is she here?* I'd seen Esti only once since my return, on the day I'd arrived. She'd been one of the people in the plaza. Esti had always been a quiet presence, even when among the Sea People. She spoke little, lending her voice only to talk with me and Izara, and to support Oroitz when he demanded it. *Well, except about Gotzon—she let Gotzon stay with the gatherers, even when Oroitz complained.*

What does Esti think of the village, I wonder?

Esti stirred, slightly. "You know my story," she said, as if picking up a conversation we'd been having. "When I was captured, I was forced by many men."

I stiffened. Esti was still, waiting for some response. I thought of Izara and Argi, and then Kerbasi. My stomach churned with the familiar mix of shame and anger. *Kerbasi was Esti's son, from her capture. If he had succeeded, he and Omer, would I have been forced to bear his child, as Esti was made to carry him?*

My arms were wrapped around my midsection again. "How did you bear it?" I asked, my voice dry and brittle. I remembered my younger self asking the same question. Esti hadn't answered then, had put me off.

Tonight, she answered me. "It is not who I am," she said. "It is only what happened to me."

That isn't what I meant, I wanted to say, but I couldn't speak the words.

"Things happen. Sometimes good things, sometimes bad things, unfair things. The sun rises, and then it sets. Life goes on." She stood up. "I tell you, you do not know what you will do when bad things happen until they happen to you."

Bad things have *happened to me*. But how could I say that?

"If you expect too much from others, you will be hurt. No one is responsible for any choices but her own." She smoothed the fabric of her tunic, then set off toward the path back to the village.

My tongue loosened when Esti was about halfway there. "But I'm headwoman's daughter, Esti!" I shouted, leaping to my feet. "I *have* to accept responsibility for others!" The anger in my voice surprised me.

Esti didn't look back; she gave no indication she had heard me at all. When she reached the path, she turned on to it, fading into the darkness.

I'm headwoman's daughter, I repeated to myself. My throat swelled with the unfairness of her words. I would never have expected Esti to take Izara's side. *It's all very well to say you're not responsible when you are a captive. But sometimes you* are *responsible. My sister claims to be a leader.*

I watched the water ebb and flow, ebb and flow. My anger slowly receded. Why had I been angry at Esti?

I'm not angry at Esti. I'm angry at Izara. And I'm angry at Abene.

But why? Were Izara and Esti—and me, too, and Abene—were we so different? Didn't each of us make the best choices, as she saw them?

I was seized by a longing for Eneko, a craving so strong I could barely breathe. If only I could see his friendly, calm face; if only I could speak and hear him answer. He had always understood me. When I couldn't find the words, or the courage to speak them, he had heard them anyway. Hodei, too. She had seen how my fear for the Sea People tore at me, even when I had hidden it so deeply within me that I hadn't seen it myself.

Suddenly I was crying, my body expressing my pain.

I was so alone.

I had left the valley, and it was possible—likely even—that I would never see them again. I was carrying a baby, a baby I'd never imagined having. My people had been changed by something new and strange, something that was butchering the spirits that nurtured us, that devoured our previous way of life like wildfire consumed brush. And Izara, my twin, my other self, was the leader of this new, strange thing, and so different from me we might never have been sisters.

Azkerta can reveal a path when all seems lost.

There was nothing else to do. I climbed back atop the boulder, dipped my finger into the reed bundle, and placed the bitter paste on my tongue.

I was in the *orei*'s cave, kneeling before the pool, my arms crossed over my chest. On the water's surface, I saw Izara and Argi sitting beside the hearth outside their structure.

I dove into the pool.

For a moment, all was black. And then I was standing on the hillside looking down at the village, the burned and cleared land, as I had earlier this afternoon. It was deep night.

Despair washed over me. Below, the fields were shining with barley, as clear as though it were daytime, as though I were waking. The barley cried, like a baby hungry for milk. The barley did not know it was a part of any destruction. It was merely trying to survive, as we all were. It was as subject to the strangers' will as a child to its mother's.

I felt a presence beside me. I turned, and there was Abene.

She was not looking at the village, nor the fields, nor at me. Her gaze was on her hands, in which she held a single mussel shell, black and pearlescent. She said to it, "This is the land my foremothers have granted us. I will not leave."

And then Izara was beside her. She took the mussel shell, she took Abene's hands, and she led her into the night.

I tried to follow them, but I could not move. The fog was coming in, swirling around me, obscuring my view. I heard the chittering of the *arhontzl*, the growl of the bear.

I tensed. If Bear came to me, would death follow?

But it was not the bear that appeared beside me in the fog—it was the *arhontzl*. It landed on my arm, wings outstretched.

And then I was enfolded in those wings, and I *was* the *arhontzl*, soaring up into the forest canopy.

The nocturnal landscape stretched out below me. I flew along the coast, and I saw that the destruction had spread far beyond what I could see on the hill—it reached far into the south, the shoreside dotted with villages and fields growing their strange plants. I looped around to the north and found more of the same. All along the coast, the strangers had grown villages just as they grew barley. Between them were small patches of forest and more clearings, clearings lined by circular ditches.

I came to land upon the beach, and I was myself again, the *arhontzl* soaring away above me to the west.

Toward the mountains.

Toward home.

I lay on my boulder, curled up like a baby, my eyes shut tight. My skin was slick with sweat and sea-spray, and I shivered with cold.

I had to get up, had to move, lest I freeze here. Reluctantly, I opened my eyes, searching out a sheltering tree, a hollow in the cliff, a nest of boulders—anywhere I might curl up out of the wind. As I scanned the shore, I saw my boulder was not the only one; there were several. There were small irregular lumps, too—driftwood and seaweed. And then there was another shape, large and low and long, that I couldn't place. A beached dolphin? It wasn't moving, whatever it was.

I crossed the beach to investigate. I was almost on top of it before I realized what it was.

A boat. A boat, turned over so its bottom faced the sky.

It wasn't like any boat I'd seen before. It was longer and wider, and it wasn't carved from a log, but constructed of thinner material stretched across a frame. I touched it, carefully. I recognized the material immediately: hide. The boat was made of animal hide, tanned and stretched over a scaffold of shaped bone. A boat made this way would be lighter, easier to maneuver. It would be capable of traveling over the sea.

A sea-traveling boat.

My eyes were suddenly wet. It had been my ability to picture sea-traveling boats in my mind that earned me my place as shaman's apprentice, just as my first true vision earned me a place as a shaman. But I wasn't a shaman anymore.

Unexpectedly, my mental voice startled me by roaring back at me: *Who says I'm not? I have the tattoo. I have traveled in the spirt world. I may have put my seer-self aside for a time, but I can reclaim it.*

Eneko told me that my path was mine to choose. Hodei said what I do with my gift is my choice. Udane, too. Being headwoman is my choice, *she said.*

My decision, no one else's.

You can always come back, you know that, yes? Eneko had said.

My legs gave way beneath me, and I sat down, hard, on the sand.

Months ago, I'd spent hours on a beach not far from this one, bereft and watching the waves. It was strange, now, to remember that girl, like remembering a person that had died. I'd still thought everything would return to normal, then, if only Abene would have me back.

But despite myself, I had found joy in another life.

When I was little, I used to wonder if Abene was really my mother, because we were so different. She was firm. Unyielding. Stubborn. Wasn't that what she had said to Izara about Nene, that Nene never wavered? Decisiveness. *That* is what made a headwoman strong, she'd taught us.

For her, this land, the connection to her foremothers—*that* was more important than the spirits of our old world. And Izara, her favored daughter, had found a way for her to stay here. The strangers might be destroying the forest, but the forest was not what mattered to Izara and Abene.

Maybe Abene couldn't imagine making choices other than the ones she had. She'd acted the only way a headwoman could—as she saw it. When the band was threatened, she prepared to fight; when her eldest daughter challenged her, she disowned her. Whatever else, she was strong, and she was determined we wouldn't lose our territory.

My mother had never been given the option to be other than what she was. But I had a choice. I had a choice because Abene had let me go. Maybe she let me go because she thought I was incapable, but she let me go, nonetheless. Something Nene had not done for her.

And I had gone, as I'd always wanted to. I had traveled to other worlds.

There were two worlds before me even now. The world of the bands, being pushed inland, and the world of the strangers, with their villages and their animals and their seeds. I could see that the second would, in time, replace the first. The view from the *arhontzl*'s eyes made that clear.

What did that mean for the spirits?

What did it mean for my sister?

Izara. I thought of my sister as a child, the girl who had teased me till we both collapsed in giggles, who played pranks on the elders that never made anyone angry, only amused. My sister, the young woman who had defended me against Kerbasi and Omer when I couldn't defend myself. Like Abene, like Nene, Izara never wavered. Even when she was wrong, even when she went entirely against tradition, she did so confidently, accepting no challenge, no argument. She was, truly, our mother's daughter.

I was something else. But that did not make me imperfect. My wavering, I realized, was *my* strength. No, not wavering—my being willing to see things in *many different ways.*

All I have ever done is "thought things through," Eneko had said.

My thoughts were coming faster and faster now. He tried to tell me that night, but I didn't understand. He tried to tell me again, before I left the mountains, when he told me the story of his own apprenticeship. He *knew* my return here would be a failure. He *knew* I could not stop what was happening, nor force my sister to think or feel as I wanted.

Why had he let me go?

Even as I thought it, I knew the answer: *Because it was my decision to make. Not his. That's what he was telling me.*

And it's still mine.

I had become a seer, but I hadn't let go of being headwoman's daughter, just as Hodei warned me... and so I hadn't been able to grow up, even after I left my family.

Izara may be destroying our old world. But she's also creating a new world out of pieces of the old one. The pieces that matter to me are as gone as the girl who stood on the beach, wondering about the strangers in their boats. I cannot reverse this change.

Who is Nahia, in this new world?

I am a shaman, I answered myself.

And for the first time, I really believed it.

I am not responsible for any choices but my own. And that means I am free to do what I *know is right.*

I woke to light on my face. As the sun crept over the horizon, its first rays fell directly across me. It was early morning, and I was cold and damp and cramped, curled into a ball next to the boat. I must have fallen asleep, eventually.

But the certainty I had found last night—I searched for it, as one might look for the first shoots of an early flower pushing through the slush—that had not disappeared.

I sat up, stretching, and shook the sand from my hair. My face was tacky with dried tears. I stood in one swift movement, raising my arms over my head to greet the day. I found myself chanting the morning protection song, the first time I'd done so since I had come to the village.

Today, I recognized my voice and knew it as mine.

THIRTY

The village was strangely empty when I returned.

Ordinarily in the morning, the paths between the structures were bustling with people heading to the fields or to the plaza. Today, there was no one. Smoke from the morning fires lingered between the houses; the drifting haze and empty alleys made the village seem abandoned, as if raiders had come and everyone had fled. But nothing was awry: the doors were all closed, the vessels made of hardened clay all neatly stacked by the storage sheds. The village was just empty.

I made my way through the maze of houses to Izara's. Izara's home, too, was clean and neat and empty. The outside hearth was cold, and the door was shut tight. Inside, the bowls for katcha, the sleeping furs, all the morning clutter had been carefully put away.

I went directly to the storage pit at the back of the house and knelt beside it. My two foraging baskets were at the bottom, beneath a couple of ceramic pots and a tangle of linen clothing. I took my baskets. They contained the few possessions I'd brought with me: my leggings and tunic, my bow, the quiver of arrows, the small leather bag.

I stepped out of the light, prickly outfit Izara had given me, folding it neatly. I pulled on my old tunic and leggings, letting their weight settle on me. I had to lace my leggings loosely to fit around my belly, but there was no other strangeness with my leathers. They felt comfortable, a part of me that had been missing.

Only my small leather pouch remained untouched. I held it for a long moment, my heart racing, before I turned it upside down and let the contents spill out. The shaman's pendant. Izara's shell necklace. The *tsairi*'s gift of hardened clay, the object I now knew to be a broken fragment of a ceramic vessel. And the claws the bear had gifted me on my journey.

I put the shaman's pendant on first. At first, it felt strange around my neck, which had grown accustomed to being unencircled... but after a moment, I didn't feel it at all.

I hesitated over Izara's shell. As I held it in my hand, images of her—my twin, the sister so close she'd almost been half of me—flashed through my mind. Izara, the irrepressible girl who was always laughing, always ready for a game; the sister who had never failed to defend me when it mattered most.

I slipped the shell pendant around my neck, too. It snuggled cozily next to the boar's tooth that marked me a shaman.

Now only the ceramic fragment lay before me. I thought, *It's a piece of the strangers. I should throw it out. Do I really want to carry around a reminder of this village?*

The answer came immediately. *No, I don't want it. But the strangers are here, and I cannot make them go away. The* tsairi *gave this to me for a reason.*

I reached into my basket and rooted within it. My fingers closed on the long slender shape of my stone awl. Carefully, I put the awl to the fragment, grinding against it until I made a small hole. There was a strip of buckskin in the bag, too, I knew. I searched again till I found it. I passed the buckskin through the hole in the fragment, tying the two ends together to make a necklace, and then I put it on.

The shell, the fragment, and the shaman's pendant lay beside each other at the base of my neck. Last of all, I tucked the bear claws back into the pouch and tied it at my waist.

I stepped outside into the quiet and empty village. The silence was oppressive. I walked carefully, looking about me, expecting someone to appear. But I saw not a single person, not one lit hearth.

I was almost at the plaza when I finally heard voices. Or rather, one voice: that of a person making a speech before a crowd. I stopped and peered around the edge of the big meetinghouse.

My breath caught in my throat. Everyone was in the plaza: the entire village, it looked like. There were familiar faces among the throng: Maia. Alaia, with her daughter in a sling. Gotzon and Tora.

Izara, too, standing ashen-faced, Argi beside her. Izara had taken his hand and was gripping it hard; I could see her knuckles shining white.

My stomach tightened. *So soon, Udane?*

Because Udane was speaking. "This situation has long been out of hand. The time has come for the Sea People to decide who their leader is. My sister abdicated, and her *second* daughter took her place. But we never had a leadership ceremony, no discussion of the girl's fitness. Now Abene's first daughter has returned to us. She is our true headwoman!"

Izara's voice, ragged. "How could we have followed those old rules, Udane? Things are different now. There are no Sea People. We have become something new."

Udane again: "Speaking such words is proof you are not fit to lead us."

Abene came to stand on Izara's other side. Her voice was low, but I could hear her perfectly. "We discussed this, as elders, many times."

There was a low murmuring among the villagers now, like the sound of wind rustling through pine needles. How much did they understand? Did they know what was happening?

Abene said, "My daughter has found a way for us to remain in the land of our foremothers. She has proven herself to be a leader. And if that leadership does not look like the way we used to do things, well, so much the better."

Udane flared. "Says the woman who forswore her duty to us, like a coward."

There was a moment of silence. Then Oroitz said, stiffly, "Everyone knows the rules. One has spoken, two more must speak."

Udane jumped in. "This is the business of the Sea People, not the rest. The speakers must therefore be of the Sea People. And they must be adults."

Esti stood up. "I speak for Izara," she said. Her voice was soft. Unlike Abene's, it didn't carry. I had to strain to hear her. "Not many could come through what she has. She has fed and sheltered us, and she has given us new dreams. Who better to lead?" She shrugged, tossing her long light hair over her shoulders, and sat down.

Oroitz said, "We must have a third speaker." He did not look at Esti.

The silence dragged. Izara didn't step forward, didn't say anything, but I could see her trembling. Her hand gripped Argi's ever tighter.

No one else would speak for my sister, I knew. Alaia did not want to stay with the village. Tora was too young to declare for anyone, and even if Maia or the other villagers understood enough to follow the debate, Udane had made sure their voices wouldn't count.

It was time. I stepped into the plaza.

"I will speak," I said.

I was at the eastern end. Heads turned, one after another, like a river suddenly changing course. The sun warmed my hair. I knew they couldn't see my face, knew I must be a shadow in the sunlight to them, but in that moment, I was powerful, tall, as if the sun were pouring directly into my body, coursing through my veins.

It was silent again, but the silence had a different texture. It wasn't heavy, but charged, like the air before a lightning strike.

"I, too, miss the old ways, and I have thought Izara a traitor. But I was wrong.

"All of you—those of you from The Sea People, and those of you from elsewhere—where would you be now if she had not had the courage to step forward and take leadership when she found herself captured? Think. I know the shape our band was in when I left it. I know that it worsened after I left. The Sea People would have dissolved, whether we joined with these villagers or not. I have traveled. I know the men who were once our hunters have been absorbed, one by one, into new peoples. This is not a change we can fight."

I wrapped my right hand around my three pendants: the thin sharp shell, the boar's tooth, the rough ceramic fragment. They seemed to beat within my hand, as if they were a living spirit. "Izara has allowed some of what we were to live on in this changed world. How many captives keep their own language? How many women, seized by men, retain power? It is thanks to Izara you even have the opportunity to challenge her."

I looked at Udane. I wanted her to know how hard this was. But she betrayed no sign of any emotion. Her face was frozen, blank.

I said, "But some of you are kept here against your will. That is wrong. Those of you who want to leave can go. No one will hinder you, and I will help you now. Alaia?"

There was a rustling as Alaia came forward.

"You, too, are born to Dania's line," I announced. "Lili, your grandmother, was Nene's sister, and would have become headwoman had Nene been unable to lead. With this token," I pressed one of the bear claws into her hand, folding her fingers around it, "Ihintza, leader of the Ibex People, will recognize you as my friend. A friend of Nahia the shaman. Will you lead those who wish to follow you?"

Alaia's eyes were wide, shocked, but a smile was spreading across her face. "I will!"

I turned back to the crowd. "There is no golden age in the interior. The world has been altered everywhere, and will become more altered yet. The spirits have shown me this. But you will be able to honor the old ways—and to live them." I took a deep breath, tightened my hand further around the shaman's pendant. "One more thing I must say. **Argi**."

Argi had been looking at Izara—trying to track what was happening, I guessed—but when I called his name, he looked up. I beckoned to him, and he stepped forward. I had no idea if he had comprehended the dispute, but this I must convey to him.

I spoke slowly, looking into his eyes. "*There will be no more raiding*," I said. "*There will be no more capture of unwilling women, or children, or of any people.* Your way of life must stand on its own. If it is as superior as you say, then you will have many who wish to join you."

Argi looked back at me, his brown eyes uncertain. I could not be sure he understood. Izara, behind him, did—but would she be able to stand against Argi and the men of the village alone, if the raids began again?

I closed my eyes and reached for the *orei*'s cave.

It was surprisingly close at hand. I stepped into the pool, found the forest.

The bear growled. The *arhontzl* chittered.

Now, I said to the *arhontzl*.

Once again I saw through the *arhontzl*'s eyes. We swooped through the forest, passing above the scarred landscape of the strangers, flying over the village.

I saw the crowd in the plaza below us.

We swooped down, our claws extended.

Shouts brought me back to myself.

I opened my eyes to see an *arhontzl* flying low, even though it was full day. It swept down, passing so close to me that the wind cast by its wings ruffled my hair. Then it circled, coming ever closer to where I stood.

I held out my arm, and it landed there.

The shouting stopped. It was perfectly quiet. My arm ached with effort, with the great bird's weight.

"**No more raids**," I said again, and my voice seemed something beyond human. "**You will let those who wish to leave be free. Or I will return. And I will bring the storm.**"

Argi stood before me. I saw respect in his eyes—and behind it, fear. Terrible, blinding, trembling fear. He bowed, over and over.

"No more," he agreed. His voice was hoarse and scratchy. "We do not force anyone!"

I turned to the *arhontzl.*

Thank you, I said silently.

Its amber eyes met mine.

And then it lifted and twisted back into the sky, blazing gold in the daylight as it winged toward the forest.

I stood looking out across the assembled group. Argi and Abene melted into the press of people in the plaza. Izara stood alone. She was staring at me, her face splotchy, her eyes wide and unsure. She seemed small and fragile, almost childlike, like the shy and unsure little girl I had been, but she never had.

Or had she? Did my sister have insecurities that I'd never seen?

Be free, Izara. Be free in your heart. I smiled at my sister, trying to send her strength and love. *Lead as you think best, in your new world. I do not understand it. But I understand that you have chosen it.*

She smiled back, shakily, and then she turned to face the wide-eyed throng. As she did, she seemed to grow taller, stronger, leaving the unsure child behind. "I am your headwoman true."

Tora ran to embrace her, and then Maia, and then Argi, and others. Tongues were loosened; voices laughed and called to each other; others murmured fearfully, and I saw many newly respectful eyes fixed on me. Alaia strode over to Udane and Oroitz, the bear claw between her fingers.

I turned and left them all behind.

I closed my ears to the joyful shouting in the plaza. I took in the village, the smell of salt from the sea so close by. The air was crisp, the trees on the hills yellow and orange, the pines between them dusty green.

This used to be my home, a land of forest and sea. Now it was someone else's home, a land of grain and sheep. It was the home of my sister and her people.

I couldn't stay and watch the woods disappear. I could accept it; I could see it was the way the future bent; I could even be glad some of the Sea People were here, in Dania's land. But I couldn't be a part of it. And I couldn't condemn my child to live in it, either.

I looked toward the western horizon. I couldn't see the mountains from here, but I knew they lay beyond. My heart lifted.

I was going to *my* home.

THIRTY-ONE

As it turned out, I did stay in the village for one more night.

I wanted to leave right away. I had said what I needed to say, and they had all heard it. But if I were to cover any distance at all before winter, I needed stores for my journey. So I spent the afternoon gathering. I collected herbs, mushrooms, and the last of the chestnuts.

In the evening, I headed back to Izara's. As I made my way through the village, the people I passed smiled at me. Some of them made the gesture I'd seen them make to Izara and Argi. I smiled back at them.

I passed Udane's house as I walked. The doorway was a dark shadow, but as I approached, she came to stand in front of it. She must have seen me, but she was silent, leaning heavily on her stick and ostentatiously looking the other direction. I sighed. I knew my choice had been the right one: Alaia would lead the split, not me, and she would do it well.

It was too much to expect Udane to be happy about it, I supposed.

A little farther down the path, I met Alaia and her daughter. She gave me a fierce hug. "Thank you," she said. "I cannot thank you enough."

I shook my head. "Thank *you*. It's not my calling to lead our people. It never has been. My path lies elsewhere."

Alaia's smile was broad. I don't think I'd ever seen her look so happy. "I am happy to do it," she said. "Take care, little sister. Travel well!"

"And you," I said. "We won't forget each other."

Behind her, I saw Gotzon. I almost didn't recognize him—the small bundle of perpetual motion had become taller, a boy rather than a child. But the shock of light hair was unmistakable.

"Gotzon!" I called, and he turned, his face lighting up in a smile. The young man I'd seen superimposed on the child fell away as he barreled toward me, his arms outstretched.

"I thought you'd left already," he said, squeezing me hard.

"Without saying goodbye?" I said, stroking his hair. "I wouldn't do that."

He pulled away. "You did last time."

What could I say? He was right, I had. "That was different," I told him. "What about you, are you leaving?"

He looked troubled. "My father says he will go with Alaia. My mother says she will not go with him."

I touched his cheek. "And you, Gotzon? What do you wish to do?"

"I want to stay here. I am good with the animals."

"Then that is what you should do," I told him. "Listen to your heart, little rabbit. But should you ever want to travel, or if you need to leave here, for any reason, and do not wish to find your father, you should come to me. I will be in the mountains. Ask for me, or for Eneko. You'll find me."

"I don't want to travel," he said. "But—" His small face was suddenly serious. "You're not ever coming back?"

There was a lump in my throat. "Probably not," I admitted. "But we don't know what life will bring… so maybe."

"I'll miss you."

"And I you, little rabbit," I said. "Be well."

He hugged me again, even tighter. And then he dashed off, not looking back.

I finally reached Izara's house. My sister was waiting for me; she stood in the entranceway, watching the path, for once not busy grinding grain or listening to one of the village's women. When I came into view, she grinned and raised her hand in greeting.

I put my basket down, and for a moment, we stood looking at each other.

Then Izara held out her arms and hugged me close. I pressed my face against her shoulder. The woven cloth of her tunic was coarse against my cheek.

After a long moment, she stepped back, smiling. Her eyes were wet, and I was startled. I could count on one hand the number of times I'd seen Izara cry. When she had, the tears she shed were of rage, not tenderness.

She reached out and touched the fragment of hardened clay that hung around my neck.

I reached up and touched it, too. "I did it this morning."

She didn't ask me where I'd come by it. "I like it," was all she said. "The three of them look good together. Let's go for a walk."

Somehow it was easy to talk again, easy in a way it hadn't been for a long time. Izara tried to convince me to stay, to become the village's shaman.

"No," I said. "I need to go back to Eneko. I left before I knew about the baby."

Izara threaded her arm through mine. "Why didn't you tell *me*?"

I sighed. "Oh, Zari... I didn't even realize myself. Udane—"

"Never mind," Izara interrupted. "I understand. But you could stay with us through the winter. That would be easier, and safer, too. I don't want to lose you so soon, or my niece. Stay till after the baby is born."

"No," I said again. "I appreciate the offer, truly. But I don't know how long Eneko will stay at the cave where I left him. The sooner I leave, the better chance I have of finding him. And whether I find him or not, I need more training. I left right after I got the tattoo. I have so much more to learn. Besides, I don't belong here. My place is out there." I hesitated. I didn't know how Izara would react, but there was something else I had to say. "You know, Izara, you could go with Alaia and the rest of them. Or you could come with me. I'd take you anywhere you wanted to go. Are you *sure* you want to stay? With . . ."

I trailed off. I didn't want to risk the peace we had only now found.

Izara gripped my hand. She didn't seem angry, to my relief. "I *do* want to stay here," she said. "Here," she repeated, and she smiled, "is my land-sense."

I shook my head. I would never understand my sister's choices, or my mother's. But I would respect them.

Izara said, "Your place is not only in the mountains, either. You *do* belong here, you know, and I will always have a place for you. Didn't you see how the women listened when you spoke? If I am to be their leader, their true leader, your support would be helpful."

Warmth spread through me, but still I had to laugh. "Oh, come on, Izara!" I said. "You need my help like you need—oh, like you need a sheep to help gather mussels. You know you've always wanted this. You were born to do it. It's time."

She gazed sadly at me. "But I'll miss you."

"And I you, Zari," I said. "Every day, every moment. Forever."

I wanted to talk to Abene, too. I wanted to tell her I forgave her, and to ask for her forgiveness in turn. But after my walk with Izara, the evening was full of activity and people, and there was no time or space for a conversation.

There was only one moment in which I might have said anything. Throughout the evening, as I packed my baskets, Izara bustled around me, adding more food, a fur, a woven net to the load. At one point, she dashed outside to the storage shed for yet more food. Abene moved slowly around the house, putting the detritus from Izara's energy back in place. Her hair was almost fully gray now, and she moved hesitantly, her stride careful.

I could have spoken then, but the words wouldn't come. We both worked quietly, comfortably, not speaking.

I just had to trust she knew.

Izara, Argi, and Abene all rose early the next morning, to see me off. We gathered before the house, eating chestnuts that Udane and I had gathered. When the sky to the east began to lighten, I stood.

"Well," I said, and then stopped. This was so awkward. What could I say?

Argi knew what to do. He bowed to me, band-fashion, saying solemnly, "I thank you, Nahia. Travel well." Then he vanished, leaving me with my mother and my sister.

Abene enfolded me in her arms. "Blessings," she said. It was just one word, but it was enough.

Izara walked me to the edge of the village's clearing, right to the foot of the big hill. The dawn air was chilly. My baskets were bulging. Last night, as I'd packed, they had forced additional food on me; I protested, but they insisted I would need it on the trail. I knew they were right.

The morning smelled damp, autumnal, and I inhaled deeply. There was brine on the breeze. I knew I would not smell the sea again for a long time, if ever.

I looked back to the village. There was sea-haze hanging over it, mixing with the wood smoke from the hearths. I knew that haze would burn off into a beautiful fall day, but for now, it made the village seem otherworldly. Almost like something from a vision.

At the edge of the forest, I put down my baskets and turned to Izara.

For a moment, we just looked at each other. Then she hugged me fiercely, holding on as if she would never let go.

When we finally separated, she held out her hands, and I grasped them in my own. I let my eyes travel over my twin's face, taking in the shining hair, the expressive mouth, the lively eyes, trying to fix her image firmly in my mind so I would never forget anything.

"I love you," I told Izara, and hugged her again.

Izara didn't say anything, just smiled, her eyes glistening. She stepped back and raised her hand in the villagers' gesture.

I swung my baskets back up on my back. Touched the three pendants that hung around my neck: Izara's shell, the shaman's pendant, and the fragment of hardened clay.

And with a final wave, I set off to the west.

A FEW NOTES ON NAHIA'S WORLD

THE MESOLITHIC-NEOLITHIC TRANSITION

Nahia is a novel, and it should not be confused with fact. But, at the same time, this book tells the story of a change that really did happen.

Western Europe was the realm of hunter-gatherers for hundreds of thousands of years—first Neanderthals, and later *Homo sapiens*, members of our own species. But beginning about 7,900 years ago, those hunter-gatherers were joined by people who practiced agriculture. Eventually, all the hunter-gatherers were either absorbed into agricultural populations, adopted agricultural practices on their own, or disappeared. Which of these happened is a matter of debate, and probably varied from region to region, but either way, eventually, no hunter-gatherers remained. Very few people today carry any DNA that can be traced back to these European hunter-gatherers.

Archaeologists call the change from foraging populations to agricultural ones the **Mesolithic-Neolithic transition**. In *Nahia*, the people of the bands are what archaeologists refer to as "Mesolithic foragers"; the strangers, or Argi's people, are agriculturalists, the people who brought the Neolithic to Europe.

We know the agriculturalists who came to Europe were originally from the Near East (a transcontinental region including the Balkans, Anatolia, Thrace, North Africa, and Western Asia). At this writing, it appears that these colonists entered Europe using two different pathways, moving from east to west. One group, who made a type of pottery we call "Linear Band Ware," came over land, up the Danube. The other group (in this book, Argi's people) made pottery decorated with the impressions of shells, called "Impressed Ware," and seem to have arrived via the Mediterranean Sea. While some foragers may have been assimilated into these farming groups, many others seem to have retreated to the north and west. Eventually, the foragers were succeeded by farmers all across Europe, a process that unfolded over the next thousand years.

The move from a foraging lifestyle to a farming one had many impacts, some immediate, some longer term. Nahia sees the immediate impacts—the clearing of land, the need to stay in one place—but some of the longer-term impacts are harder to show. Tooth decay is one: a reliable archaeological sign of a population's shift to agricultural production is cavities! (Nahia does see this among some of Argi's people, who have grown up eating grains.)

I am an archaeologist, and I used archaeological data to inform *Nahia*, but I also think the first responsibility of any novelist is to tell a good story. So when the archaeological record isn't clear on what happened at a particular point, I didn't let the lack of information stop me. At the time I'm writing this, ancient DNA analyses tell us that the first agriculturalists in Iberia were new arrivals, and the patterning of Neolithic sites along the coast (as well as the speed of settlement) suggests that these new arrivals did use boats to colonize. The physical appearance of the people of the bands (including the presence of people with dark skin and blue eyes) and of the strangers also matches what ancient DNA and bioarchaeological studies have told us. Raids, abductions, and hybrid villages composed of both foragers and farmers, such as the one Izara founded, on the other hand, are hypothesized by some archaeologists, but there is not yet clear evidence.

We also don't know what language either the foragers of the Mesolithic or the agriculturalists of the Neolithic spoke, except that neither was likely a member of the Indo-European language family (the family to which most modern European languages belong). As I write this, there is increasing consensus that Indo-European languages came to Europe in the Bronze Age, several thousand years after this story takes place. It's probable that the Mesolithic foragers and initial Neolithic colonists spoke completely different languages from each other (languages which are also entirely distinct from any today).

One non-Indo-European language *does* exist in Western Europe today: Basque. For this reason, I used modern Basque as a (very loose) base for the language spoken by Nahia and her people. However, it is very unlikely that Mesolithic hunter-gatherers spoke Basque or anything like it. My choice to use Basque as a basis for the Sea People's language was an artistic decision, not a scientific one.

In short, I took the facts as they were understood as I was writing, and I searched for a story between those facts. As research continues, it may turn out that parts of the story I found are contradicted by the data. What we think we know can change very quickly.

But imagining the past is a funny endeavor, and sometimes, it works out the other way—new research confirms what we imagined.

In 2023, long after I wrote the first draft of *Nahia*, I happened to visit the State Museum of Prehistory in Halle, Germany. In the "Human Succession" section of this museum is an exhibit focused on the Bad Dürrenberg shaman, a thirty- to forty-year-old woman who died and was buried about nine thousand years ago. The grave goods that were found alongside her remains suggest that she was a religious specialist, a Mesolithic forager who acted as an intermediary between her people and the spirit world.

Nahia was not based on the Bad Dürrenberg shaman. I had no knowledge of this burial when I wrote this novel. But many aspects of what we know about the Bad Dürrenberg shaman line up with Nahia's story. This is the magic of imagination.

It is probably best to think of Nahia's world as fictional, just as Nahia, her family, and the people she encounters are fictional. Even though this world is based on what we know of Northern Spain at the Mesolithic-Neolithic transition, there are many things the archaeological record cannot tell us, and imagination doesn't always lead us in the right direction.

But no matter how fictional this story may be (or may turn out to be), I hope it does speak truth in a larger sense. The transition from foraging societies to agricultural ones was undeniably one of the most significant events in human history. Real people lived through this change, and saw their worlds altered beyond recognition as a result.

Nahia and her people are made-up characters...but the changes they experienced really did take place.

PLANTS AND ANIMALS

In her journey, Nahia interacts with many plants and animals, some of which may be unfamiliar to readers of this book. I mostly refer to them by their English names, but sometimes I use a word from Nahia's language instead. In some cases, as with the *arhontzl* and the *orei*, I did this because the English terms for the species Nahia encounters are technical in a way that would interfere with the story. In other cases, most often with plants, I made this decision for another reason.

Plants are amazing. Many people don't realize how many pharmaceutical medicines have their origins in plants used by traditional healers. The birth control pill, aspirin, and quinine are just three of the many pharmaceutical drugs used today that are derived from plants used in traditional medicine. Like all systems of medicine, herbal medicine requires training. Getting surgery from someone whose only prior experience was reading a book is not something I would want to do. Similarly, attempting to practice herbal medicine without training from a qualified practitioner is risky at best. The plants that form the basis of traditional medicine can be dangerous. Using them without training can be fatal.

I am not a qualified practitioner. I am an archaeologist who has studied herbal medicine in a general way, as an outsider, and who has a knowledge of some of the plant species that were used by prehistoric Europeans. So while I had specific plants in mind as I wrote about herbal medicine in *Nahia*, I don't want to advocate the use of those plants as remedies. I especially want to caution that there are plants that, while we know that prehistoric people used them, we don't know how they prepared them. For many medicines, preparation is critical to the medicine having its intended effect.

If you want to learn more about plants and their medicinal properties, there are many terrific herbal training programs around the world! There are also many sources to learn about plants in general, as well as about wild animals. But if you just want to know a little more about some of the plants and animals I had in mind as I wrote *Nahia*, the following list may be of interest to you.

Nahia encounters the following animals in her journey:

- *Arhontzl*: the Eurasian eagle-owl (also known as the eagle-owl or the uhu), one of the largest owl species in the world (*Bubo bubo*)
- Bear: the Eurasian brown bear (*Ursus arctos arctos*)
- Boar: the European wild boar (*Sus scrofa*)
- Chamois: a small wild member of the goat-antelope family that lives in the mountains (*Rupicapra rupicapra*)
- Domestic dogs (*Canis familiaris* or *Canis lupus familiaris*): both Mesolithic foragers and Neolithic agriculturalists had domestic dogs, but they were from different stock and likely differed from each other in appearance (and we know they differed substantially from domestic dogs today)
- Eurasian hoopoe (*Upupa epops*): this bird makes a distinctive *hoop-hoop-hoop* call, which is a common springtime sound along the Spanish Mediterranean coast today
- Iberian ibex: a species of wild goat (*Capra pyrenaica*)

✦ Land snails: many different species were eaten by Mesolithic foragers, but one of the types most frequently found in archaeological sites is the grove snail, also called the lemon snail (*Cepaea nemoralis*)

✦ *Orei*: known in Europe as red deer (*Cervus elaphus*), this animal is closely related to the American elk/wapiti

✦ Rabbit: the European wild rabbit (*Oryctolagus cuniculus*), the ancestor of the domestic rabbit

✦ Roe deer/roebuck: a small deer (*Capreolus capreolus*) that is widespread in Europe. The roe deer is a member of the same family as white-tailed and mule deer. A roebuck is an adult male

The following are some of the plants I had in mind while writing *Nahia*. Plants are often harder to identify in the archaeological record than are animals, and we frequently know less about which ones were used in prehistory. However, the following wild plants are ones that likely would have grown on the Iberian Peninsula during Nahia's time. They all have a documented history of use in later periods (as food, as medicine, as raw material, in ceremony, or in a combination of these), and some we know were used in prehistory as well.

✦ *Artemisia alba* and *Artemisia herba-alba*: these plants are distinct species with different properties, but they are often called by the same English common names, which include white artemisia, white mugwort, and white wormwood (these names are sometimes used for other plant species in other parts of the world as well)

✦ Common mallow (*Malva neglecta*)

- Dandelion (multiple species in the genus *Taraxacum*)
- Dwarf elder (*Sambucus ebulus*)
- Elder (*Sambucus nigra*)
- European crabapple (*Malus sylvestris*)
- Heather (*Calluna vulgaris*)
- Hawthorn (*Crataegus monogyna*)
- Hazel (*Corylus avellana*)
- Onionweed (*Asphodelus tenuifolius*)
- Oyster thistle (*Scolymus hispanicus)*
- Plantain (multiple species in the genus *Plantago*)
- Roman chamomile (*Chamaemelum nobile*)
- Sage (multiple species in the genus *Salvia*)
- Soapwort (*Saponaria officinalis*)
- Silver thistle (*Carlina acaulis*)
- Snowy mespilus or European serviceberry (*Amelanchier ovalis*)
- Spanish or Portuguese heath (*Erica lusitanica*)
- Spanish salsify (*Scorzonera hispanica*)
- Vervain (*Verbena officinalis*)
- Wild cherry (*Prunus avium*)
- Wild fennel (*Foeniculum vulgare*)
- Wild thyme (*Thymus praecox*)
- Willow (multiple species in the genus *Salix*)
- Yarrow (*Achillea millefolium*)

Some of the toxic or otherwise dangerous plants that would have grown in Nahia's world are listed below. In some cases, these species have been identified in the archaeological record; in others, we know about their use later in time, but they likely were used earlier.

- Belladonna (*Atropa belladonna*)
- Henbane (*Hyoscyamus niger*)
- Joint pine (*Ephedra fragilis*)
- Mandrake (*Mandragora autumnalis*)
- Monkshood (*Aconitum napellus*)
- Opium poppy: This is an especially interesting one! The poppy (*Papaver somniferum*) is native to the western Mediterranean. It's a good guess that the psychoactive properties of this plant were known to Mesolithic foragers, although (at this writing) there is no direct evidence of this. In the early Neolithic, however, poppy use became widespread across Europe, including in areas far from where this species grows naturally.

ARCHAEOLOGICAL BACKGROUND

This section is for those of you who would like to know more about the archaeology that inspired parts of Nahia's story. Still, there is so much more to the archaeology of the Mesolithic-Neolithic transition than I can include here! I hope this teaser will inspire some of you to investigate deeper.

ALCOHOL

It's long been suspected that brewing alcohol went hand in hand with the spread of the Neolithic in Europe. Some recent archaeological work has found traces of possible alcoholic beverages on the surfaces of ceramics from Neolithic sites. One ceramic vessel dated to the early Neolithic, recovered in a site outside Barcelona, Spain, has been argued to have traces of a fermented barley drink; farther south, in a site near Toledo, there's an early Neolithic vessel with residues suggesting it contained mead. The pioneering researcher on this topic was the late Professor Andrew Sherratt; more recently, scholars such as Professor Elisa Guerra-Doce have published informative and promising studies. It's this work that inspired the beer drinking that Nahia observes in the strangers' village.

There's been less research into Mesolithic people and alcohol. Since they didn't grow domestic grains, it is less likely that they would have brewed beer. However, you don't have to brew alcohol to drink it—in many situations, fruit or honey will ferment on its own. Honey harvesting, the taking of honey from wild beehives, is a practice that likely goes back deep into prehistory, and there is concrete evidence for it as well. Rock art in Spain, dated to about 7,500 years ago (just a little after Nahia's time) illustrates honey hunting in great detail. (For more information on this, look up the site of Barranco Gómez!)

If people were honey hunting, they certainly encountered fermented honey. Based on this, it's been argued that people have been drinking naturally fermented honey for more than ten thousand years. While I refer to what Herri and his companions were drinking as "honey wine," the term "wine" is shorthand: they are drinking fermented honey that they harvested from a wild beehive, not wine that they brewed themselves.

Architecture

In *Nahia*, Nahia lives first in a seasonal camp made up of tents, then in a cave, and later in the strangers' village with permanent structures. While I did base these settings on the archaeological record, I don't want to suggest that Neolithic people brought architecture to Europe, or that they always lived in villages themselves! Neolithic Iberians also lived in caves; Mesolithic Iberians sometimes constructed more permanent structures; and the history of more permanent, constructed structures in European sites goes *way* back into prehistory, possibly to hundreds of thousands of years ago.

There *is* evidence for an increase in the ubiquity and number of permanent structures once the Neolithic came in, but that likely reflects the fact that Neolithic people were more sedentary. It's not an indicator that they were the first people to develop architecture, or that hunter-gatherers didn't know how to construct permanent shelters.

Art

Southwestern Europe (and many other parts of the world, too) is filled with rock art, some of which dates back forty thousand years or more—long before Nahia's time.

The *orei*'s cave, while not based on any specific place, *is* inspired by Paleolithic cave art. While I've never had visions like Nahia's, seeing such cave art in person has been one of the peak experiences of my life. During one of my first field experiences, when I was working with a team excavating a site in southwestern France, I had the chance to visit Lascaux—one of the most famous of these caves. The guide leading the small group I was with (at that time, only four people were allowed in per day) made her flashlight flicker, so we could see the paintings as they would have looked by torchlight. Looking up at the animals ranging across the cave walls, seeming to move in the flickering light, I was transported into another world. Since that first visit, I've had the privilege to visit many other art caves, and every time, I've had a similar experience. These visits inspired the *orei*'s cave.

Art-making, in one form or another, seems to be fundamental to the human experience. While there isn't much mention of it in this book, Iberian Mesolithic and Neolithic people made art of various kinds; in addition to the jewelry and ornamentation that feature in this story, there are also paintings, carvings, and figurines from these time periods.

A final kind of art that I want to mention (one that does appear in *Nahia*!) is tattoos. Because tattoos are on skin, which doesn't usually preserve, the first direct evidence of tattooing in prehistoric Europe doesn't appear until we have mummies (such as Ötzi, the ice mummy, who lived more than five thousand years ago, or over two thousand years after Nahia's time). We do know that tattooing and shamanic practice were linked in prehistory, due to the discovery of tattoo kits with individuals like the Upton Lovell shaman, who died in the Neolithic. Whether tattooing existed prior to that—and if so, how much prior—remains a matter of debate. I took artistic liberty in *Nahia* in assuming that tattoos did exist. They certainly *could* have existed—but for the time being, at least, we don't know for certain.

Baskets, Ceramics, and Cooking

Ceramic technology was present in Europe at least as far back as twenty thousand years ago (that is, long before Nahia's time), but Mesolithic hunter-gatherers in western Europe, like hunter-gatherers in many other times and places, don't seem to have used it to make vessels (though recent research suggests the story may be different in eastern and central Europe). Instead, they made baskets (the baskets from Cueva de los Murciélagos in southern Spain are a great example), bags of hide, and wood containers. Neolithic people, on the other hand, invested heavily in making ceramic pots.

One impact this would have had on everyday life is on cooking! If ceramic vessels have been fired at high heat, they can later be placed straight into a fire to heat their contents. Waterproofed baskets and hide bags, on the other hand, cannot. Hunter-gatherers without ceramics have historically heated water by placing stones in a fire, filling a basket or bag with water, and then, when the stones get hot, placing them in the water to heat it. Fire-cracked cobbles, a byproduct of this method, are common in Mesolithic sites. Food can be cooked in a similar way; it can also be roasted directly in the fire or placed in pits for slow cooking (there's evidence for both in the archaeological record). There is also evidence of smoking food (likely fish) from Iberian Mesolithic sites.

In *Nahia*, the Sea People use both hide bags and waterproofed baskets to hold water and to heat it. They cook food in baskets with heated rocks; they also cook directly on the fire and in cooking pits. In the village, we only see people cooking with ceramics, but we know that even people who had ceramics used some of these other methods as well (even to boil water).

FIRE AND LIGHT

Fire is important to human cultures everywhere, throughout time: it's a source of heat, of protection, and of light, as well as being important for cooking food. A common feature of both Mesolithic and Neolithic sites is demarcated hearths, the areas that held fires. These fires were probably banked when not in use, so as to be easily started later.

If you are traveling, though, keeping your fire banked is not an option. This is where what are sometimes called "fire-making kits" come in. Fire-making kits are collections of flint, iron pyrite, tinder, and/or other materials that will make a spark, and they are found in archaeological contexts from all over the world (including in prehistoric Europe). Those of us with ready access to matches or a lighter often don't think about the difficulty of starting a fire without such tools. For the Sea People and the villagers in *Nahia*, being able to start a fire from flint and tinder would have been a matter of life and death.

Lamps (formed from ground stone and, later, from ceramics), which would have burned animal fats, are also known from European archaeological sites; the oldest known such lamp is more than twenty thousand years old. Torches are also well-known in the archaeological record.

Learning more

If reading *Nahia* has inspired you to want to learn more about European prehistory, or prehistory anywhere in the world, I am thrilled! Here are a few places you might start.

- Books, articles, museums, and archaeological sites: These are the most direct way to learn more, but there are so many of them that they can be overwhelming! Visit museums at home or anywhere you might travel. Visit museum websites, too—they frequently have online exhibits. Many archaeological sites can be visited in person, and they may have associated museums/websites. (The official websites for the art caves of Lascaux and Chauvet are particularly good!) Make use of your local library and the internet to track down current research. Ask a librarian for help if you get lost in the weeds. If you have access to a college or university library, you may find it, and its librarians, to be especially helpful. Many university libraries are open to community members, so even if you are not a student, you may be able to access them.

♦ Classes and lectures: In the USA, formal classes on archaeology and prehistory are most likely to be found in the anthropology departments of colleges and universities. Even if you aren't enrolled in such an institution, you may be able to sit in on a class. There are some online classes available out there as well, so if you want to try this but don't live near an institution with relevant offerings, don't give up! University anthropology departments, museums, and local archaeological organizations also often have lecture series (sometimes available online as well as in person) that are open to the public.

♦ Local archaeological organizations: These are some of the best places to learn. While they typically will focus on the archaeology of their particular location, you may find attending their meetings to be helpful (even if you are interested in European prehistory and don't live in Europe). These organizations often can put you in touch with people who are working in areas that are of interest to you. They also may have projects going on for which you can volunteer.

ACKNOWLEDGMENTS

I was supported by a vast community in writing this book. When I think about everyone and everything that contributed to the novel you now hold in your hands, I'm humbled, overwhelmed, and most of all, profoundly grateful. So let me start these acknowledgments by offering gratitude to all of you (for if you are reading this, you too are part of this community!).

Nahia had a long journey from first draft to publication. Learning to write as a novelist, rather than an academic, has been a wild ride. Dee Garretson, Kelly, Summer Hayes, Amy Lin, April Mazza, Jenna Nelson, Cindy Pon, Caroline Starr Rose, Ellanie Sampson, and Will Taylor all read drafts of *Nahia* and offered invaluable advice. The writers of Purgatory and the New Mexico chapter of SCBWI were incredibly supportive, too. Whenever I burned out, Natalie Goldberg helped rekindle the flame. Two guides deserve special thanks: My agent Russ Galen read an early draft and made a critical suggestion that was fundamental to the story it became. And my editor Mora Couch worked tirelessly, offering her time, her knowledge (of writing, of publishing, and of prehistory), her patience, and her wisdom as she guided *Nahia* from a loosely conceived story to a polished novel. Thank you, thank you, thank you! Thanks also to everyone at Holiday House: editor Della Farrell; the amazing marketers and publicists, including Michelle Montague, Sara DiSalvo, Terry Borzumato-Greenberg, Tiffany Coelho, and Alison Tarnofsky; designer Chelsea Hunter; and Emma Swan and Rebecca Godan. I'm especially grateful to Fernanda Suarez, who created the gorgeous cover.

There are many people who did not know I was writing a novel, but who nonetheless supported and inspired me: the researchers who study Mesolithic and Neolithic Europe, particularly the Iberian archaeological community; my students, a never-ending source of inspiration; the former and current members of the UNM Zooarchaeology Lab; and my family, biological and non, especially my parents (very fortunately for me, my mother is *nothing* like Abene). And finally, *Nahia* would not exist without David, who is family and more than family. Thank you, all of you. I am more grateful than I can say.

ABOUT THE AUTHOR

I am a professor and an archaeologist. More specifically, I'm what's called a *zooarchaeologist* (or *archaeozoologist*)—I study animal remains from archaeological sites, with the goal of learning about past relationships between people and their environments. For example, an analysis of bones at a given site can give us information about our ancestors' diets, trade networks, hunting strategies, and, in some cases, their religion or their worldview. Archaeozoological investigation helps us understand what past environments looked like, too. This paints a more complete picture of ancient life.

When I tell people what I do, they often respond, "Wow, how did you get into that?" As a kid, I was a difficult combination of passionate, anxious, and irritable. School was tough for me. I wanted to be outside, or reading a book for fun, or better yet, reading a fun book outside. (This is still true.) But I was always interested in the past, and I was also curious about the natural world in a way I now know is called "biology." Still, becoming an archaeologist never occurred to me until I took an archaeology class in college—I had heard a rumor that the professor might take us on a trip to Egypt! It wasn't true, but I was surprised at how much I liked the material. I loved the idea of *hands-on* history, of *actually touching* the past. So, I took another class. And another.

I discovered zooarchaeology specifically thanks to my undergraduate professor Dr. Anne Pike-Tay, a zooarchaeologist whose focus was Paleolithic France and Spain. Working in Anne's lab as a research assistant showed me how to integrate my interests in the past *and* the natural world, something I'd had no idea how to do. Thanks to her mentorship, by the time I graduated, I knew I was interested in how people responded to the Pleistocene-Holocene transition—the transition from the last ice age to a climate more like today's. After college, I worked in cultural resource management archaeology (in this role, archaeologists make sure no important site is unknowingly destroyed in the course of construction or development), and as a project archaeologist for the Pueblo of Zuni in New Mexico. For my Ph.D., I went to the University of Washington in Seattle. I spent my summers working on Paleolithic excavations in the Dordogne region of France—including six months as a Chateaubriand Fellow in Bordeaux—while completing my dissertation research on changing diets at the Pleistocene-Holocene transition. I also worked as a graduate teaching assistant and was astonished to discover that I *loved* teaching—having struggled when I was a student helped me figure out how to reach my own students. Life is surprising sometimes! After earning my Ph.D., I began teaching at Diné College, a tribal college on the Navajo Nation, eventually transitioning to Utah State University and then to the University of New Mexico, where I am a professor today. I've continued exploring how people's relationship to the environment changed throughout the end of the Pleistocene, particularly in the Iberian Peninsula (where *Nahia* is set).

In 2017, I was honored to receive a Fulbright scholarship to Spain. For four months, I lived in Cantabria and worked with colleagues on the examination and identification of animal remains at El Mirón Cave. This is a famous place: Here, scientists have discovered beautifully engraved art on animal bones, an ancient stone workbench, and the Red Lady—an 18,700-year-old woman of the Magdalenian Culture who was buried under a limestone block. The animal bones discarded here seem to have been used not for food, but for the creation of tools or, possibly, ornaments or other art. One of the most exciting experiences I had was identifying an engraved red deer scapula. I'll never forget the time I spent in Cantabria. It helped inspire me to write *Nahia*. I was not the first to be so inspired; El Mirón Cave is one of the sites that inspired Jean Auel when she wrote *Clan of the Cave Bear*.

I continue to work in Europe, but these days I work in North America as well, mostly as a museum and lab-based researcher. For some years, I and colleagues have been exploring how the introduction of domestic animals of European origin (for example, sheep and cattle) changed human-environment relationships here. And, through collaboration with my many amazing students, I'm involved in a suite of other projects all over the globe. None of this is anything I could have imagined when I was an anxious child struggling in school. And while the day to day of being an academic archaeologist does (like any job!) have its ups and downs, mostly I have to say: I love what I do, and I'm grateful to have the chance to do it.